Previously published Worldwide Suspense titles by
PAUL CARR

LONG WAY DOWN
THE CAYMAN SWITCH
THE BLACK PALMETTO
BAD WAY OUT

DEAD MAN'S TAKE

PAUL CARR

W☉RLDWIDE

TORONTO • NEW YORK • LONDON
AMSTERDAM • PARIS • SYDNEY • HAMBURG
STOCKHOLM • ATHENS • TOKYO • MILAN
MADRID • WARSAW • BUDAPEST • AUCKLAND

W☰RLDWIDE™

ISBN-13: 978-1-335-41751-0

Dead Man's Take

First published in 2018 by The Wild Rose Press, Inc.
This edition published in 2021.

This edition published by arrangement with Harlequin Books S.A.

For questions and comments about the quality of this book, please contact us at CustomerService@Harlequin.com.

Harlequin Enterprises ULC
22 Adelaide St. West, 40th Floor
Toronto, Ontario M5H 4E3, Canada
www.ReaderService.com

Printed in U.S.A.

Recycling programs
for this product may
not exist in your area.

DEAD MAN'S TAKE

I want to thank the people at The Wild Rose Press, Inc., especially my editor Laura Kelly, whose wonderful work made my story better. I also want to thank my wife, Elaine, and my friends in the writing community for their help and support.

ONE

THE BODY LAY face down in the reeds near the shore of Little Basin. A uniformed deputy stood a few feet away wiping perspiration from the back of his neck, the Islamorada sun already sizzling before 9:00 a.m. An iguana scampered through the scrub, sending the deputy backward as if jolted by electrical shock.

Detective Dalton approached as a second deputy stretched crime scene tape around the area.

"Hey, hey," the deputy said, "you can't come over here."

"Monroe County Sheriff." Dalton held up his badge and the man stepped over for a look.

"So, you're the new detective. Michael Dalton. I heard about you."

"You get a look at the body?"

The deputy's nametag read Ted Colson. He nodded. "I think it's a gunshot wound to the head. We didn't touch anything. Crime scene guys will be here soon."

"Any footprints, other than your friend's over there fouling the scene?"

The deputy frowned and turned to his partner. "Hey, Jim, get out of there. Make sure you step on solid ground."

"A fisherman on a boat found him this morning,"

Colson said. "Looks like he hasn't been here long. The wildlife hasn't bothered him much."

Dalton took out his phone and zoomed in with the camera. He could see congealed blood on the side of the man's head. Longish blond hair, going to gray. Slender with knobby elbows. His T-shirt and jeans were dark, maybe black. Some sort of image on the back of his shirt. No way to guess at his age. He snapped a photo. "You have the name of the fisherman who found him?"

"Hold on. I'll get it," Colson said. He used the radio clipped to his shirt and called the station.

The name came back, along with an address, and Dalton jotted the information in a pocket notebook.

"He say why he couldn't hang around until you got here?" Dalton asked.

"The 911 operator said he had to go to work. He's a car salesman."

Crime scene investigators, a man and a woman, arrived with the medical examiner. Dalton introduced himself, his eyes lingering a few seconds longer on the woman. Her name was Robin Marlowe, and she gave him a smile.

The crew took several photos of the surrounding area. Deputy Jim told them where he had stepped, leaving an unintended trail.

"I don't see any other shoe prints here," the woman said. "The victim must've gone in the water somewhere else."

The medical examiner stepped closer. "Okay, get him out of there."

Within a few minutes, they had the man on top of

a body bag. He looked about forty, his eyes wide as if expecting a surprise. Bullet hole on the forehead, left side. Dalton snapped another photo. The shirt had Key West stenciled across the front. Probably one of many thousands sold in the gift shops in the Keys.

Lifting the man's head, the ME examined the bullet wound. "Hard to peg the caliber of the weapon. I'll need to see the bullet." He checked for a wallet and found none. No keys either, or a phone. Just a couple of coins. After he ascertained water and body temp they zipped the bag and carried it through the brush to a van.

Dalton went to the office to complete his new employee paperwork. Starting work that morning, he'd arrived early and was getting set up when the commander, Lieutenant Cobb, assigned him the case. After making notes about the homicide in his notebook, he dragged the stack of employment forms in front of him.

"You the new guy?" A man said from a few feet away. Dalton hadn't heard him come in. He looked about thirty or so, dressed in khakis and a pullover shirt with a star on it. Maybe an inch or so shorter than Dalton's six-two and musclebound. He sported a crew cut, and beads of perspiration dotted his forehead and neck, as if he'd just come from the gym.

Dalton stood and introduced himself. "Michael Dalton. Just started today."

"Steve Chase." He didn't offer his hand, but raised an eyebrow. "I heard you got the homicide called in this morning."

"Yeah, I did. Just got back from the scene. Looked like the guy took a round to the head."

Chase smirked. "Wonder why you got the case instead of me. I been here five years."

"You'd have to ask the lieutenant about that."

"Yeah, I'll do that." Chase turned and headed toward Cobb's office.

Dalton went back to his forms. The other detective came back a few minutes later, his face red, and went to his desk in the cubicle across the office. He sat there for a few minutes before stepping back over.

"He said you closed a lot of homicides in your previous job. Some kind of hotshot."

Dalton felt his pulse drum up in his ears.

"He told me to assist you if you need help," Chase continued. "I guess that means I get you coffee and do your reports."

Raising an eyebrow, Dalton said, "I do my own reports, but you're welcome to help on the case."

"Oh yeah? Think I'll pass." He stood there for a couple of beats. "If you were so good where you came from, why'd you leave?"

Dalton stared. "None of your business, Detective."

Chase turned and headed toward his desk.

Before he got out of earshot, Dalton said, "One cream, no sugar."

The detective spun and said, "What?"

"That's how I take my coffee."

Chase gave him a scowl, his face red, and stomped away.

Dalton finished his forms, turned them in, and went in to see the Medical Examiner. The body lay on the table, the ME studying the man's ankles. He glanced up. "Detective Dalton, it'll be a while before I can tell you anything."

"Sure, I just wanted to take a better look."

"Okay, fine."

The ankles of the deceased had marks on them, maybe from ligatures. And there were cuts on his fingers.

"What do you think caused those marks?" Dalton asked, pointing to the victim's ankles.

"It appears that something was used to tie him up. Something that pressed into his skin, but didn't cut. Like cord or wire."

"I noticed the cuts on his fingers, too. Maybe the wire was hooked up to an anchor, and he cut his hands trying to get out of it."

Shrugging, the ME said, "That's possible, I suppose. It would mean he was still alive when he went in the bay. I'll check his lungs for seawater."

Dalton thanked him and left. On his way out, he spotted the female CSI in the break room getting coffee. Robin Marlowe. He stepped inside.

"You have a minute?" Dalton asked.

She stepped over to a table. "Sure, have a seat."

He poured himself a cup and joined her.

"You're Dalton, right?"

"Yes. My friends call me Mick. And I remember you're Robin." Robin. Beautiful eyes and smile, could've been a model. How did the sheriff's office lure her?

"Okay, Mick it is. You finding your way around?"

He shrugged. "No problem there."

She grinned. "I saw Steve Chase giving you a hard time earlier."

The way she mentioned it, he wondered if there might be a relationship. "I might feel the same way if I was in his situation. You been here long?"

"Almost a year. I was with the Miami PD before that. More expensive down here, but it's nicer. How about you?"

"Chicago Homicide. Like you said, it's nicer down here." After a beat, he said, "You learn anything about that body yet?"

"Not really. I ran his prints, but didn't get a match on the Florida database. I put in a search request on AFIS. I should hear back from the Feds pretty soon."

Dalton thanked her, went to his car, and called the man who had reported the body. Randy Lloyd answered and said he could spare a few minutes if the detective wanted to come by the dealership where he worked.

"DID YOU KNOW the man in the water?" Dalton asked Lloyd. They sat in the salesman's tiny office with a picture window on the outside wall.

Lloyd hesitated for a beat. "I don't think so. I got close enough to see that he was dead and called 911, but I couldn't see his face."

The detective pulled out his phone and showed him the photo of the victim.

Shaking his head, Lloyd said, "Doesn't look familiar to me."

Dalton stared for a moment. "What kind of fish do you catch around here?"

"You a transplant?"

"Yeah, Chicago."

"I catch snapper, grouper, whatever bites. They're all good to eat."

Dalton took his time, scanned over the lack of activity outside the window. "You get any fish this morning?"

Lloyd chuckled, as if to say *Nice try*. "Yeah, I got a cooler full. You can come by my house and take a look if you want. I was on my way back to the marina when I spotted the body. That was about eight o'clock. I had to be at work at nine, and I told all that to the 911 lady."

The detective didn't think there was anything else to be learned from the salesman. He got the name of the marina where Lloyd kept his boat and left.

CSI Robin called as Dalton pulled out of the car dealership. "I got a hit on the database. The victim is Carl Myron. He was a guest in a Georgia prison until eight months ago for burglary."

"You have an address?"

She told him where Myron had lived when he'd gotten his Florida auto license. He thanked her, hung up, and arrived at the place on the fringe of Islamorada a few minutes later. The house sat at the end of a dead-end street near a marsh. Thousands of peeled gray paint flakes outlined the sinking foundation. Probably a rental. An old sedan sat in the dirt driveway. Dalton rapped on the door and got no answer.

He called Robin back. "See if you can find out the owner and get him over here." Waiting in the car with the air running, his phone chirped a few minutes later.

Robin said the landlord lived next door and would be there right away.

An older woman dressed in baggy shorts and a tee shirt ambled up. Dalton shut the car off and got out.

"What's this about?" the woman asked, dropping a cigarette to the ground and grinding it out with the toe of her flip flop. She had a couple of teeth missing in front, and her words whistled when she spoke.

Dalton showed her his badge. "The guy who lived here has been murdered. I need to take a look inside."

"Aw, man, he owed me back rent. Kept putting me off. I guess I won't ever get it now."

Got that right, Dalton thought. She opened the door, said she had things to do, and left.

Stretching on vinyl gloves, he pushed inside. A threadbare sofa sat in the middle of the room next to a lamp stand. He opened the one drawer on the stand and found magazines, utility bills, charge receipts, and a couple of mobile phone bills. Myron's name appeared on the bills and receipts. The tile floor was cracked and dirty. One spot had a faint stain on it, as if someone had made a half-hearted attempt to scrub something away. Maybe blood.

Moving to the first of two bedrooms, he found more papers on the floor, along with several articles of clothing. The clothes pockets were empty. Not much of significance in the papers, except for a pay stub from Pound Construction Company. He noted the name and left it. The bed looked as if it hadn't been made in a long time. Dirty sheets and pillow cases. A couple of shirts and a pair of jeans hung in the closet. Nothing in the pockets. The second bedroom was neater, having only a bed with no covers and a couple of bags of clothes from Goodwill atop the mattress.

He called Robin back and asked her to come over and go through the place. They arrived a half-hour later and went inside with their equipment. Dalton's phone chirped. Lt. Cobb. *What did he want?*

"I need to talk to you right away," his supervisor said. "In person."

COBB WAVED HIM to his office when he entered the work area. He went in and took a seat in the chair opposite the lieutenant's desk.

"I got some news on you I didn't expect," Cobb said, a frown on his face.

"Oh, yeah, what's that?"

The man glanced at his computer screen. "I'm looking at a story here on Chicago news that says you shot a Cook County Commissioner. Why didn't you mention that before?"

Dalton shrugged. "It was police business. I didn't think it was important."

Cobb's eyes narrowed. "The article says there're lots of unanswered questions, and the police haven't cooperated."

"Maybe you should talk to the police chief."

"I called him, and he said the records are sealed."

"Okay, that's why I didn't say anything."

"You're not making this any easier. I need to know what happened."

Shrugging, Dalton said, "I got cleared, and that's

all I can say. If that isn't good enough, do what you have to do."

The lieutenant stared for a moment, then shook his head. "Okay, that's all for now."

He got up and walked out, passing Steve Chase on his way to his desk.

The muscle head grinned. "Everything okay?"

So, he had found the story and told the lieutenant about it.

Fixing him with a smirk, Dalton said, "Nice going, rookie. I'll have to think about how to repay you."

Chase's eyes widened as the grin leaked away.

TWO

When Dalton got to his desk, he found an email from Robin with the victim's driver's license photo attached. After downloading it to his phone, he noticed a voice-mail light blinking on his desk phone. The M.E., saying to stop by.

The nameplate next to the open door read Dr. Everett Lake, M.D., Medical Examiner. The occupant sat behind his desk, working at the keyboard. Dalton tapped on the jamb.

"Ah, come in. Just about to send you a message."

He entered and took a seat.

"I finished the autopsy. The bullet was a soft-nosed 9mm, but it didn't kill him. Hit his skull at an angle and caused some damage, but didn't penetrate the brain. The trajectory of the bullet indicated that the shooter fired from about the same height as the victim's head, and was probably facing him. As you suspected, he was alive when he went overboard and had water in his lungs. Based on the body and water temps, and the condition of the tissues, I put the time of death between 5:00 and 10:00 p.m. yesterday."

"That recently, huh?"

"Yes, there was little deterioration." While Dalton took notes, Lake continued. "The tears in the skin of the fingers could have been made by the sharp ends of wire bindings. They were superficial, and a broken piece of wire was stuck in the hem of his jeans. So, maybe you were right about him undoing himself from some kind of weight."

"Can I see the wire?"

"Sure, step back here."

They went into the autopsy room and Lake picked up a plastic evidence bag with the wire inside. It would measure about two inches. Maybe 16 gauge. Easily twisted, and breakable if bent back and forth a few times. Dalton laid a dime next to it and snapped a photo with his phone. He thanked the ME and headed out.

The victim, maybe thought to be dead by the shooter, probably regained consciousness when he hit the water. He'd worked at his bindings and got them undone, but not in time to keep from drowning. Just thinking about it, Dalton drew a couple of deep breaths.

THE MARINA WHERE the 911 caller said he kept his boat was about a mile from where the body ended up. The dock master sat at a computer behind the counter in the office. His nameplate read *Mark*.

"Can I help you?" Mark asked, looking up from the screen.

"Sheriff's office." Dalton badged him and asked if he could confirm the timeline of car salesman Randy Lloyd.

"Sure, I was here when he left and returned. He takes his boat out a couple mornings a week. Heads out around 6:00 and comes back by 8:00 or so, usually with a bunch of fish. Offered me three or four pounds of them last week."

Given the distance from where the body was found, this marina could have been the place where the murderer had left from. Dalton showed Mark the license photo. "You know this man?"

The dock master studied the image. "Yeah, he maintains one of the boats for the owner. Something happen to him?"

"He's dead. Lloyd found him floating down the coast from here. You seen him lately?"

Mark frowned. "Dead, huh? That's too bad. He was here yesterday. Left in the boat an hour or so before dark, said he needed to check out the engine. The owner, Joe Pound, wasn't with him, but I didn't think anything about it. I'm not usually here that late, but I had to stay and help my night guy unload some supplies."

Pound was the name of the construction company that employed Myron, according to the pay stub in Myron's rented house.

Dalton gazed out over the marina. "Is the boat out there now?"

The dock master glanced at his security monitors. "No, it isn't. Guess it didn't come back in."

"Do you know how he got here?" Dalton asked, recalling the clunker parked at Myron's rented house.

"Couldn't say. He just passed by and told me he was taking the boat."

"You have any idea who might have wanted him dead?"

The man's eyes grew large. "Me? No, I didn't even know him except when he came in here."

Dalton got the boat registration number and left. In the car he searched his phone for Joe Pound, and found a home address and one for his construction company.

POUND LIVED A few blocks off US-1 on what appeared to be about an acre of land bordering Florida Bay. A boat dock was visible from the street. Dalton wondered if Pound's boat was tied up there. The house, a one-story stucco, spanned about half of the property with a wrought iron fence out front. A squawk box stood next to a drive-through gate.

Stopping at the microphone, Dalton pressed the button and waited. Nobody answered and he pressed it again. A female voice said, "Yes, who is it?"

"Monroe County Sheriff. I need to see Joe Pound."

"He's at his office. What's this about?"

"Just some questions I need to ask. No need for alarm." *Not yet, anyway.*

Dalton backed out and headed toward the company address on Plantation Key, about four miles north. A few minutes later he stepped into the offices of Pound Construction and faced a young blonde woman at a reception desk.

"Can I help you?"

He showed her his badge and said he needed to talk with the owner. Her eyes widened and she got up and went to an open office in the corner. A tall, overweight man dressed in khakis and a long-sleeve designer shirt stepped out.

"Sheriff's office? My wife called about you coming by. What do you need with me?"

"Can we talk privately?"

The man raised an eyebrow and waved him to his door. "Sure, by all means."

Inside, Pound took a seat behind his desk, leaned back and crossed his legs.

Dalton sat in a guest chair. "I wondered if you know the location of the boat you keep in Islamorada."

"Far as I know, it's at the marina. Why?"

"I noticed a dock at your home. Why don't you keep it there?"

Pound's eyes narrowed. "That's a company boat. I let clients use it. I keep my private boat in my boathouse. What's this all about?"

"Carl Myron took your boat out late yesterday and didn't come back."

"He's supposed to ask permission before taking it out."

Nodding, Dalton said, "He turned up dead this morning in the edge of Little Basin near Islamorada. Murdered."

The man frowned, his face coloring. He uncrossed his legs and leaned forward, elbows on his desk. "Are you kidding?"

"No, the sheriff's office doesn't kid."

Pound reached his hand up and massaged his neck, as if he had a sudden pain. "He's my wife's cousin, and she'll probably find a way to blame me."

"Is there a reason why she'd blame you?"

"No, no. It's just that I didn't want to hire him, and we had a big argument over it."

He didn't say any more, and after an awkward pause, Dalton broke the silence. "He have any other relatives close around?"

"No, his parents are dead. He has a sister in Ohio."

"You have her name? I'll need to let her know."

"No, but I can get it for you."

Dalton handed him a generic card from the sheriff's office with his cell number written in. It would be a week or so before he'd get some with his name on them.

"You know where he hung out, or who his friends were?"

Pound shook his head. "No. We weren't close at all. I just cut him a paycheck each week."

"So, you don't know of any reason he would take the boat?"

"No, I haven't seen it in a couple of weeks. I don't go down to the marina unless I need to meet with a client."

"Then I guess your boat is missing, and Myron could've been murdered on it. When's the last time you saw him?"

The big man ran his fingers through his hair and sighed. "I think it was day before yesterday. He does odd jobs for us. Hold on." He picked up his phone, made a call, and put it on speaker. A man answered, and Pound said, "Hey, Sid, didn't Carl Myron pick up some plans from the architect a couple of days ago and bring them by the site?"

"Yes, he did. I've got them right here."

"Have you seen him since then?"

Sid paused, as if thinking. "Don't think so. He left right away. Why do you ask?"

"He's dead."

"Huh, that's too bad. He seemed a little out of kilter, maybe a bad hangover. Was it pills and booze?"

"No. According to the sheriff's office, he was murdered."

Sid whistled. "Well, he was living out there on the edge."

"A detective is here asking questions. You know where he hung out or who he was friends with?"

"No. He seemed to be a loner."

Pound thanked him and hung up the phone.

"What did he mean about living on the edge?" Dalton asked.

The big man shrugged. "He was late a few times and we had to send somebody over to get him out of bed. We figured he was abusing drugs and alcohol. I would've cut him loose if my wife wasn't in the picture." He shook his head. "And now my boat's gone."

"You know of anybody who might have a reason to kill him?"

"Nooo. Like I said, we weren't close at all."

Dalton told him to call the sheriff's office if he thought of anything else, or heard anything about his missing boat. "The body's at the Medical Examiner's office in Islamorada, in case your wife wants to see him. We already have a positive ID on him, so it isn't necessary." Pound led him to the front door, as if eager for him to leave. Maybe thinking about what his wife would say.

Back in the car, Dalton wondered if the guy was telling the truth. He did appear surprised about the news, but seemed more concerned about his boat than the man's death. He also hadn't asked how Myron had been killed.

DALTON HAD A late lunch at a seafood restaurant. The place looked a hundred years old and weather-beaten, but his fish sandwich was maybe the best he'd ever had.

There didn't seem to be any other leads at the moment, so he decided to go back to his desk and research Pound's construction company, in case there might be some news stories that dished dirt about his business. The CSIs were returning as he entered the office. He waited for Robin to come by and asked what they'd found.

"Not much. I'll stop in after we've had a chance to go over everything."

At his desk, he ran searches and found a story about one of Pound's employees getting thrown in jail for drunk and disorderly conduct. The guy had gotten loaded in a bar, picked a fight, and broke some things. Not Myron, so he moved on. Another story detailed a lawsuit against Pound. He'd constructed a building for a man who skipped out without paying. It turned out the guy didn't have clear title and the owner wanted the building removed at Pound's expense. Nothing pertaining to criminal activity. There were lots of reviews on the company, most of them positive, only a few negative. All the negative ones were about trivial things.

Robin stepped in and took a seat by his desk. "I heard you had to go in to see the LT? Everything okay?"

Dalton waved it away. "Just some administrative stuff."

She raised an eyebrow. "Somebody said Cobb was all red-faced."

"I told you, it was nothing." *Everybody's pretty nosy down here.*

"Okaaay." After an awkward couple of beats, she looked over her notes and gave him a rundown of the crime scene, most of which he already knew. They'd found few fingerprints other than the victim's, but hadn't been able to identify them yet. No blood. The stain turned out to be red wine. She got up to leave.

No one else was in the room at the moment. "Wait," he said, "maybe we could talk later. You want to get a drink after work?"

She turned back, her eyes narrowed. "That your best pick-up line?"

He hoped she was kidding and smiled. "No, I just thought I might've been a little abrupt a few minutes ago."

"So your idea of apologizing is to invite me for a drink?"

"Well, I'm sorry, too. How's that?"

A smile crept back into her face. "Okay, apology accepted." She told him a place they could meet.

Dalton headed home a few minutes later. He lived in a guest cottage at a marina owned by his uncle on Little Torch Key. When he'd come to the keys a few months before for a security job, Uncle Eric had offered for him to stay until he could find a home of his own. It was a pretty nice situation, and Dalton hadn't looked very hard for another place. Besides, Eric, who was getting on in age, seemed to like having him there to help out with the marina.

He turned off the road to the long winding drive that led down to the water and the canopy of mangroves surrounding the marina. Houseboats and cruisers filled a couple of dozen mooring slips. Eric sat outside in the shade of the deck, an icy drink on the table at his elbow. Cupcake, their pet cat, sat on the deck by his chair. When Dalton exited the car and headed toward the deck, Cupcake ran to him, sprang up on his rear legs, and hugged him around the neck. A fully grown cougar, the cat probably weighed around one-sixty, but put surprisingly little weight on Dalton's shoulders.

"Rowww."

"Hey buddy, you having fun out here with Uncle Eric?" Dalton scratched behind its ears and the animal dropped down and ambled back to the shade. "He probably shouldn't be out here." He had rescued the big cat a few months before from Florida Wildlife, where it would have been euthanized.

"Don't worry about it. He likes everybody."

"Okay, I'll remind you of that when your regulars move somewhere else."

Eric took a sip from his glass, probably gin and tonic, his drink of choice, and waved away the comment. "How'd your first day go?"

Gazing out over the water of Pine Channel, Dalton inhaled the salty air and let it out slowly. "Think I'll need a cold beer before getting into that." He headed for his guest cottage next to the main house where Eric lived and operated the marina. Another five cottages dotted the landscape between Dalton's place and the water. Fishermen rented them by the day and week. They also rented fishing boats, bait, and saltwater tackle. Eric kept the slips and cottages booked most of the year.

He returned to the deck with his beer and took a chair next to his uncle. Before having a swallow, he held it to his forehead for a few seconds, enjoying the icy sting. Cupcake raised his head and parked it on the arm of his chair. He scratched the cat's ears and took a long pull on the beer.

"Rowww."

Dalton poured a few ounces in a bowl they kept on the deck. The cat lapped up the beer and then lay down in the shade, purring. He told his uncle about his case and about the other deputy's reaction at not getting the assignment. "Already made an enemy on my first day."

Eric scratched behind Cupcake's ears and sipped his gin. "Must not be much of a detective if they didn't give him the case."

Dalton thought he was probably right, and made a mental note to look into Chase's record and background. The deputy going after him on the first day wasn't a good sign.

A Sheriff's cruiser came into view down the driveway. Dalton wondered what that could be about. He got up from his chair and sauntered over as Lt. Cobb braked to a stop and got out, a scowl on his face.

"I talked with the sheriff. She said to pull your badge and service weapon until we get this Chicago thing sorted out."

THREE

"WHAT WAS THAT all about?" Eric asked.

Dalton shook his head. "I just got suspended."

"This is your first day."

"Yep." Dalton told him about his conversation earlier in the day with the lieutenant.

"So even though you were cleared in the Chicago shooting, they want to hold that against you?"

"I think the other detective I mentioned stirred it up. He probably found the news stories and gave them to the LT."

Eric drained his glass and set it down. He looked out over the marina, the sun drifting down behind the mangroves. "Because he didn't get the case. Sounds like a real loser."

"I need to look into his background. He might have some skeletons of his own."

He went inside and cranked up the laptop. A search on Steve Chase and the Monroe County Sheriff brought up several hits. Most were about minor arrests he had made, but one, a letter from the opinion page in the local newspaper, criticized his employment with the sheriff's office. It highlighted his promotion to detective after only five years as a uniformed deputy. The author, identified only as Concerned Citizen, said Chase had attended a private college for less than a year before getting kicked out for a drunken fight with another classmate. His father was a wealthy restaurant owner, and the author thought Chase had been given special treatment in his hire and his promotion.

Maybe he'd never investigated a homicide. That could explain why the lieutenant hadn't given him the murder case. Dalton wondered who had promoted him, and if that person had any connection to Chase's father.

Remembering his drink date with Robin, he glanced at the time. Already ten minutes late. He closed the computer and headed out. When he reached the bar, Robin's car stood waiting to turn out into the street. He pulled in and lowered his window. She looked steamed, but ran her window down as well.

"Hey, sorry I'm late, but I need to talk."

She stared for a couple of beats, then nodded and backed up and parked. He pulled in a few cars from hers and hurried back to her door.

"So I guess you have a good excuse," she said, her eyes narrowed.

"Yeah, I do. Let's go in."

The place was almost full, but they were able to get a table on the deck outside. The sun completely gone, a crescent moon shone high over the water. A waiter came and they ordered: margarita for her, beer for him. The man came right back with the drinks and she took a sip through the straw.

When they were alone, Dalton said, "The LT came by my place right after I got home and suspended me."

He watched her face for any recognition that she might already know.

She raised an eyebrow. "You just started today. What did you do?"

"I didn't do anything, but I think Steve might have sabotaged me with a story about my stint in Chicago." He told her about the meeting with the lieutenant and the discussion about his shooting of the Cook County official.

"Why wouldn't you tell him about it? You said you were cleared."

"The case is still open, and I signed a non-disclosure when I left."

"I don't understand. If it was still open, why did you leave?"

"It wasn't my case, and that's all I can say about it."

She frowned and took a long sip from her glass. "Okay, so what are you going to do now?"

"Guess I'll wait and see what happens."

Shaking her head, she said, "Huh, one day on the job." She leaned back and peered out over the water. "I've never been here. It's nice."

"Yeah, the crowd looks mostly like locals, maybe a few tourists." She just nodded, and after a protracted silence, he said, "Do you know why Steve would want to get rid of me?"

"Probably just jealousy. He's kind of a joke in the office. Nobody thinks much of his cop skills."

"How'd he get to be a detective?"

"Good question." She flashed a cagey smile. "It was

right before I came down here, and I heard a couple of deputies quit when he got the job."

They made small talk for a few minutes, then finished their drinks and left. He agreed to keep her posted on his situation.

DALTON WENT TO sleep around midnight, and sometime later woke to a clanging noise in the kitchen. He got out of bed, picked up his personal 9mm from the nightstand, and eased to the edge of the doorway. When he flipped on the light, Cupcake came in the back door, which stood ajar. He was sure he'd locked it before bed. The yard was fenced, and the cat had a pet door that let him in and out whenever he wanted.

Dalton grabbed a flashlight and went out to the gate, which he kept latched. It didn't have a lock on it, but he didn't think there was a need with a cougar on the grounds. Somebody had opened it, and the latch was still undone. Spatters of blood dotted the post and edge of the gate about a foot from the ground. He secured it and went back inside.

Cupcake met him at the door. He knelt and examined the cat's front paws. One had blood on the claws, as well as fabric threads. The cat had probably grabbed onto the leg of the intruder on his way out of the gate.

He retrieved a sandwich bag from the cabinet and pulled off several of the threads. Probably wouldn't ever get a chance to use the evidence, but it wouldn't hurt to keep it just in case. Using a tissue, he cleaned the blood off the paw and put that in the bag, too.

Why would someone break in? Whoever it was probably didn't know about the cougar. That left out every-body in the marina, because they all knew and stayed clear. The kitchen looked as it had when he'd turned off the lights, except for the coffeemaker, which was turned over on the counter. He supposed that had been the noise that woke him. Nothing appeared to be stolen. The door jamb and lock seemed to be intact, though an amateur could probably get inside using a credit card.

The cat had already stretched out on the floor and seemed to be snoozing. If nothing had been stolen, he wondered if there might be another reason for a break-in. A quick search of the cabinets yielded no answers. Nothing out of order. Items in the refrigerator were as he had remembered leaving them. Then he opened the freezer section. Everything seemed okay there, too. A couple of pizza boxes sat on the bottom, and several frozen food bags lay on them. The day before, when he'd returned from the market, he'd shoved the bags in on top of the boxes. Only one problem, the bag in front was one he'd purchased a week or so before. Upon re-moving all the contents, he spotted the reason why: a small plastic bag of white powder lay in the corner. He pulled it out and replaced the other items.

THE NEXT MORNING, he made coffee and took it out to the deck where Eric sat. A box of doughnuts lay open on the table.

"Help yourself," Eric said.

Several doughnuts were missing from the box, and the cougar lay next to Eric, licking his paws, as if he'd just ingested a couple of the treats.

Dalton took one and sat down. He told his uncle about the break-in.

Eric's eyes widened. "I don't believe it was anybody from the marina. All these people are pretty well heeled."

"I have a pretty good idea who did it." When he'd gotten back to bed the night before, he lay there wondering why Steve Chase would go to such lengths to get him booted from the murder case. One thing was for sure: it went far beyond professional jealousy. The guy *really* wanted him gone, so something else was in play. Could Chase have had some kind of involvement in the murder? It seemed farfetched, but so did evidence-planting.

He ate his doughnut and sipped the coffee.

A Sheriff's cruiser eased down the long driveway and stopped close to the deck. Dalton kept his seat. The deputies inside were the same two he'd seen at the scene where the body had been found. Colson, the one who'd done all the talking, sat behind the wheel. He got out and stepped over first. Deputy Jim followed.

"I heard you got suspended," Colson said.

"Something like that. What brings you out here?"

The deputy's expression turned serious. "We got a report that you have a controlled substance in your cabin."

"What are you talking about? Who called?"

"Anonymous. We need to take a look inside."

Dalton gave him a stare. "What if I don't let you?"

Colson shrugged. "We can get a warrant sent out, but we'll have to stay with you until it's delivered. Be simpler if you just let us have a look."

Cupcake rose up and the deputies jumped back.

"Whoa, where'd he come from?" Deputy Jim said.

Dalton reached over and rubbed the cat's ears. "Don't worry, he's harmless."

"You have a permit for him?"

"Of course." *Not.*

Dalton hadn't rescued the animal through strictly legal means, and hadn't pursued a permit for fear he would attract unwanted attention from Florida Wildlife.

Eric said, "Let'em in. You don't have anything to hide."

Dalton sighed and gazed out over the marina. "Okay, you can have your look, but don't take all day." He got up and led them to his door. Deputy Jim walked backward, keeping an eye on the cat.

Inside, the deputies went straight to the kitchen, glanced around for a few seconds, then opened the freezer. They rummaged around in there for a while, but didn't find anything but frozen food. Colson gave Dalton a smirk. After a search of the cabinet drawers, they went to the bedroom. The place being small, there were few places where something could be hidden. Then they scoured the small living room, and finally looked at each other and shrugged.

"Okay," Colson said, "caller must've gotten the address wrong."

Dalton nodded. "Yeah, must have. Did the caller say my name?"

Colson nodded. "He did, but it doesn't matter since we didn't find anything."

"It matters to me," Dalton said. "I want caller's number."

"Sorry, it was blocked."

"Okay, then, I'd like to listen to the recording."

The deputies glanced at each other and Colson said, "I don't know if you can do that."

"Sure I can. I'll stop by later."

When they got outside, he followed them to the cruiser. "Say, you know Steve Chase?"

Colson gave him a sidelong glance as he opened the driver's door. "Yeah, I know everybody there. Why?"

"I just wondered. He seemed pretty upset about me catching the murder case. You think he's a good detective?"

The deputy's eyes narrowed. "I guess he's okay. Listen, we have to get going. Sorry for the intrusion." He got into the car and they left.

Dalton went back to the deck.

"Everything okay?" Eric asked.

"Oh, yeah, fine. I'm going for another cup. You want one?"

Eric shook his head. "No, I already had two."

Cupcake got up and followed him.

Inside, he poured the coffee and sat down at the kitchen table. The cat lay at his feet, purring. It sounded like small boat motor. He scratched its ears and sat there thinking about what he might do. Things had gone downhill since he'd finished at the office the day before. Lt. Cobb didn't say what they would do to resolve the suspension problem, and the situation could easily deteriorate further if Chase had his way.

Being on the outside limited his options. He couldn't keep up with the murder investigation and determine if Chase really did have a connection. A call to the Chicago PD might help, but he wanted to do that only as a last resort. Still, he didn't want to wait for the deputy's plan B. It might be worse than planting the drugs, and he might not see it coming. There *was* something he could do, maybe pretty risky. After bouncing it around for a few minutes, weighing the ramifications, he took out his phone and punched in a number.

SAM MACKENZIE SAT under the awning on the rear deck of his boat, sipping on his second cup of coffee and perusing the newspaper.

"Hey, good morning," Jack Craft said from the dock. "Mind if I join you?" Jack lived aboard his yacht down the dock.

"Sure, come on over."

The older man stepped onto the boat and ambled over, his coffee mug in hand, and took a seat. "You remember the guy that helped out on that last job a few weeks ago, Mick Dalton?"

That last job had been one of Jack's con games, and Dalton had saved Sam's life by shooting a man about to kill him. "Sure, I remember him. Why?"

"Funniest thing. He got a job with the Monroe County Sheriff's Office."

Giving him a frown, Sam said, "Tell me you're joking."

Jack chuckled. "No, I couldn't believe it myself. I

knew he had a background in law enforcement, so I suppose it shouldn't come as such a surprise."

"Huh, how'd you find out about that?"

"That's why I'm here. He called a few minutes ago and said he's got a problem with the job. They assigned him a murder case on his first day, and then suspended him for what he thinks is a trumped up reason. And last night somebody broke into his place and planted drugs for the police to find."

"Somebody wants to get rid of him."

"Right, and he thinks it's another detective in the office."

Sam stared for a moment. "So, what does that have to do with me?"

Jack grinned. "He wants you and J.T. to give him a hand with his problem."

FOUR

DALTON SAT ON the deck overlooking the marina, finishing a BLT. The mangroves provided a mottled shade from the early-afternoon sun. A pleasant stirring of salt air, not quite a breeze, cooled the skin.

It had been three days since his suspension, and he'd had no further word on it. The trip to the sheriff's office to listen to the 911 caller had been fruitless; the caller's voice was unrecognizable, almost a whisper.

Jack Craft had called back and said Sam and J.T. would be willing to help. Sam's boat *Slipstream* was due in the late afternoon. One of the regulars had pulled out the day before to go cruising and wasn't expected back for a month or so. Eric had reserved the slip for Sam. It lay between two houseboats toward the end of the dock. This was the high season, and the marina stayed full most of the time.

When the boat arrived, Dalton ambled down and waited for J.T. to toss the tie lines. Once secure, Sam invited him aboard for a beer. They settled into chairs on the rear deck under the awning.

"I admired this place that time we visited you," Sam said glancing around the docks. "It's out of the way, but still within easy range of the other keys." He uncapped beers and handed them out.

"I appreciate you two coming down. I know this isn't your usual kind of gig. But I think you can help me out of this jam, especially with computer help from J.T."

He and J.T. hadn't had the warmest conversation the last time they'd seen each other, so Dalton was hoping they would be able to get along, at least until he could get the information he needed. "I suspect you have better databases than the sheriff's office."

"You suspect right," J.T. said. A smile teased at the corner of his mouth.

Dalton gave them a rundown on what had happened.

"What about this business in Chicago?" Sam asked. "You think that's going to get cleared up?"

"Oh, yeah. Chase just got them stirred up for no reason."

Sam raised an eyebrow. "No reason, huh?"

Shrugging, Dalton said, "Well, he had enough reason to plant drugs in my cottage. I just don't know what it is."

J.T. took a sip from his bottle and gave him a smirk. "You sure you want this job?"

Dalton thought for a moment. Did he really want the job? He wasn't sure. Like his previous position, it would be good and bad. "I'm not letting them railroad me."

"Okay," Sam said, "I owe you, so tell us what you want done."

"Steve Chase's background seems a little thin, so I want a full workup on him. And get all you can on the murdered guy Carl Myron. I have a hunch his death might be connected somehow to Chase."

"I can do that," J.T. said. "Nothing I hate worse than a dirty cop."

Dalton stared for a beat, wondering if J.T. might be referring to him, too. He turned to Sam. "I also want to canvass the bars with the murdered guy's picture. You can help me out with that."

J.T. brought up a list of all the bars in the area and Dalton and Sam agreed to split them up. Dalton sent Myron's driver's license photo to Sam's phone and gave him the keys to his car. He'd gotten permission from his uncle to use his pickup for a day or two. Before they left, he asked J.T. if he had a way to locate Pound's missing boat.

"Maybe, if I have the registration number."

Dalton gave it to him, along with Joe Pound's address, and they headed out, leaving J.T. tapping keys on his computer.

Dalton started with the places closest to Myron's rented home. The weather had cooled a little with an overcast sky. It made getting in and out of the air conditioned vehicle more tolerable. He found a bartender in the third place he entered who knew the dead man.

"Yeah, he comes in here every week or two. You a cop?"

"No, he owes me some money, and I need it."

The bartender, a skinny man with longish, frizzy hair just nodded, and Dalton wondered if he believed him. "You think any of your regulars would know where he is?"

"They might. He hangs around with a couple of guys. They're not here right now. Usually come in about six, but I haven't seen them in a few days. I think they work somewhere around here, though."

"You know their names?"

"They call one of them Buster. I don't know if it's his real name, though."

Dalton laid a bill on the counter. "How about calling me if they come in again?"

The skinny man grinned as he picked it up. "He must owe you a lot."

"Yeah, he does."

He left his phone number and headed to the truck.

Sam called before he reached the next bar on the list.

"J.T. said he struck out on the boat location. They probably found the GPS transponder and disconnected it. He did find the number of a phone registered to Carl Myron, though, and it's currently located somewhere out in Florida Bay. That might also be the location of the missing boat."

"Okay, I'm on my way back."

FORTY MINUTES LATER the three were on the water, dragging a dinghy behind and closing in on the location of Myron's phone. The GPS coordinates put it about five miles north of Islamorada in Florida Bay, and the map indicated a small island adjacent to it. About a mile out, a land mass appeared on the horizon. As they got closer, they could see palms and mangroves, but still no boat. Sam eased back on the throttle and said the depth finder showed just a few feet of water below the hull.

Dalton went to the bow and peered below for obstacles. A couple of minutes later he hurried back to the wheel house. "Probably should stop here. I can see a sandbar up ahead."

They set the hook, and Sam and Dalton got into the dinghy armed with handguns. Sam ran the motor and Dalton sat up front. He had brought J.T.'s handheld GPS unit and monitored it as they neared the coordinates.

"Go around to the other side," Dalton said.

As they rounded the little island, Dalton spotted an inlet shrouded with mangroves. "Turn in here. I think it's in this cove."

The boat came into view, nosed between two overhanging limbs. Sam cut the motor to an idle and they drifted to within thirty feet of the craft. The registration number painted on the hull matched that of Joe Pound's boat.

"Hello," Dalton called toward the craft, "anybody there?" After waiting a few seconds without an answer, he said to Sam, "Let's tie up on the shore."

After securing the line to a tree root, Dalton handed Sam vinyl gloves and stretched on a pair himself. The boat didn't appear to be secured, just wedged into the tree roots. A ripple of a wave rolled in and the hull rocked and scraped against one of the limbs. It let out a screech and Dalton's pulse fired up in his ears. He called out one more time before they stepped out of the dinghy. Sam covered him as he climbed onto the bow of the boat, and then followed him aboard.

The first thing Dalton noticed was blood spatter on the windscreen, and then the unmistakable odor. They eased along the port side and glanced into the wheelhouse and the open door of the salon. A man lay there, face-down on the deck, a crimson spot the size of a dime on the back of his head. Blood puddled underneath and decorated a wide area on the far side. Navigational charts lay on a nearby table, also spattered.

Muffled music played somewhere below deck. They passed through the salon and descended the ladder to a passageway with a berth on either side. The door to the captain's quarters at the end stood open. A man lay in a pool of congealed blood just inside. He appeared to have been executed like the man in the wheel house: bullet to the back of the head. The music had stopped, and an announcer offered a $500 discount on mattress sets if they could get to the store before ten.

Dalton pulled the dead man's wallet and found a Florida driver's license for Floyd Sparks. He snapped a photo of it with his phone and returned the wallet to the man's pocket. The front pocket contained a phone and some change, and he took the phone. Back topside, he got the other man's phone and took a photo of his license, too. His name was Eldon Perl, and he had smiled for the camera.

"We need Myron's phone," Dalton said.

After looking around for a few minutes without success, Sam said, "J.T. gave me the number." He called it, and the phone they'd taken from the man down below rang out with a loud rap song. "Okay, we have it. Let's get out of here." As they made their way to the bow, Dalton spotted a roll of wire on the deck next to the rail. It appeared to be the same gauge as the piece the ME had found stuck to Carl Myron's jeans. He pulled a dime from his pocket, held it close to the loose end of the wire, and snapped a photo.

Back on Sam's boat, J.T. weighed anchor, and Sam

and Dalton headed to the wheelhouse. "What do you think happened back there?" Dalton asked.

Sam started the engine. "That bunch probably did a drug deal or stole something and got double-crossed."

"Yeah, that's my impression. Carl Myron was probably in on it, but something went wrong and he got shot. I'm pretty sure that roll of wire I saw on the bow matches up with a piece of wire stuck in the hem of Myron's jeans. They used it to tie a weight to his ankles and threw him overboard, hoping nobody would ever find him. Then somebody got greedy and killed off those two on the boat. It had to be someone seemingly friendly to them. How else would he take both by surprise with a bullet to the back of the head?"

"Would've had to use a noise suppressor," Sam said. "And it might've been two shooters, instead of just one." He rammed the throttle all the way up to full power, as if eager to put distance between them and the dead men.

"No doubt, two would've made for a less risky operation. Pop them at the same time. But that would mean both the dead men knew and trusted two people who turned against them. That seems like a stretch. It's curious, though, that the killer didn't get rid of those bodies like they did with Myron."

"Maybe he was in a hurry."

Dalton stared out through the windscreen as they sped into the sun's glare. "Or didn't care. He had to know those guys would be identified when found, and must've been confident their trail wouldn't lead back to him."

When they got back to the marina, Dalton said, "I

need somebody to call in that boat location to the sheriff's office. Either of you have a burner?"

J.T. opened a travel bag and pulled out a flip phone. Dalton gave him the number, and he punched keys for several seconds, maybe twice as many as for the sheriff. When he got an answer, he said, "I was out fishing and saw a big boat that looked abandoned." He gave the person on the other end the coordinates and hung up.

"Why'd you enter all those numbers?" Dalton asked.

J.T. gave him a grin. "I called a transfer service I use on the internet. That way nobody can trace the call location back to the cell tower I pinged."

"Pretty clever."

"I think it is."

Dalton invited them to have a beer on the deck by the guest cottages. They ambled down the dock and headed for the shaded chairs where Eric and Cupcake sat.

J.T. spotted the animal up ahead and stopped. "Hey, what's that cougar doing over there?"

"Don't worry, he won't bother you," Dalton said.

"The last time I saw a cat like that, he knocked me down and sat on my chest. I almost had a heart attack."

"It's the same one," Sam said. "Dalton told me he adopted him. He never hurt you."

"Yeah, well, just the same, I think I'll go back to the boat and work on those phones." He turned and hurried off.

Dalton introduced Sam to Eric.

"Mick says you're a former SEAL, like him," Eric said.

Nodding, Sam took a seat. "That's right. Been a few years, though."

"Well, you watch his back. I think he has some enemies."

"I will. He saved my life a few months ago."

Eric gave Dalton a glance, his eyes narrowed. "How'd he do that?"

Sam hesitated, maybe trying to decide how much he should tell.

Dalton said, "I'll get us a beer," and headed for his cottage.

An hour later they were back on the boat to see what J.T. had found.

"I went through the calls on both phones," J.T. said. "They talked back and forth to each other the day before Myron's body was found. And there were calls on both phones to the same number the night Myron took the boat out. I tried to identify the owner of that number, but couldn't find an account associated with it. Probably a burner."

"You try calling it?"

"Yeah, no answer."

"That's interesting," Sam said. "Myron wasn't afraid of using his own phone, but the person he called didn't want to be identified. Maybe the fourth person in the mix."

"The one who double-crossed everybody," Dalton said. He pondered that for a few beats, wondering if Chase could have been the fourth man. "You learn anything about the deputy I mentioned, Steve Chase?"

J.T. shook his head. "Not much. I scanned his arrests, but didn't find any links to Myron or the two dead men. His father is wealthy and probably has a lot of local connections, so I need to dig into that a little more. Myron isn't from this area, but I looked into his background, too. He grew up in Ohio. His parents are dead. Dad's name was Bruce Myron, mother's maiden name, Louise Nash. He has a sister who still lives there."

"That matches with what Joe Pound told me," Dalton said.

"I also got some history on Floyd Sparks and Eldon Perl, the two dead men. Both served time in prison with Carl Myron. It appears they were all on the same burglary that went bad."

"You see any nicknames for either of them?"

"Yeah, Perl goes by Buster, instead of Eldon."

"A bartender I talked with said one of the men Myron hung out with was called Buster."

"Probably these guys, then."

Eric phoned and said he was having a cookout with burgers and beans. The three headed over to the deck for an early dinner, and J.T. seemed pleased that the cougar wasn't in attendance. After eating, J.T. went back to his computer, and Dalton and Sam headed out to cover the rest of the bars on their lists.

An hour or so later, Sam called Dalton. "Hey, one of the bartenders remembered Carl Myron coming in a few days ago and meeting a woman. It stuck in his mind because the woman was a real looker, and they seemed like such an unlikely pair. He didn't recall either of them ever coming in there before, and they didn't stay long. The timeframe matches up with the night before Myron left with the boat."

FIVE

WONDERING ABOUT THE woman Myron had met at the bar, Dalton drove back to the landlady's home next to the dead man's rented house.

"You remember me?" he asked through the screen door.

"Yeah, I remember. What's wrong now?"

"Your former tenant is still dead. Just trying to tie up some loose ends. You have a few minutes?"

The woman had a beer can in her hand, starting early. "Yeah, I guess so. Come on in."

He entered and stood in the center of the drab living room.

"Sit anywhere. You want a drink, a beer maybe?" She held up her can for him to see, as if to convince him she had the good stuff.

"Yeah, sounds good." Dalton thought she might be more forthcoming with information if he shared a drink with her. He took a seat on a threadbare sofa and she headed down the hall, flip-flops smacking the backs of her heels.

When she returned and handed him a can, she said, "You can pop your own top."

"Sure thing. Thanks." He snapped the tab and took a sip.

She sat in an easy chair across from him, a saucer-sized ashtray filled with dead butts at her elbow. "I like a cop who'll have a drink on duty." Some of her words whistled through the gap between her front teeth.

Dalton nodded. She probably had no way of knowing about his suspension. "Do you know if Myron ever had guests over to his house?"

"Right down to business, huh?" When Dalton didn't respond, she continued. "He had a visitor every now and then. Don't know if I would call them guests, though. Usually it was somebody bringing him home when he was in the tank. Couple of times they sat on the porch and had a few more beers."

"Can you describe the people you saw?"

"Nah, I never paid much attention. It was always late, after my talk shows. In the dim light they all just looked like bums."

"What about women visitors?"

She started to shake her head but stopped. "You know, he did have a woman come by a week or so ago, around five in the evening. I thought maybe she was somebody trying to sell him something. Stayed about twenty minutes and left."

Maybe the same woman the bartender had told Sam about. "Can you describe her?"

"Long blonde hair, shapely, and looked like a lot of class. Not somebody who'd be visiting him unless she wanted something." She frowned. "Ain't you going to drink your beer?"

"Oh, yeah." Dalton smiled and took a long swallow. Her frown disappeared. Though she liked having a cop take a drink with her, she obviously didn't want any of it wasted.

"You remember what kind of car she drove?"

"Yeah, a Mercedes, and it looked brand new." Her words began to slur.

ON HIS WAY home to the marina, Dalton thought about the woman with the Mercedes. The landlady was the second person to say she outclassed Myron. Maybe his cousin, Joe Pound's wife? That would account for her dropping by to check on him. He wondered, though, why she would meet him in a bar at night. Maybe to give him money? Joe Pound had said he didn't want to hire her ex-con cousin, and had done so only upon his wife's insistence. If she gave him money, too, she probably did it without her husband knowing.

At the marina he found a note on his door from Eric saying he was down on Sam's boat having drinks. He headed that way and found them on the rear deck.

"These guys are all right," Eric said. Several empties sat on the table next to his chair. "C'mon, join us. I was just telling them how I know Jack Craft."

Funny, his uncle had never told him how he knew the man. He'd just given him his phone number when he arrived in The Keys and told him he might be a good source for finding employment until his paperwork with the sheriff went through. Sure enough, Jack had given him some assignments, not all of which were legal.

"He and I flew missions together in Southeast Asia," Eric said.

J.T. said, "You mean Vietnam?"

Eric shrugged. "There, and some other places."

"What kind of missions?" Sam asked.

The older man seemed to mull that over, maybe deciding what he could tell. "We transported things. Jack was the pilot. I was navigator."

"I didn't know Jack was ever a pilot, or in the military?" Sam said.

"He was an excellent pilot, but we were private, not military." He paused, and then turned up his beer for a long drink, as if to indicate that was all he would say about that. "We've kept in touch all these years. He helped me get established down here." Eric finished his drink, bade them goodnight, and headed up the dock.

Dalton said to J.T., "I've been thinking about Joe Pound's wife. She's Myron's cousin, and she might be the one Sam mentioned who met with him at the bar. I talked with his landlady and she said a woman driving a new Mercedes visited him about a week ago."

"I looked up the Pounds when I first got here," J.T. said. "They've been married a little over a year. He looks older than her in their wedding photo. Hold on." He went inside and got his computer. "Here, take a look."

The wedding photo had been taken under an arbor next to the shore. Joe Pound appeared stuffed in the tux, his face flush as if embarrassed. His new bride, in all-white, radiated youth and beauty, but also seemed uncomfortable in front of the camera, maybe for a different reason than her husband. He looked mid-fifties, and J.T. was right about the age difference: she was probably thirty, at the most. She had long blonde hair.

"Did the newspaper do a story on the wedding?"

"I didn't find one," J.T. said. "This photo is from Joe Pound's social media pages. She didn't seem to have any accounts."

"Huh. She could be the link to Deputy Chase and Myron. Dig deeper on her."

SAM CALLED AT nine the next morning and said J.T. had some information if Dalton wanted to drop by. He'd gotten up an hour earlier and had coffee and a bear claw on the deck with Eric and a couple of the marina guests. His uncle had taken his advice and kept the cougar inside the fence while guests were expected. After a last sip of coffee, he headed to Sam's boat.

The two sat on the rear deck under the shade of the awning, J.T. at his computer.

"You were right," J.T. said. "Joe Pound's wife drives a new Mercedes."

"So she's probably the woman who met Carl Myron."

"Probably, but I found something else. It took some digging. She has a Florida driver's license issued a couple of years ago under the name Heather Scott, and the information on it agrees with the birth certificate she provided for her marriage license. Both indicated her age as twenty-eight at the time. So far so good. Then I searched for her birth record in her hometown in Ohio, and it checked out. Only one problem: I also ran across an obit for a Heather Scott who died in an auto accident in that same town two years ago. Everything matched up."

Dalton smiled. "So Heather Scott is an alias."

"I'm pretty certain."

"That means she might not be Myron's cousin, either," Sam said.

J.T. nodded. "Probably right. So maybe she was pulling Myron's strings on this job, whatever it is, and he ended up dead. Then she killed the other two on that boat and took whatever they stole."

"If they trusted her enough to let her board," Sam said, "she could've shot both of them. I still think another person might have been involved, though. She could've distracted them while the other took them out, one at a time. Or they could've each taken a shot. Could be her husband, or maybe Deputy Chase."

Dalton nodded. "Maybe. It would help if we knew what the dead men had on that boat that led to their murders." He turned to J.T. "Did you look up news stories on crimes during that time."

"Yep. I didn't find anything that fit. Since you know when Myron left with the boat and when he turned up dead, that nails down the timeframe. Several places got robbed that day in Miami, and even a couple of convenience stores in the Keys. Nothing stood out as a big haul like this must've been, though, and none of them seemed to involve the use of a boat."

"How about home invasions?" Dalton asked. "Lots of wealthy people live next to the water on these islands and around Miami."

J.T. shook his head. "If it happened, it didn't get the attention of law enforcement or the news."

"Whatever got stolen," Sam said, "was from somebody who couldn't afford to report it."

Dalton mused over that for a minute or so, and then said, "We need to find out Heather Pound's real name." Turning to J.T. he said, "You have a phone number for her?" J.T. nodded and gave it to him. He used one of the burner phones to call her. A woman answered. It sounded like the same voice he'd heard on the intercom at their gate the day he'd visited, so he hung up. "She's home, so I'm going to stake out her house and follow her if she leaves. It might be a big waste of time, but I don't have anything else going on right now."

Sam said, "While you do that, we could take a look inside the deputy's home."

"You're kidding, right? That would be pretty risky." It did sound tempting, though.

Sam shrugged. "Maybe for you. If a witness sees us it isn't a problem. Nobody knows us around here." He glanced at the time on his phone. "He's probably at work right now, and we can be in and out in a few minutes."

"You okay with that?" Dalton asked J.T.

"Sure, I'm going stir crazy on this miserable tub."

"Hey," Sam said, scowling.

"Oh, sorry." J.T. smiled. "I meant to say *this luxury yacht*."

"That's better."

Dalton swung by the landlady's house on his way and got a snappish reception. Probably still had a hangover from the night before. He showed her the Pound's wedding photo with the husband cropped out of it.

"Is this the woman you saw visiting Carl Myron?"

"That looks like her. You think she killed him?"

"Probably not, but she might know who did."

He left and headed to Heather Pound's home. When he reached to within a block of the address, he searched for a spot where he could pull to the side of the road without being easily noticed. A vacant lot with a *For Sale* sign on the far side of the street provided the cover he needed, with a palmetto thicket standing a foot or so over the roof of the truck. He backed into the drooping fronds, leaving enough visibility so he could still see the entrance to Pound's property.

More than an hour passed without any activity, and then the gate swung open and a Mercedes sped out onto the street. He waited until she got a couple of blocks down before following. She went over to US-1 and drove a mile or so before turning into a shopping center and then a restaurant with an outdoor dining deck. Heather joined a couple of other women at a table on the deck. She grabbed a waiter as he passed.

Dalton got out of his car and took the nearest vacant table. He ordered the fish, which the menu purported as fresh daily, and a beer. While his table was too far away to hear what the women said, he had a clear view of them from his seat. They appeared to all know each other and went straight to their menus while they drank. The waiter brought them a second round before taking their order. Maybe a regular luncheon for them.

The fish arrived within a minute or two of the time the women got their food. Dalton took his time eating, and after a few minutes the waiter brought the check. As he finished, the women paid and left. He dropped a bill next to his plate and hurried by their table, grabbing Heather's glass inside a napkin as he went past.

SAM AND J.T. drove to a car rental agency to pick up a nondescript vehicle. They found Chase's address and made their way north on US-1 to the condo complex where he lived in unit 231. They parked in a visitor space close to the door, noting that Chase's spot was marked with his condo number. No residents seemed to be around, maybe all of them at work.

The rear of the condo bordered the ocean, which was visible through the breezeway next to the stairwell. If not for his wealthy father, Sam would have wondered how the deputy could afford the place on a law enforcement salary.

They stretched on vinyl gloves before climbing the stairs to the second floor. Sam knocked on the door and rang the bell. Nobody answered, so he pulled his picks from his bag and worked them in the lock. A minute later they slipped inside. The place didn't appear to have an alarm; the owner was a Sheriff's deputy and probably thought he didn't need one.

The kitchen lay on the right, a living room on the left, all one large open space. Sliding glass doors led from the living area onto an expansive balcony and a panoramic view of the Atlantic. A hallway pointed to the rest of the house. They eased down it and found an office on the right. Bookcases lined one wall, but there were few books, all adventure novels. A desk held a laptop computer and a printer. A gun safe about five feet tall stood in the corner.

J.T. went to work on the computer while Sam checked the desk. Bills for utilities, insurance, and condo maintenance littered the surface. A piece of note paper containing what appeared to be a phone number lay on the corner. Sam put it in his pocket. Older monthly bills were stuffed in the top drawer. Gun magazines filled the bottom drawer, one for each month going back a couple of years.

Sam knelt in front of the safe and took his gear from his bag. He stuck listening cups around the lock and snapped on the power to the smart-phone-sized gadget. Spinning the dials, right first, then left, he watched the display for indications of the sound of the tumblers falling into place. Within a couple of minutes he popped the door open. Two handguns lay on the floor of the safe. Rifles, two carbines and one assault, hung from brackets on the walls. A sawed off shotgun also hung there. The deputy liked his guns.

A handgun would be the most likely weapon for killing the men on the boat. He checked the magazines on both, one a 9mm and the other a .45, and found three rounds missing from the 9mm. He sniffed the barrel tip and thought the gun had been fired recently, but couldn't say for sure. A full box of 9mm cartridges lay in the corner of the safe, so the deputy hadn't failed to reload because of lack of ammo.

He headed down the hall, passing a bathroom, to a master bedroom on the left. An unmade king bed stood in the center of the room, an open closet opposite it. Shirts and pants hung on the hangers. What appeared to be dirty clothes and a couple of pairs of running shoes lay on the floor of the closet. No boxes, bags, or anything else that might contain booty. The top drawer of the nightstand next to the bed held a couple of gold

chains that might have cost a hundred dollars each. Fit-
ness mags lay in the bottom drawer.

A guestroom across the hall had a bed and a nightstand. The room looked as if no one had ever slept there.
Sam took a cursory look inside and found nothing of
importance. He sighed and headed back to the office.

"How's it going?" he asked J.T.

"Almost finished."

"Okay, we've already been here twenty minutes."

"I'm working as fast as I can."

Sam stepped over to the window and peered down.
A minute or so later he saw a car turn in and park.

"Time to go. Chase just pulled into his parking
space."

SIX

"I TOLD YOU Chase is on his way up," Sam said. "You need to cut it off, now."

J.T. glanced at him. "Almost done."

"Okay, I'm leaving." He started toward the door.

J.T. gave him a scowl, but jerked the flash drive from the computer and punched the power button.

They exited the condo, unable to spend time relocking the deadbolt, and hurried up the stairs to the third level. Sam leaned around the corner so he could see Chase's door.

The deputy trudged up the landing and inserted his key into the keyhole. When he twisted it, he stopped for a beat, and then turned it back and forth a couple of times, maybe wondering if he'd left it unlocked. Shrugging, he pushed inside and closed the door behind him. Sam and J.T. stayed where they were for a minute or so, and then Chase came back out and locked the door. He twisted the knob a couple of times, maybe to be double sure, and headed down the stairs. Sam and J.T. waited until he started his car and pulled out of the parking lot before leaving.

ON DALTON'S WAY back to the marina, after getting the glass with the fingerprints, Eric phoned. He said he was watching TV when a news alert came on talking about two men who had been murdered on a boat.

"They said the police are at Hingle Marina right now, investigating the scene. You know anything about that?"

He didn't like lying to his uncle, but the less he knew about those bodies the better. "No, but Hingle is only a mile or so from where I am, so I'll swing by there and take a look." He thanked him for the call and hung up.

The marina parking lot was nearly full, and twenty or more men and women stood behind yellow crime scene tape gawking at the boat about fifty feet away. The Medical Examiner's van stood close by. Dalton edged his way to the front.

Deputy Chase pushed through the crowd and ducked under the tape. He headed to the boat and stayed a few minutes before returning. "Nothing to see here, folks. You need to make room; we're coming through."

A couple of minutes later, the ME's team rolled two gurneys up the dock. Each contained a black body bag with a lumpy shape inside. Robin Marlowe trailed behind the group, seeming lost in thought.

"Get back," Chase said to the crowd as the investigators pushed underneath the tape and loaded the bodies onto the van.

Robin caught Dalton's eye and mouthed the words *Call me.* Chase seemed to notice the interaction and turned to see the recipient of her message. He stepped under the tape and headed over to Dalton. "What're you doing here?"

"I heard about it on the news and thought I'd stop by."

The deputy motioned for him to follow, and they made their way to a spot outside earshot of the crowd.

"You need to leave. This doesn't concern you."

"I'll be coming back to work in a day or two, and this'll be my case again. I need to know what's going on."

Chase narrowed his eyes. "You're on suspension. Lt. Cobb hasn't said anything to me about getting that lifted."

Dalton huffed a laugh. "Sounds like you're not in the loop."

The deputy's face reddened. He grabbed Dalton by his shirt front. "Why don't you take a swing at me? It'd be a shame if you got locked up for attacking an officer of the law."

One of the onlookers videoing them with his phone caught Dalton's eye. "I think you have it backwards." He nodded in the direction of the camera.

When Chase saw what was happening, he released his grip, took a deep breath, and strode away.

Dalton drove home and carried Heather Pound's cocktail glass into his cottage. He dusted it for prints and lifted several that looked promising. When he finished, he glanced out the window. Sam and J.T. were getting out of the car, and he went out to meet them. "What'd you find?"

"Not much," Sam said. "J.T. has some computer files. Maybe something will be on them."

"You have any trouble?"

"Chase drove into the parking lot as we finished up, and I didn't have time to lock the deadbolt going out. I watched him open it, and it was pretty obvious he noticed it was unlocked. He didn't appear to think anything of it, though. We left everything as it was."

Dalton shrugged. "No big deal."

"I'm gonna get started on these files," J.T. said, holding up a flash drive. He turned and headed toward the dock.

Sam pulled a piece of paper from his pocket and showed it to Dalton. "I found this on Chase's desk."

"Looks like a phone number."

"I think it is, but it doesn't match any of the numbers on the dead guys' phones. We'll check it out." Sam put the note in his pocket. "How about you? You get any track on the Pound woman?"

"I followed her to a restaurant and got some fingerprints from a glass. Don't know how much help they'll be, though. She'd have to have prints on file somewhere to get a match. You know if J.T. can get into AFIS?"

"Huh, good question," Sam said, "I'll ask him."

"Okay, let me know. I'm going inside and make a call."

As Sam sauntered off down toward the dock, Dalton punched up Robin's number and headed back to his cottage.

"Hey," she said, "I haven't heard from you in days. Are you okay?" Robin with the beautiful eyes, concerned about him.

"Sure, doing fine. Just waiting for the lieutenant to get me cleared to go back to work. You heard anything about it?"

"No, I ran into him in the hall yesterday and asked when you would be returning. He gave me a dirty look and said, 'Why do you want to know?' I told him I didn't mean to pry, and then he seemed to soften up and apologized, said he had a lot on his mind."

"Yeah, I imagine he does, especially if Chase is running the investigation."

"Well, that's the thing. Cobb is running it himself."

"Huh. I didn't see him at the marina."

"He was there earlier and left. I heard him call Steve and ask where he was, that he needed him there for crowd control."

Probably just using the deputy for errands and leg work.

"Who did investigations before I was hired?" Dalton asked.

"The last detective, a man named Foskey, got killed on the job. That was early last year. From what I understand, he'd been here about ten years. Came down from somewhere up north, like you. After that, several detectives rotated in from other places to fill in. They never closed Foskey's case, though, maybe because nobody stayed long enough."

"They identify any suspects?"

"No. He was killed in a drugstore parking lot. There were no witnesses, and the store's cameras were too far away. Bullet to the back of the head."

It sounded like an execution. "You have any other murders since him?"

"There were a couple of drug killings, and one guy got murdered by his wife. The rotation guys solved them because the killers were dumb, left DNA and prints in the wrong places. We also have an infrequent body wash up on the Gulf shore after a bad storm. Most are immigrants from Cuba, and the cause of death is usually drowning. No bullet wounds like our man Myron."

"How did those guys on the boat die?" Although he already knew, he thought it would seem odd to Robin if he didn't ask.

She hesitated, maybe wondering if she should tell him since he was on suspension. "Both shot in the head."

He thought about Heather Pound's prints. Robin might run them for him as a favor, but it would get her in trouble if anybody at the office found out about it. Even if exposing the woman's true identity helped solve the murders, Cobb would want to know where she got the prints.

"You still there?" she asked.

Back to Robin of the beautiful eyes. "Yes, still here. You want to get a drink later, maybe dinner?"

"All these questions, I wondered if you were going to get around to asking."

He could see her smiling in his mind's eye, and something fluttered in his chest. "So, what's your answer?"

"I can go at seven."

"I promise not to be late this time."

They made plans to meet at the same restaurant they'd been to before. He hung up, got a beer, and headed down to *Slipstream*.

Sam sat on the rear deck, a beer in his hand, the sun reclining off to the west. The remains of a sandwich lay on a table near his chair. "J.T. said it's a no-go on AFIS. The last time he tried getting in there, the FBI got onto his trail, and he doesn't want a repeat of that."

A dolphin swam by, rolling its dorsal fin to the surface every few feet, maybe searching for mullet or shrimp.

"No problem," Dalton said. "I thought it was a long shot, anyway. He find anything on Chase's computer?"

Sam drank from his beer bottle and set it down. "I'll let him tell you about it. Wait here; he needs a break." He went inside and returned with J.T. in tow.

"Not much on the computer," J.T. said, setting the laptop on a table. "He didn't send many emails. There were a few to his supervisor, Cobb, saying he couldn't come in because he was sick. Usually on Mondays. A recent message to a person with a user name *RollT* just said, 'Call me.' One message to somebody named Robin invited her to go out, but I didn't find a reply. Most of the emails he received seem to be spam marketing that he didn't delete."

So Chase had attempted inroads with Robin. She might've ignored the invitation, or saw him at the office and gave her answer. The thought of them being together seemed a little unsettling, but not really important in the scheme of things. "This *RollT*, any way to figure out who he is?"

"Maybe, I'll give it a shot."

"How about social media. He have any accounts?"

"Just Facebook. Only has a few friends, just family and a few cop connections. His messages are pretty lame, just turning down invitations to family get-togethers, stuff like that. His documents folder was almost empty, just a resume going back several years, and some photos of himself."

"Huh, I thought there would be more," Dalton said.

"There was an email from his phone carrier a couple of years ago indicating he had selected a data plan, which means he has a smart phone. Probably uses text and voice for most of his communications. Speaking of phones, I checked out the number on this note paper." He held up the note Sam had shown Dalton earlier. "It belongs to a CPA in Islamorada named Rudy Banks."

"I wonder why he would've written down a CPA's number."

J.T. sighed. "Don't know, but there's nothing unusual about that. Somebody probably referred him, and Chase got his number." He closed the computer, stood, and headed back inside.

Sam gave Dalton a grin. "I think he's getting impatient. He said he has some things to attend to and needs to leave tomorrow. I told him I'd drop him at the airport."

Dalton's phone chimed and he took it out and glanced at the display. He rejected the call and stood. "Gotta get going. I have a date. See you two in the morning. Eric might have breakfast on the deck about eight."

Sam gave him a questioning look. "Okay, sounds good."

Dalton strode to his cottage and returned the call.

"Hey, I couldn't talk."

The voice on the other end said, "I haven't heard from you since you got canned."

"Not much to report."

Silence. A couple of seconds passed. "You need to get back in there. I can intervene—"

"No, that's okay." Dalton paused for a couple of beats. "I need you to run some prints, though."

"Send them to me." The connection died.

SEVEN

DALTON'S PHONE CHIMED. He didn't recognize the local number, but answered anyway.

"Is this Michael Dalton?"

"Yes, who's calling?"

"This is Lola Ann, Channel 6 News. I wondered if I could interview you on these recent murders."

"I'm not with the sheriff's office right now."

"I know! I heard about that. Can you tell me what happened? My sources tell me you worked on the job for only one day before being suspended."

"Who gave you my number?"

"Someone at the sheriff's office."

Probably Steve Chase, thinking Dalton would get himself into more hot water if he spouted off to the TV station.

She said, "We could meet and talk for a few minutes. Off the record, of course."

Off the record. Fat chance. In addition to the murders, she probably wanted to pick at him about why he got suspended. Dalton had seen her in action on TV. A beautiful woman, but a barracuda if there ever was one. He thought about it for a few seconds and wondered if he might flip the action around.

"Okay, I guess I could spare a few minutes."

They made arrangements to meet at ten the next morning. Dalton hung up and headed out for his date with Robin.

She sat in her car waiting as he drove into the parking lot. When she got out, she smiled and said, "Right on time."

The host gave them a table on the deck outside, near the spot they'd sat the time before. Both ordered beer. He chose fried jumbo shrimp, she a shrimp salad.

When he told her about the interview she said, "Tell me you're not serious. Lola Ann is a smear queen. She trashes all her guests."

"Yeah, I know. I'll keep that in mind."

Robin's smile said, *You're an idiot.*

"I wonder who gave her my phone number?"

She shook her head. "Wasn't me, that's for sure. Maybe HR."

"I don't think they would hand out personal phone numbers. They worry too much about lawsuits."

"Yeah, you're right. I don't know, then."

The food arrived and Dalton took a couple of bites. "These shrimp are delicious."

"I know, mine are, too. So, what have you been doing with all your free time?"

"Mostly, helping my uncle with the marina." A lie. He had done almost nothing for Eric since he'd lost his badge and felt a little guilty about it.

"What kinds of things are there to do at a marina?"

He told her about assisting the customers with their boat moorings, keeping the docks repaired and clean, helping keep the store stocked with supplies, and taking care of their pet cougar.

"A cougar, really? Where did you get a cougar?"

"I adopted him shortly after coming to the Keys. His name is Cupcake." He told her the story about the owner getting killed and the state's plan to euthanize the cat. "I had to fence off an area when we got him. He's pretty domesticated, but I didn't want him to go wandering off terrifying the customers."

"So he doesn't bite?"

"Never known him to."

She leaned forward in her chair and laid her arms on the table, her eyes aglitter with excitement. "I want to see him! Can we go by there tonight?"

"You bet."

A while later she laid her fork down on her plate. "Steve Chase came by this morning and said somebody has been rounding the bars asking questions about Carl Myron and his friends. You know anything about that?"

He furrowed his brow. "What, you think it was me?"

Shrugging, she said, "I hadn't really thought about it, but Steve thinks it was you, said you were telling bartenders Myron owed you money. He told Cobb, so he might call you about it."

They left a while later and she followed him to the marina. He invited her into his cottage and made coffee. While she sat on the sofa, he brought the cat in from outside through the kitchen. Cupcake rubbed his head against Dalton's knee as they made their way to the living room. When the cougar saw Robin, he got to within a couple of feet of her and sat. Leaning toward her, he sniffed the air.

Robin seemed nervous, but excited all at once. "Hello, Cupcake."

Almost a whisper, the cat said, *"Rowww."*

THE NEXT MORNING, Sam took J.T. to the airport. When he returned, they had ham biscuits and coffee on the deck with Eric. The customers had already come in for breakfast and left, so Eric let Cupcake out to join them. He ate the meat from two biscuits, leaving most of the bread behind, and stared at Eric until he gave him a third helping.

When Eric took the cat back inside the fence, Sam said, "J.T. gets bored pretty quick if there's no money involved."

"I understand. This isn't his cup of tea. Yours either for that matter."

"If we need more research, though, he'll do it." Sam took a sip of coffee and glanced out over the water where a pelican dived for a meal. "I gotta say, though, you might be barking up the wrong tree trying to nail this deputy. We haven't found anything that suggests he's involved in these murders."

Dalton nodded. That didn't mean Chase was innocent. They just hadn't found the right thread to pull. "Maybe later today we can check out the CPA who owned the telephone number you found in Chase's condo."

Sam gave him a grin and a shrug. "Sure, just let me know." He stood and headed to his boat, and Dalton left for his appointment with Lola Ann.

THE REPORTER SAT at a deck table outside a restaurant, a cameraman setting up a few feet away. So much for *Off the Record*. Dalton parked and headed over.

Lola Ann stood when he approached and shook his hand. She was even more beautiful in person, with the long auburn hair, inviting blue eyes, perfect white teeth. "Thanks for agreeing to meet with me. Are you okay with the camera rolling?"

He gave her a smile. "Sure, that's fine."

She paused, as if surprised he would agree so easily, then turned to the cameraman and gave him a nod. They took a seat at the table and Lola Ann turned toward the lens and gave her beaming smile. "I have suspended deputy Michael Dalton with me today, and hopefully he will give us some answers we haven't been able to get from the local sheriff's office." Turning to Dalton, she said, "So, Mr. Dalton, I understand that—"

"Mick."

"Pardon me?"

"You can call me Mick."

She looked toward the camera and gave a big grin, showcasing those beautiful teeth. Barracuda. "All, right, then, Mick it is. So, Mick, I understand that you were a deputy with the sheriff's office for one day before being sent home. Can you tell us a bit about that?"

He gave her a dismissing wave. "It's just some administrative thing with the application process. Should be cleared up in a day or two."

"You say it was an administrative thing. Can you be more specific? Our researchers at Channel 6 news say it has something to do with a case you worked in Chicago before coming here."

"I'd say your researchers don't have much to do, Lola Ann. I'm not saying any more about that."

"There must be more to the story—"

"Move on."

The reporter narrowed her eyes, glanced at the cameraman, and ran her index finger across her throat: *cut it*. "Okay, Mr. Dalton—"

"Mick."

She sighed, "All right, *Mick*, let's get something straight. I control the interview and I'll ask the questions that I deem important. Is that clear?"

"Hey, you asked me for an interview. We can end it now if you want."

After staring for a moment, she gave him a smirk that said *I'll get you later*. Nodding to the cameraman, she turned back with the TV smile. "All right, Mick, can you tell us about this murder case? Since last week, three murders have been discovered. Do you think they're related?"

"The first murder victim left the marina in a boat the day of his murder. A couple of days later, two more murder victims were found on the same boat. So, I'd say they're related."

"Do you know if the sheriff's office has any suspects who might have perpetrated these cold blooded killings?"

Dalton shook his head. "I don't know the answer to that. But I hope to be back at work soon. I know they have their hands full at the sheriff's office, and I can solve these murders."

"Do you know something they don't know?"

Dalton gave her a smile. "I have a lot of experience closing homicide cases."

"Tell me more about that, all those cases you've solved." She gave him a smug grin, as if he'd given her an opening she wanted.

"Ask those researchers you mentioned. I'm sure they'll fill you in." He stood and strode away.

ON HIS WAY home, his phone chimed. Lola Ann.

"That was a pretty nasty thing you did," she said.

"Sorry, I didn't care to have my background laid open on network news. That wasn't part of the deal."

"Well, I don't know how much of the interview I can use."

"You're a pro. I'm sure you'll figure it out."

She remained silent for a few beats, and then said, "You got in a plug about all your homicide experience, telling them they need you back."

"Sorry it didn't work out the way you wanted."

"You're not sorry, but hey, I actually like your style. My folks pulled up a number of interviews you gave while in Chicago, and I could tell you were working the press, rather than the other way around. Normally I don't get anything out of law enforcement around here. We could probably help each other when you go back to work. Why don't we get a drink and talk about it?"

"Sure, I'm game."

He hung up as he arrived back at the marina. Sam

and Eric sat on the deck, a large pitcher of lemonade on the table between them.

"How'd it go?" Eric asked, pouring him an icy glassful.

"Not bad. It'll probably be on the news tonight." He sat down and took a long drink from the already sweating glass. It hit the spot, so cold it gave him brain freeze. Turning to Sam, he said, "Let's go check out that guy we talked about." Before leaving, he went inside and got his personal handgun from the drawer in his nightstand.

Rudy Banks, CPA, had an office in a shady strip mall a block from the Overseas Highway. Sam agreed to go inside and pretend to need accounting services for a new business. He came back within a few minutes.

"His receptionist caught me as I went in the door and told me if I had an appointment Rudy wouldn't be able to see me today. She said he sent her a text a few days ago saying he would be out of town for a while, and she had to cancel all his appointments." Sam stared out through the windshield for a few beats, and then said, "This might be the link you've been looking for."

"Why do you say that?"

"The receptionist said he's never texted her before, and he hasn't answered any of her calls since then."

EIGHT

"I GUESS BANKS doesn't do that well in the accounting business," Dalton said.

They sat in the idling car across the street from a small, rundown home in Tavernier. A rotting picket fence surrounded the front yard.

"He's young, probably just starting out. Here's a photo." Sam held up his phone and showed him an image of the CPA's website. A dark-haired man, maybe a couple of years shy of thirty, smiled back at them.

The house didn't have a garage, and no vehicles were present. Next door stood a two-story quad apartment building with a couple of rusted cars out front. It, too, looked in bad repair. A palmetto thicket separated it from the house.

"Maybe we should take a look inside," Dalton said. "Can you open the door?"

Sam nodded. "Shouldn't be a problem."

Dalton turned into a parking spot outside the fence and they stretched on vinyl gloves before getting out.

At the door, Sam knocked a couple of times without an answer. He opened the cheap lock using a credit card while Dalton watched for onlookers. They pushed inside to a small entry hall. The living room lay to the right. A cheap sofa sat alongside the interior wall opposite a large-screen TV playing a muted sports program.

A table appeared askew next to the end of the sofa. It held a lamp with a busted shade. Two beer cans and shards from a broken light bulb lay underneath the table.

They pulled their handguns and eased through the rest of the house, but didn't find anybody. Everything appeared orderly, the beds made. A pair of socks rolled together lay on the floor next to a chest of drawers. Two lightweight suits hung in the closet. In the corner sat a small desk, and a light film of dust on its surface outlined a spot where a computer might have rested.

Dalton looked inside the drawer of a bedside table while Sam searched the chest of drawers, neither finding anything of significance. A search of the bathroom yielded only toilet articles. They retraced their steps to the front door and left.

In the car, Sam said, "Looks like something happened to Banks while he watched the ball game."

"Yes, it does. They were careful to put the lamp back on the table, but missed the broken bulb. Banks is a neatnik, and I don't think he would've left it that way. I believe they searched the place, too, and his computer was gone."

"So he knew something about one of his clients that he shouldn't have known."

"I'd say."

"I guess the question is: why did the deputy have Banks' phone number on a piece of paper?"

Dalton had thought about it. "The guy could've left a voicemail on Chase's work phone, and he wrote it down to call later."

Sam stared for a moment, maybe wondering why Dalton was easing up on the guy. "Why would he call *him*, though? If he wanted to report some criminal activity, it would seem likely he would call the sheriff's number."

"I don't know," Dalton said. "He might know him personally, and wanted to keep his call low key. Most people in that position wouldn't want it known that they squealed on a client. We need to know who the client is."

"From the looks of his home, he might not have many. We could visit his office tonight and have a look at his files."

Dalton nodded, staring through the windshield as he drove back toward the marina. If he was still with the sheriff's office, he would have to get a warrant and everybody would know about it. This would be a lot simpler, and if they didn't find anything, nobody would know they even looked.

They stopped at a café and had burgers and beer. Dalton's phone chirped as he finished his sandwich. He glanced at the display and answered.

The voice on the other end said, "The prints you sent belong to a woman named Wendy Nash, convicted of passing bad checks in Ohio."

"Okay, thanks."

"Keep me posted." The connection dropped.

He told Sam about Heather Pound's identity.

"Nash? J.T. said Carl Myron's mother was a Nash. So maybe they were cousins after all."

Dalton wasn't sure this new information would help. The woman could've changed her name to clean the slate, so she could marry a semi-wealthy builder in the Florida Keys. Nothing seemed to be panning out. His leads so far, suspicious on the surface, could be explained away. On the other hand, Wendy Nash could be a career criminal with the capability to kill three men, and the reason why the deputy wrote down Banks' phone number might not be so innocent. Dalton kept going back to the cocaine somebody had planted at his cottage. There was nothing innocent about that. Somebody wanted him off the case.

DALTON AND SAM waited until dark, although the CPA's receptionist had been gone for more than an hour. A popular restaurant and a couple of trendy shops provided the strip mall with plenty of business at that time of day. They parked on the block behind the area and walked around to the end of the development. Nobody appeared to be hanging around the rear of the offices, but they donned ski masks in the case of cameras. Sam provided vinyl gloves, and they stretched them on before heading to the back door to Banks' office.

Sam worked at the lock for a few minutes and they were in. The back room appeared to be where they kept a coffee maker and office supplies. The reception area lay directly ahead, down a short hall. Light from the outside shone through a window, casting a shadowy glow. They found Banks' private office and entered and closed the door. He had a window that provided a view of the green area that separated the strip mall from the back yards of the residential area behind it. There were no drapes over the window, so they used penlights.

A keyboard and monitor sat on the desk. Loose wires lay in the well underneath where a computer had resided. Behind the desk chair, against the wall, stood a file cabinet, but all the drawers were empty of any files. The cabinet looked well-used. Miscellaneous scraps of paper, dust, and paper clips lay in the bottoms of the drawers.

The desk had a lock that secured the drawers, but Sam opened it with a twist of his pick. As Dalton expected, they found nothing of value inside. They exited the office and eased to the receptionist's desk. An appointment book lay open with entries scratched through, probably where she had canceled meetings with clients. Whoever had searched the office had left her computer in place, maybe thinking it wouldn't have any client files on it, and maybe not wanting to alert her that her boss was gone for good.

Sam booted up the machine. There was no password, and he went straight to email. A few messages to clients apologized for not being able to meet as scheduled, that Mr. Banks had to leave on an emergency. Other emails appeared to be communications with the receptionist's personal acquaintances and businesses. Sam ran the word processing program and found a few letters to clients that seemed innocuous. The spreadsheet program had only one file named "Client List." He brought it up and printed it.

BACK AT THE MARINA, Sam followed Dalton to his cottage and they looked over the list. There were only a dozen or so, and only one name stood out as familiar: Lyndon Chase. It had to be the deputy's father, who owned restaurants in the area. Landing that client had to be quite a coup for Banks, a relative newcomer to the business. Dalton did a computer search and found that he owned three local eating establishments and two in Miami.

"He could be the one," Sam said. "Has to be worth a fortune, and probably didn't make it all legitimately."

"Yes, could be. But it might explain why Banks might know Steve Chase and called him to keep his whistleblowing on the down low. Since he wouldn't call him about something his father did, we need to search on the others, too."

Sam shook his head. "Wish J.T. was still here. He could help with that, for sure. I'll call and give him the names. If he's where he can use his computer, I'm sure he'll run them down for us."

Dalton's phone chirped and he glanced at the display: Lt. Cobb. "I need to take this."

Nodding, Sam picked up the list and headed out the door as Dalton answered.

"I caught your news debut tonight with Lola Ann," Cobb said, louder than necessary.

"I suppose you didn't care for it."

"No, I didn't. You should've mentioned this to me before doing it. We have a strict policy on personnel giving press interviews."

Dalton gave it a couple of beats before saying, "You remember, I am on suspension."

"Doesn't matter. You should've asked first."

"Okay. Is that all? I was in the middle of something."

Silence for several seconds. Maybe Cobb was fuming, trying to get his temper under control. "No, it isn't. The sheriff saw the news, too. I guess she liked your little show, because she called and said to put you back on. Report to my office Monday morning." He hung up.

NINE

"GOOD TO HAVE you back, Detective," Cobb said to Dalton from across his desk.

"Nice to be back, Sir."

Cobb handed him his badge and service weapon and then picked up a file. He paged through it, a look of concentration on his face. "I want you to pick up this convenience store robbery. It happened early this morning."

"Sure, glad to."

"The clerk pulled a gun and the robber shot him and cleaned out the register. The clerk is still alive in the hospital. Uniforms went out on the call and wrote it up. The report says the store has security footage."

The lieutenant leaned back in his chair. "We need to find this guy soon. It's got the business community scared he'll hit another store."

"What about the murder I was working on?"

Cobb paused for a few seconds. "Did you see the news last night?"

"No, what happened?"

"Joseph Pound committed suicide. Shot himself with a nine mil. He left a note claiming responsibility for the killings."

Dalton's pulse thumped in his ears. How could that

be? The guy hadn't even been on his radar. "Was that all the note said?"

"He said those guys were stealing from him. The ME is still examining the body, but the sheriff said to close the case if it turns out to be suicide."

"Did you interview the wife?"

"Yes, she was in tears. Said her husband seemed worried about something. He went to his office about ten Saturday night saying he had to take care of something. An employee found him the next morning in his office chair. Apparently, he'd been drinking, and a half-empty bottle of booze sat on his desk."

Something didn't sound right. "So you're keeping the case."

Cobb nodded. "For now."

Dalton suppressed an urge to roll his eyes. "Is there anything else?"

"No, that's all." He handed him the robbery file. "Oh, yeah, one more thing." He gave him a smirk. "No more press interviews without prior approval from me."

Dalton stared for a couple of beats, and then nodded and left.

At his desk he perused the robbery file. Not much else he could do before going out and viewing the video. He pushed the file aside and got a cup of coffee from the break room. On his way back he stopped in to see Robin. A typed piece of paper, enclosed in a clear evidence bag, lay in front of her. Her eyes looked weak, her hair frazzled, as if she'd been up all night.

She smiled. "Hey, you on the job again?"

"Yep, Cobb assigned me a robbery that happened

this morning." He pointed at the evidence bag. "That Joe Pound's suicide note?"

She nodded and glanced outside her workspace. The other CSIs appeared to be away on a break. "You want to sit down and take a look?"

He took the chair next to her desk and she handed him the note. It read: *Heather, I'm sorry about your cousin. I didn't mean to kill him or the others. They were stealing me blind and I had to do something. I caught them in the act and things got out of control. I hope you will forgive me. Joe*

"Typed," Dalton said. "Anybody could've written it."

"It was written on the computer in his office. The document was still on the screen when we got there, and the hardcopy was in the printer tray."

"You check him for gunshot residue?"

"Yes. He had it all over his shoulder and the sleeve of his right arm."

"How about his wife?"

She gave him a stare. "You get the case back?"

He shook his head. "No, Cobb's keeping it."

"Steve stopped by earlier and said Cobb is ticked off about you doing that press interview, and he didn't think the case would land in your court again. He seemed pretty gleeful about it."

"Yeah, he would be. You check the wife for GSR?"

"Yeah, we did. She didn't have any."

"Was the gun registered to Pound?"

"No, the serial number was filed. It might be the same gun that killed Myron and the others. We'll have to wait and see if there's a match on the slug the ME pulls out of Pound."

He glanced at the note again. "Any prints on the paper?"

"No, none. Apparently, he didn't touch it after printing it out."

"How about prints on the computer keys?"

She raised an eyebrow. "Only his."

Dalton laid the document on her desk, took a sip of the coffee, and stood. "So, you think he did it himself?"

"Sure looks that way. I can't say I'll be disappointed if this one gets closed."

"Were you here all night?"

She gave him a pained smile. "That obvious, huh?"

"Yeah, why don't you go home and get some sleep."

Dr. Lake sat behind his desk signing a document. Dalton rapped on the open door.

The ME looked up and motioned for him to enter. "You have a nice vacation?" He, too, looked tired, and he wore tattered clothes that he probably reserved for yard work on the weekend.

Dalton smiled. "Not really. I heard about Joe Pound. Did you make your determination yet?"

Lake gave him a twisted frown. "Getting there. I need to take another look at the body."

"Why is that?"

"Just a minor detail, but it bugs me. According to the report, alcohol was involved. He certainly smelled of it, but I didn't find any in his blood."

Back at his desk, Dalton mulled it over. Did any of

the circumstantial information he'd gathered since being suspended disprove the suicide theory? Even if it did, he couldn't use it as evidence. Whatever happened to the CPA might have nothing to do with the murders. His phone number on a note in Steve Chase's condo didn't incriminate anybody, either. Joe Pound's wife using a fake name didn't mean she had anything to do with the murders or his alleged suicide. The suicide seemed open and shut, except for the alcohol level, but Pound's wife could say she was mistaken about how much he'd been drinking. He wondered if he should just move on and let them close the case. Then he remembered the cocaine.

Dalton looked up the location of the evidence room and headed down the hall. The custodian, a sergeant, sat at a desk inside the cage.

He showed the man his badge and introduced himself.

"I heard you were on board and then got sent home. You're back now?"

"Yes, as of this morning."

The sergeant nodded. "So, what can I do for you?"

"I wanted to ask about some evidence that might be linked to a case I'm working. You have anything back there from a recent drug bust?"

The man in the cage opened a book and ran his finger down a list. "Yeah, looks like we seized some cocaine a couple of weeks ago. It must've come in at night, because I don't remember it."

"Does your list say who brought it in?"

"Yeah, Detective Chase."

"Can I have a look at it?"

The sergeant shrugged. "Sure, why not." He found the location on his list, and then opened the cage door for Dalton to enter. They wandered through a maze of metal shelves until the custodian found the box and pulled it down. He laid it on a table in the rear of the room and opened it. It was full of small plastic zip bags containing the drug. All ready for distribution. The bags looked a lot like the one someone had planted at his cottage.

Dalton checked the evidence sheet taped to the top of the box. It indicated that there were 25 bags logged in. "I guess nobody has removed any of these bags for any purpose."

The custodian took the box top from him and glanced at the entries. "Nope. Nobody has touched this box since it came in. You have a reason for asking?"

Shrugging, Dalton said, "Not really. It's just that a small amount of cocaine showed up somewhere, and I wondered if this might've been the source."

"It didn't come from this box." The sergeant frowned, as if his integrity had been questioned.

"You mind if I count the bags?"

Rolling his eyes, the man said, "Knock yourself out. I'll stand here and watch."

Dalton stretched on vinyl gloves. He took them out one by one, counting out loud as he did so, and placed them on the table. The total came to 24. "One short."

"I don't see how. The records show nobody's opened this box."

"You want to count them?" Dalton asked.

"No, I watched you. The count must've been off when the deputy brought them in."

Dalton stared for a couple of beats. "Yeah, that's probably what happened."

"What case did you say you're working on?"

"A robbery." He turned and headed for the door, and the sergeant let him out.

ACCORDING TO THE REPORT, uniformed deputies had questioned the store clerk on the scene before being carried off by EMTs, and he couldn't identify the robber. Dalton swung by the hospital to ask again if he'd remembered anything that might help identify the man. He found the patient sleeping and decided to come back later.

The convenience store was only a couple of miles away. The store manager, a man with graying hair, led him to a backroom and set up the security video for him to view. It showed a man walking into the store wearing a hoodie, shielding his face from the camera, and then disappearing from view to the rear of the store. There was never a clear image of his face. A minute or so later he appeared at the counter wearing a ski mask and holding a gun. A couple of seconds passed, the two staring at each other. No audio, but the man in the mask thrust the gun at the clerk, and must've given him an order. He opened the register, paused for a second, and grabbed a handgun from under the counter. Before he could bring it up, the man with the mask fired. It appeared that the round hit the clerk's shoulder, and he fell back against the cigarette shelf and dropped down out of sight. The shooter leaned over the counter and peered at the man on the floor, and then emptied the register and ran out of the store.

Dalton's phone chirped. When he answered, Sam said J.T. had gone over the names on the CPA's client list. Dalton told him to hold on and walked outside so he could have a private conversation.

"All of them are small-time except for the deputy's father and a woman named Lucinda Toole. She owns Toole Parts, a wholesale auto parts business that sells throughout Florida."

"Huh. Wonder how Banks got her account?"

"I don't know, but she's headquartered in Key Largo, and J.T. said there's something fishy about her business."

"Yeah? What?"

"Said she doesn't have a web presence."

"No website?"

"Nothing on the internet, at all. He said he had to get the information from her business license records with the city."

"That does sound curious. I need to check her out."

"You need my help?"

"Yes." He told him about the alleged suicide and the sheriff wanting to close the case. "Everything seems to fit a little too perfectly."

"You don't buy it?"

Dalton sighed. "I suppose it ties up all the loose ends, at least the ones the sheriff's office knows about. But they don't know about Heather Pound using a fake ID, or about Banks disappearing and Chase having his phone number written down. They also don't know about the cocaine somebody planted at my cottage."

Sam remained silent for several seconds, and then said, "You know, I'll be glad to stay and help as long as you need me, but is it possible you're following these seemingly suspicious leads down a dead end?"

"I don't think so. There are too many coincidences. I'm convinced whatever happened to Banks is related to these murders."

"Okay, you're the detective. Just let me know what you want to do next."

"We need to visit Lucinda."

"Well…if you're determined to go with this. There *is* something J.T. found that's interesting. Lucinda's ex-husband is a man named Leonard Orlov."

"Orlov. That name sounds familiar."

"Yeah, he was in the news last year, accused of killing a Miami shop owner."

TEN

DALTON WENT BACK inside the store to finish the video. He ran it through several times. There was also footage from a camera with an outside view. It showed the robber approaching on foot from around the corner of the store and leaving the same way. Neither view provided even a partial image of the robber's face. Dalton froze the frame as he reached for the money. His hands were pale in the dim light, and he wore clear vinyl gloves. Tattooed letters on the knuckles of his right hand spelled P-U-R-E. Probably jailhouse ink. If so, he would be in the system. Dalton printed a copy of the screen and then got the manager to burn him a copy of the video.

He noted the time the shooter entered the store and when he exited. Outside, he ambled around the corner to the rear of the building where he found only a narrow space between the store and a raised natural area. A getaway car couldn't have parked in such a small space, but a bike or scooter could. Also, the robber could have walked from the access road about a quarter mile away.

The store was located in a U-shaped shopping area with trees in the center. He drove around to the opposite side and scanned for cameras. Though he spotted several, the distance and the trees would likely render any video images unusable. As he drove toward US-1 on the access road, he spotted a gas station tucked back in the trees and turned in.

He went inside and held up his badge for the clerk. "I'm investigating this morning's robbery of the store over in the shopping center. You have video of the road outside?"

The young man behind the counter nodded. "I think so, but I don't know how to operate it. You want me to call the manager?"

"Yes, please do."

The clerk got on the phone and spoke for a minute or so before turning to Dalton. "He wants to talk to you."

Dalton explained about the robbery again and why he needed the video. The manager said he could let him view it, but couldn't get there until later in the day. They agreed to meet there at 5:00 p.m.

As he left, he noticed a camera mounted directly inside the plate glass window pointing at the gas bays and the access road beyond it. The robber would probably have had to go by on that road.

SAM MET DALTON in Key Largo. They rode in Dalton's car and found the address of the Toole Parts Company. Though in a commercial area, it sat at the edge of Blackwater Sound. Sam had agreed to go inside, look the place over, and hopefully talk with Lucinda Toole. There was no sign out front. A Mercedes SUV sat in the driveway.

Sam opened the door and stepped inside. It didn't look like much, just a small room with a desk and an empty chair. An open door on the left led to what appeared to be a private office. Shuffling sounds emanated from the doorway.

"Hello, anybody here?" Sam called.

A beautiful woman in snug jeans came out. She had dark hair, large eyes, and full lips, and she seemed short of breath. Drops of perspiration dotted her forehead. "I thought I heard somebody come in. What can I do for you?"

Sam smiled. "I'm opening an auto repair business and need to set up a parts account. Are you the owner?"

The woman hesitated, then said, "Yes, but we're in the process of moving to a new location. If you'll leave your name and number, I'll have someone call you once we're settled in the new place."

"Sure, that'll work."

She picked up a pen and a pad from the desk. "Okay, shoot."

He gave her the name Daryl Moore and the number of one of the burner phones J.T. had left behind. "You moving close by?"

"Not too far." She glanced at a watch on her wrist.

"Okay, I hope you get moved soon. I plan to open shop in a couple of weeks."

"Yeah, should be a matter of days."

When he headed toward the door, she said, "By the way, how did you hear about us?"

He turned back and said, "Found you on the internet."

Her eyes widened, and she remained silent for a beat too long. "Oh, okay, good. We'll call you."

Back in the car, Sam said, "Lucinda looks like a

movie star, but I think she wanted to get rid of me." He related his conversation.

Dalton nodded. "Sounds like she could be skipping out. Maybe she's the one the CPA got in trouble over. We need to wait a while and see where she goes." He drove down a block and turned the car around so they could watch for her exit. "You said she seemed surprised when you said you found her on the internet?"

"Yes, she did."

"Since she doesn't have a website, she knows somebody is onto her."

"I'd say."

An hour passed before she came out the door, loaded three boxes into the Mercedes, and drove away. They let her get down the street a couple of blocks before following.

She went about three miles before turning into a neighborhood, and then entered the driveway of a residence. A small moving van sat out front, and two men were loading furniture.

Dalton said, "Get the address and ask J.T. to find out who owns the place." He kept going past, and neither the woman nor the men appeared to notice them.

Sam dialed up J.T. and gave him the information. He said he would have to call them back later. Dalton took Sam back to his car and headed for his appointment with the gas station manager.

THE MANAGER MET Dalton as planned and set him up with the video for the last 24 hours. Dalton zeroed in on the timeframe he'd written in his notebook. He guessed it would take a few minutes each side of those times for the robber to walk through the wooded area between the crime scene and the gas station. During that window he viewed more than fifty vehicles on the access road. Some of them turned into the station and headed toward the pumps. No motor bikes or scooters were in the bunch. One car pulled over to the side of the station, outside the camera's view. It was an older sedan that appeared dark blue or black and had only the driver inside. The car remained there about ten minutes before leaving. Because of the angle of its entrance and exit, he couldn't see the driver's face, and got only part of the license plate number. It appeared to be a Florida plate, and he wrote down the part he could read. He reran the videos again before leaving, but didn't find anything else of note. The manager burned him a copy of the selected timeframe and he left.

On his way to the office, he swung by the hospital to see the store clerk. Terry Munson was awake and had just finished a meal. He appeared to be late teens. Dalton showed him his badge. "Now that you've had some time to think about what happened, tell me what you remember about the man who shot you."

"He wore a mask, so I couldn't see his face."

"How about when he entered the store? Did you get a glimpse of him then?"

The young man frowned for a couple of beats. "I think I was ringing up a customer, because I didn't notice him coming in. He just appeared at the counter with the mask and pointed the gun at me."

"You think he was young or old?"

"Old. Maybe thirty or forty."

Dalton grinned. "Did you notice the tattoos on his knuckles?"

His eyes widened. "Yeah, I did! One hand had PURE tattooed on the knuckles, and the other had EVIL. I'd forgotten all about that."

Dalton made a note in his pad. "Okay, anything else? Do you remember his eye color, and eyebrows?"

"I think his eyes were like this real light blue, and his eyebrows were blondish. I could see them through the holes in the mask."

Nodding, Dalton said, "That's good." Sounded like the man was probably fair skinned and fair haired, unless he'd bleached his brows and wore colored contacts. He asked a few more questions, but the kid couldn't come up with anything else.

It was after six when Dalton arrived back at the office. Everyone appeared to have gone for the day, except Cobb, who came out and sauntered over. "You make any headway on the robbery?"

Dalton nodded. "A little. The video didn't reveal much, but I did get this." He showed him the printed copy of the tattoo image of P-U-R-E on the man's knuckles. "I also spoke with the store clerk, and he said the other knuckle had E-V-I-L tattooed on it. He told me the guy had blue eyes and blondish eyebrows. I figure his ink is from prison, so we might find him in a database."

Cobb grinned and tapped on the side of the workstation. "Good work. Keep at it and get this guy." He turned and walked away.

Dalton brought up the Florida Department of Highway Safety database and entered a search for the partial license number he'd seen on video. It yielded more than thirty plates. About half were registered to males, and only four of them lived in the Keys. There was no assurance the robber was driving his own vehicle, but he thought he'd start there. All of them were retirement age or older, except one. Lance Holder, age 36, lived in Marathon. He owned a 2005 black Chevy Impala.

A search of the DMV brought up Holder's photograph. Blond hair, blue eyes. Dalton thought he was probably looking at the robber. He printed the screen, and then punched up the FBI's database and entered Holder's name. It found him in a matter of seconds. Same guy, although he looked a little different with short hair. He'd served a couple of years for assault. Dalton phoned the sheriff's office in Marathon and asked them to pick the guy up on suspicion of armed robbery. "Tell the deputies to use caution. He shot the clerk at the store he robbed."

"You're sure he's the guy?" the watch commander asked.

"Maybe 98 percent."

"Okay, we'll get him if he's still here. I'll let you know."

The office was bare, except for the duty sergeant up front and a couple of uniformed deputies. Cobb had been gone for an hour or so. Dalton eased over to Steve Chase's desk and pressed the voicemail button on his phone. It asked for a password. He surveyed the desk for potential places Chase might have written one down. When he didn't find any scraps of paper or anything taped under the phone, he checked the center desk drawer and found a pad. Thumbing through it, he found a note that read VM 8686. Voicemail took the password and said he had no new messages and two saved messages.

The first saved message was from the HR office saying he needed to stop by and fill out a new form for insurance. When it ended, the second message started up: "Hey, Steve, this is Rudy Banks. I'm your dad's CPA. I have a problem I need to talk to somebody about. One of my clients, I'm pretty sure, is doing something illegal, and I don't know what to do about it. It's making me nervous. Please call me." He left his number.

Dalton hung up and went back to his desk. So the guy had called Chase to report a crime. That could shoot a hole in his theory that Chase had the number for some conspiratorial reason. The question, though, was what did the deputy do about it? It was unlikely, given the message Banks had left, that he just wrote down the number and forgot about it. Of course, he could've called and Banks was unable to answer. In which case, the deputy might've forgotten about it, assuming the guy would call again if he really had a problem.

The duty sergeant at the front desk rang his phone and said a deputy from Marathon was on the line for him.

"This is Dobson, down in Marathon. We're at the address on Lance Holder's license, but nobody's here. It's a rental house with a sign out front. Looks like nobody's been here for a while; a pile of mail is on the porch."

Dalton thanked him and hung up. It had seemed too easy, and it was. Tracking the guy down might be more difficult than figuring out the face behind the mask. On his way out, he stopped at the duty sergeant's desk and asked him to put out an APB on Holder's vehicle.

When he got home, he headed down the dock to Sam's boat. "It's time to force the issue on Banks' disappearance," he said to Sam.

"How do you intend to do that? Nobody knows he's missing but us."

"I have a plan."

THE NEXT MORNING, Sam borrowed Eric's pickup and drove to Banks' office. Inside, he met the same receptionist as before. "Your boss back yet? I really need to see an accountant."

She shook her head. "No, and I'm getting worried. I can't get him to return my calls."

"Huh, maybe you need to report it. Better safe than sorry."

"Should I call 911?"

"Probably be better to call the sheriff's office directly. I think I still have a card a detective gave me." He searched through his wallet and pulled out Dalton's card.

DALTON CHECKED IN at the office and briefed Lt. Cobb on the robbery suspect. "I'm going down to Marathon in a few minutes and hit the bars and stores with his photo. Somebody has seen him and will tell us where he's gone." Cobb seemed pleased that he'd identified the guy.

He went back to his desk and glanced at the time on his computer: 9:15 a.m. Sam had said he would be at Banks' office at 9:20, and if things worked as planned the woman would call within minutes after that. The expected time came and went, and Dalton began to wonder if the employee had decided to wait a little longer for her boss to return. Then, at 9:40, his desk phone rang.

"Is this Detective Dalton?"

"Yes, who is this?"

"This is Barbara Spain. I work for Rudy Banks, the CPA, and I think something might have happened to him. He's been gone for over a week and I can't get in touch with him. He'll kill me for calling if he's okay, but I'd feel a lot better if somebody would check on him. I went by his house, but he wasn't there."

"Okay, give me your address, and I'll drop by."

Ten minutes later he arrived at Banks' office and went inside. Ms. Spain told him about the text Banks had sent her the week before.

"Can I see it?"

She brought it up and handed him her phone. It read: *I'll be out of town for a few days. Cancel my appointments.* Anybody who had Banks' phone could've sent it.

"You haven't heard from him since?"

She shook her head. "No, and I've texted several times without a response. I've called, too, but he didn't answer. It isn't like him to ignore my calls."

Dalton nodded. Under normal circumstances, he probably never ignored her calls. She was in charge of his office, but she was also an attractive young woman.

"The last time you saw him, did he seem worried about anything?"

Her eyes narrowed for a moment. "As a matter of fact, he did seem concerned about something. He'd been out to visit a client. When he came back, he went in his office and closed his door. He almost never closes his door."

"When was that?"

"It was about 4:00, the day before I got the text from him."

Dalton took out his notepad and compared the time and date with that of the voicemail he'd heard on Chase's phone. It matched up within a window of about ten minutes.

"Did he say anything about his client visit?"

"No, he just came in and went to his office."

"Do you know who he went to see?"

"Umm, I don't know. Let me think." She seemed to puzzle over that for a moment, her eyes narrowed, and then smiled. "Oh, yeah, I remember. It was Toole Parts. Ms. Toole was a new client who wanted him to do a financial statement, and he had some questions about her inventory. He couldn't get her on the phone and said he thought he'd drive up to Key Largo and take a look at her warehouse."

Dalton didn't remember seeing a warehouse anywhere around Toole's office, and that might've been the problem Banks wanted to talk with Steve Chase about.

"Do you have the address?" She gave it to him and he made notes. "Can I see his computer?"

She stared for a moment, and then sighed. "I really

hope nothing is wrong. If he's just on vacation or something, he'll be awfully upset if I let somebody look into his computer."

"This doesn't sound like he's on vacation, Ms. Spain. You were right to call."

Shaking her head, she stood and went into the CPA's office. She stepped behind his desk and came right back, her eyes wide. "His computer is gone. He's never taken it home with him."

Since he and Sam had broken in a few nights before, he knew already knew about the missing computer, but wanted her to go on record as noticing it, too. The same applied to the client files. By the time she saw all the empty drawers, she seemed convinced that her boss was in some kind of trouble.

"I'll need to get a search warrant for his home, unless he's a renter and the owner can let me in."

"He rents a house. I can give you the information on the landlord, because I pay his rent each month." She opened a file on her computer and printed off a page.

Dalton called and arranged to meet the owner at Banks' residence. He left and arrived at the house a few minutes later. After a quick look inside, he called Robin in the CSI unit.

"Hey, I've got a missing person case, and the guy's home looks like there was a struggle. Maybe an abduction. I think you should come out and do your thing." She agreed and told him to wait there until they arrived.

The landlord gave him a key and left. As he got back into his car, his phone chirped, and he glanced at the display: Cobb. He pressed the Decline button.

Robin and two others showed up twenty minutes later.

"Cobb didn't like it much that you took on another case," she said, her face pinched with concern.

Dalton shrugged. "I'll brief him when I get back. He'll be fine with it."

She shook her head and smiled. "Okay, you seem to know what you're doing."

The phone chimed. Cobb again.

Decline.

ELEVEN

DALTON BROUGHT UP the map of Marathon on his phone and the bars surrounding Lance Holder's former address and headed that way on the Overseas Highway. The first three closest to the rental house were a bust. On the fourth, the bartender said he'd seen Holder in the place before. It had been a while, though. Maybe a month or so.

"You remember if you or anybody else spoke with him?" Dalton asked.

"What'd he do?"

"Robbed a store and shot the clerk."

The bartender seemed to mull that over and then shrugged. "Yeah, I spoke to him the last time he was here. He came in about five and didn't leave until after midnight. Ran a tab, and I made him pay up after four or five beers. It made him a little mad, but he paid, and then stayed on for four or five more. The last couple, he bummed off guys he seemed to know, and then stiffed us for the rest. Went to the restroom and didn't come back."

"The guys he knew, do you remember any of them?"

"Yeah, they're regulars." He lowered his voice and said, "One of them is down the bar, there. Last one on the end. Don't say I fingered him."

Dalton eased down the bar. The man on the end sat next to a shapely woman with tattoos. When asked about Lance Holder's photo, the man glanced at it and said, "Never seen the guy." He looked straight ahead, a frown on his face.

"You sure? He comes in here a lot."

This time the man looked straight at him. "Yeah, I'm sure. Go flash your badge somewhere else."

"Okay. You remember him, give me a call. I'd appreciate it." He laid one of his cards on the bar and headed out the door.

By the time he reached his car, the tattooed woman from the bar rounded the far corner of the place. Probably went out the back door. He waited, and she caught up. "Hey, I know Lance. He in some kind of trouble?"

Dalton turned and looked at her. She had a pretty face, heavy on the makeup. "Maybe. You know where he is?"

"He couldn't pay his rent and moved in with my friend in there," she said, gesturing toward the bar with her thumb. "What'd he do?"

"I believe he robbed a store up around Islamorada and shot the guy behind the counter. Where's your friend live?"

She gave him an address a few blocks away. "Maybe he's there. I haven't seen him since yesterday, but I'd like it if he left for good. He's a bad influence on Roland." She glanced toward the bar. "I gotta get back. Don't tell anybody I squealed on him."

He handed her a card. "Call me if you see or hear of him."

She nodded and stuck the card in her jeans pocket. Stalking back to the door, she said over her shoulder. "Lock him up."

"Don't worry, I will."

The last of the sun rays bore in on the mobile home at the address the woman had given him. No Impala sat out front. He knocked on the door, but nobody answered. All the lights appeared to be off inside. When he got back in the car, he called the sheriff's office in Marathon and gave the address. They said they'd check later in case he came back.

Dalton headed south, toward home. As he entered Seven Mile Bridge, Sam called and said J.T. had found the owner of Lucinda Toole's home.

"It's owned by a company. J.T. thought it might be a shell and did some digging. It turns out the company is owned by her ex-husband, Leonard Orlov."

That didn't seem too surprising. "So maybe Orlov isn't her ex after all. The Toole Parts business might be his creation. You said he was accused of killing a Miami store owner. You think he's in the protection racket?"

"As I recall, he was suspected of racketeering and drug distribution, but nobody could pin anything on him. The guy who died was somebody who went to the cops and accused him of extorting protection money. The next day an employee found the man dead inside his store. Shot in the head."

"Sounds like Orlov could've had a mole in the Miami PD."

"Yeah, maybe he was paying for protection, himself."

Dalton thought for a moment. "Okay, so that brings

us back to Toole Parts. I wonder if it's a front for laundering Orlov's racket and drug money."

"How would that work with a wholesale operation, where customers probably wouldn't pay with cash?"

"I don't know, but it would be easy to set up bank accounts for phony auto repair shops. Those places take all kinds of payments. The cash could be deposited into their accounts on a regular basis and then paid to Toole Parts to represent purchases. Nobody tracks it if it's less than ten thousand. That way, Orlov's money would get an electronic trail that looks legit. He would also have cash in those accounts to tap into if he had to make a run for it."

"Sounds pretty elaborate, but I guess it could work that way. You figured out how it relates to the murders?"

Dalton sighed. "Not yet. But it's tied in somehow."

THE NEXT MORNING Dalton drove to Key Largo. No cars sat in the driveway of the Toole Parts Company, and no one answered the door. A dirt drive continued around the building to the rear of the property. He strode down it to a wooded area bordering a cove on Blackwater Sound. Though a dock ran out from the shore, it lay empty, and a large cruiser was wedged partially hidden among mangroves about fifty feet away. It swayed on slack lines in the breeze. The boat's name had been obscured by fresh paint. It did have a registration number emblazoned on the hull, but that paint appeared to be fresh, too. *Maybe stolen?*

Nobody appeared to be aboard. He stretched on vinyl gloves, climbed onto the deck, and found the main hatch locked. Same with the one at the stern. Scanning the area to see if anyone might be watching, all he saw was water and trees. He pulled a pick from his wallet and worked it in the lock. When it snapped open, he pushed through, his 9mm leading the way.

A ladder straight ahead led below to the cabins. Sidling the rail around the ladder well, he headed into the salon. It looked as if it had been used recently. Empty beer cans and plastic cups littered a table, an ashtray overflowed with cigarette butts, and three or four articles of clothing lay about on the seats.

A vinyl pocket attached to the bulkhead near the forward hatch held a title. It named the owner of the vessel as Nathan Beam with an address on Big Pine. He snapped a photo of the title with his phone and headed below deck.

In the master cabin located to the rear, he found another mess. An unmade bed with dirty sheets, soiled clothing on the floor, and empty cups and beer cans. More of the same in a mid-cabin with bunk beds. The forward cabin seemed different. Someone had removed the bed and attached a couple of steel grommets to the deck. Knotted pieces of rope were attached, their free ends frayed as if severed with a dull knife. Spots of blood dotted the area around the ropes. Someone had been held there, maybe the CPA, and Dalton wondered what had happened to him after the ropes were cut. Whatever it was, it had to be bad. He snapped a photo of the scene and proceeded back up the ladder. After locking the door on his way out, he stepped onto the bank and got a pic of the side of the craft.

He went back to the car, pulled out, and drove away. It appeared that nobody had bothered to clean up, so the CSIs could probably get some good prints. As he approached a curve in the street, a BMW containing two men passed. Slowing, he watched it in the rearview mirror. It turned into the driveway he had just left from and disappeared down the side of the building. After making a quick U-turn, he swung back down the street and into a vacant driveway a few doors from the Toole address. By the time he got out and headed their way, the car backed out and sped away, too quick to get the plate number. Continuing on toward the boat, he heard a motor start up. Through the trees he watched the craft glide out of the cove.

Cobb CALLED AGAIN, so Dalton thought he'd head to the office and didn't arrive until almost eleven. He stepped over and rapped on Cobb's door jamb. His supervisor looked up from a file, frowned, and motioned him in. "Close the door."

Dalton did as asked and took a seat in front of the desk.

"I've been trying to reach you. You don't answer your phone." The scowl remained in place.

Nodding, Dalton said, "Yeah, I noticed you called. I must've been out of range."

"I don't think so. I called several times."

"You saying you don't believe me?" Dalton asked, an eyebrow raised.

Cobb leaned back in his high-back chair, and then

his expression softened. "Well, no, I'm not saying that, but you need to stay in touch."

"Sure thing. I wanted to update you on the robbery case." He told him about finding the robber's new address and alerting the Marathon office on the location.

"You think he's coming back to it, or he's in the wind?"

"I think he'll be back. The woman who told me about him said she wants him out, so she'll probably call me when he shows up again."

"Well, that's okay, but I want you down there beating the bushes and find the guy. The case doesn't belong to those guys in Marathon, so they don't really care about it."

Dalton nodded, and Cobb continued, "What about this missing person case you picked up on your own?"

"Oh, yeah, he's a CPA named Rudy Banks. He has an office close by. His employee somehow had my number and called, said the guy has been out of touch for several days and she's worried about him."

"That name sounds familiar." He stared into space for a moment, and then said, "Oh yeah, Steve came in last week and said a man named Banks had left a voicemail saying one of his clients was doing something fishy."

"I need to listen to it, if he still has it. Did he call him?"

"Yes, a couple of times. Said he didn't get an answer."

"That's because something happened to him."

Cocking his head, Cobb said, "What makes you so sure?"

"The woman said he went to visit a client in Key Largo and acted strange when he came back, like something had happened. When he left a little while later, she didn't see him again. She's called him numerous times without an answer. His landlord opened up his house for me and I took a look inside. It appeared somebody had been in there and knocked over stuff, like there was some kind of struggle. That's when I called in the CSIs."

"You visit the client in Key Largo?"

"Yes, this morning. But there didn't seem to be anybody there. It's supposed to be a wholesale auto parts business, but I didn't see a warehouse, and they don't even have a sign out front. Made me wonder if it's some kind of money laundering operation, and Banks found out about it." He didn't see any reason to mention the ropes and blood on the boat, since it had sailed away to who knew where...and he'd accessed it illegally.

Cobb waited a moment, as if there might be more to tell, then shrugged and said, "That's a stretch, but I guess we need to find the guy. You talked with the CSIs yet?"

"No, I thought I'd go over when I leave here."

"Okay, stay on it, but also find that robber before he shoots somebody else." He went back to his file, and without looking up said, "Make sure you keep me posted."

Dalton turned back, as if on an afterthought. "Oh, yeah, whatever happened on the murder/suicide case?"

Cobb frowned again. "Still open. The ME said he

isn't sure about the suicide." He huffed and waved his hand in a dismissive gesture. "Something about Pound not having much alcohol in his blood. I think he's just being stubborn."

At Robin's desk, Dalton said, "You find any prints at the CPA's house?"

"We did, but they were all one person, probably Banks. They didn't come up on any databases."

No help there. The guys who had abducted Banks had worn gloves. He hadn't really expected much, because they were professionals. *Professional criminals.*

"We also found a few spatters of blood on the wall and sent them off for DNA analysis. It might belong to Banks as the result of a fight with his abductors."

Dalton nodded and remained silent for a moment, and then said, "Did you finish the ballistics on the slug that killed Joe Pound?"

"Oh, yeah, it came from the same gun that killed the men on the boat. It also matched the one the ME took out of the first murder victim, Carl Myron."

"Pound's suicide note claimed he killed all those guys, so I guess that clinches it."

"Yeah, guess so."

Dalton decided he should change the subject. "How about getting dinner tonight?"

"Sure, that would be fun. There's a new place I want to try, if you're game."

"You bet I'm game."

They discussed the time and location, and as he left, she squeezed his hand. He felt his face flush and wondered where their flirtations might lead. Nothing good usually came of an office romance, and he was pretty sure there was a rule against interoffice dating. But he wasn't going to let that get in his way.

Steve Chase sat at his desk peering at something on his computer screen. Dalton approached and asked him about the voicemail from Rudy Banks.

"Yeah, Cobb just called, said you might stop by." He picked up the phone handset, brought up his messages and pressed the speaker button.

After the message played, Chase turned off the phone and said, "Cobb told me you're onto the client Banks was talking about."

"The Toole Parts Company." He told him about the conversation with Banks' employee and about visiting the business location in Key Largo that morning.

"You think the Toole people did something to Banks?"

"Yes."

Chase leaned back in his chair and stared for a few beats, his face flush, and then said, "Cobb chewed me out for not following up on this. Said maybe I could've prevented something from happening."

Shrugging, Dalton said, "We don't know what happened, yet."

"Well, let me know if I can help in any way."

Dalton nodded and walked away, wondering if this was the same guy who had grabbed him by the shirt and threatened him a few days before. Or planted a bag of coke in his freezer.

TWELVE

Dalton dropped by the medical examiner's office and found him in the autopsy room looking over a body. He glanced up from the table and snapped a switch on his recording machine.

"Help you with something, Detective?"

"Who's on the table?"

"Floater. Washed up on the beach this morning."

"A drowning?"

"Yes, I haven't found anything that spells foul play. Probably tried to make it on a raft from Cuba."

"I wondered if you'd made a call on the Joe Pound case."

The doctor shook his head and sighed. "He had ample whiskey in his mouth and on his shirtfront, but there was no alcohol in his blood. I ran the test twice."

Dalton thought he knew the answer, but asked the question anyway. "You think he could've taken a big drink and then shot himself?"

"No, he didn't swallow any of it. Somebody poured it into his mouth postmortem. I know they want to close this case, but…" The words lay there between them for a few beats, and then Dr. Lake turned and went back to work examining the floater. Higher-ups would be unhappy if he called Pound's death a murder. They might say he was on thin ice with the alcohol dilemma, but in the end, he would prevail. It meant the man's killer wrote the suicide note, and Pound probably didn't kill anybody. The killer, or killers were still out there.

"You release the body yet?" Dalton asked.

"Not yet, maybe tomorrow."

Dalton went back to the lieutenant's office and he waved him in.

"I just talked with the ME. He's pretty convinced Joe Pound was murdered." He related the conversation.

The lieutenant stared for a moment. "Huh, he say he was going to make it official?"

"No, but it sounds like he will."

Cobb stood. "Okay, I'll go talk to him."

ABOUT A HALF-HOUR LATER, the lieutenant stepped over to Dalton's desk with a file in his hand. "You were right. He's putting it down as murder. You think you can handle the investigation, along with the robbery and the missing person case?"

Dalton shrugged. "Sure." Especially since the missing person case was probably related to the murders.

"Okay, use Steve if you need him. He can do leg work for you." The lieutenant laid the file on the desk and walked away.

He thumbed through it. Not much had been done since he'd had the case. Cobb probably had his hands full, but he had questioned Joe Pound about the two bodies found on his boat, Floyd Sparks and Eldon Perl. All Pound offered was that both had worked for him. That fit with the bogus suicide note, so whoever wrote it knew the situation. Fingerprints found on the boat were for the owner, Joe Pound, the two dead men, and Carl Myron. Blood DNA had been sent off to the lab. Dalton recalled that there had been lots of blood on that boat. Probably all of it belonged to the dead men. They had found traces of cocaine and cannabis in several places, and Joe Pound denied having any knowledge of it. If they had pursued that any further, there was no mention of it in the report. A few days later, Pound was dead.

Nothing else of significance emerged from the report. He ran the dead men's names and found where they had served time at the same institution and about the same time as Carl Myron. That corresponded with what J.T. had found. There were no additional hits.

Since Cobb thought Joe Pound had committed suicide, he had done the minimum on that case. It appeared there had been no further investigation beyond the initial crime scene. No prints had been found at the scene, except for the dead man's and a couple of the employees. Dalton thought he'd better take a closer look and headed toward the construction office, stopping for a quick burger along the way.

Joe Pound's office manager, Rita Coe, met him at the door and recognized him from his previous visit.

"Nobody's here but me," Coe said. "We've shut the office down for a few days out of respect for Joe."

Crime scene tape zigzagged over the closed door of Pound's office.

"I'd like to see Mr. Pound's financial records."

Coe gave him a questioning look. "Why? The business has been very profitable."

"That's good, but I need to look them over." He didn't see any reason at that point to let her know her boss had been murdered. "In a death like this, I don't need a warrant."

"Oh. All right." She led him into a back office and sat down in front of a computer. Dalton dragged up a chair next to her.

She brought up income statements for the past two years. Both indicated profits exceeding $2 million.

"Let me see his bank deposits for the past six months," Dalton said.

She opened a file, and Dalton asked if he could run the keyboard. Shrugging, she got up and changed seats with him. He scrolled through the entries. Most were for odd amounts, and he asked her if she knew about the larger ones. She identified most of them as payments from clients for specific building projects, but she hedged when it came to the origin of a number of recurring deposits of $50,000 each.

"One of our clients, Southpoint Progress, is an organization involved in charity cases. They don't want any credit for their good deeds, and they asked Joe to be discreet. It's for work on elderly people's homes in the Keys who can't afford to keep them up. Those deposits are for that."

Dalton turned to face her. "Do you know anything about the jobs done for Southpoint Progress?"

She remained silent for a moment, her face coloring, maybe wondering for the first time if this might be a problem. "I never get involved in the work delivery end of the business. Joe just gave me the checks to deposit and told me to enter the revenue into South-point's account."

Dalton brought up deposits from the previous six months and the entries were the same: $50k every two-to-three weeks. About a million for the year. Nice income from an anonymous benefactor. Or maybe something else.

"Did he ever mention who he dealt with at South-point?"

"No." She paused for several seconds, seemingly transfixed on the computer screen, and then said, "Am I going to need a lawyer?"

Ignoring the question, he said, "Can you bring up the check image for one of the deposits?"

"Sure."

They switched seats again, and she clicked a few keys. The picture of a check popped onto the screen. He asked her to print it for him.

"I also need a digital copy of all the customer accounts for the past year."

She copied the files onto a flash drive and he left with it.

When he reached his car, he sat there mulling over what he'd found. Maybe the office manager bought the story about a donor, and maybe she didn't. Hard to say, but she was quick to ask about a lawyer, so something must've clicked in her mind that it might not be entirely legit. If it turned out to be payoffs for a crime, the DA might consider her culpable, especially since Pound was no longer around to take the rap.

He headed back to his office and arrived there a little after three. Flashing back on the boat in Key Largo that had sailed away, he pulled up the photo from his phone. According to the registration certificate in the wheelhouse, it belonged to Nathan Beam on Big Pine. A search of the sheriff's database pulled up Beam's theft report. The boat had been stolen the week before, about the same time the murders began. He was convinced that the thieves had taken it to get rid of Banks. From the looks of it, they had stayed on it for a day or so, maybe sweating the CPA on what he might have seen and told others. Dalton had a feeling they would never find the vessel. The guy was probably on his way to scuttle it that morning. Easier to do that than to remove traces of the occupants. The CPA probably ended up at the bottom of the Gulf with steel chains wrapped around his body.

Dalton wondered how the deaths of Carl Myron and the other two men were connected to the abduction of the CPA. Steve Chase had explained away the CPA's phone number as something he just didn't follow up on, but Dalton kept going back to Chase's obvious displeasure with him being handed the murder case. And the planted cocaine. The first three murdered men worked for Pound, and the cursory examination of his financial records indicated that he might have been doing something illegal. And then he was murdered, too.

More information about Orlov's business might help tie it all together, he thought. After a few fruitless internet searches on Leonard Orlov, he gave up and dialed the Miami-Dade PD. Twenty minutes and several tranfers later, he got to the voicemail of Detective Thomas

Diaz. Diaz had investigated the Miami murder case the previous year, in which Orlov had been a suspect. He left a message introducing himself and asked if he could get a copy of the murder file.

His phone chirped and the display indicated the sheriff's office in Marathon.

"Hey, this is Morell in Marathon. We got your robber. We found him at that trailer about an hour ago. What do you want us to do with him?"

"Lock him in an interview room. I'm coming down there."

He swung by Cobb's office and told him about the apprehension. That put a smile on his face. Upon gathering his papers, he headed to his car and drove south. When he arrived at the Marathon office, he asked for Morell, and a uniformed officer led him to a cubicle. The deputy stood an inch or so taller than Dalton. His uniform hung loosely on him, as if he'd recently lost a lot of weight.

"He lawyered up after I talked to you," Morell said on their way to the interview room.

Dalton shrugged. "That's okay."

Morell twisted the knob on the door and pushed through, followed by Dalton. Lance Holder sat at the table, his wrists cuffed to eyelets in the surface. A graying man in a suit sat beside him, obviously his attorney, a frown on his face.

Morell said, "This is Detective Dalton from the Islamorada office," and turned and left, closing the door behind him. Dalton took a seat across from Holder and the suit and laid his papers face-down on the table.

The lawyer introduced himself as Burns Bailey. "You have a card?" he asked.

"Sure." Dalton pulled one from his pocket and pushed it across the table.

Bailey glanced at the handwritten information on it and gave him a condescending smile. "So, you're new."

Nodding, he said, "Yes, new to Florida. Lots of years in Chicago PD homicide before this."

The lawyer's expression dimmed a few watts.

"You got the wrong guy," Holder said.

Dalton smiled and looked from Holder to Bailey and back. "Oh, we got the right guy, Lancelot. We have you on video."

The suspect gave him a smug grin. "Good try. I heard the robber wore a mask."

Dalton pulled the printed photo of the tattooed knuckles from his stack and laid it next to the man's hands. "Take a look."

The grin leaked away as he stared at the image. "That don't mean anything. There's plenty of guys have that same tattoo."

Selecting another page, Dalton said, "We also have video of your vehicle leaving the scene." He laid the piece of paper down so Holder could see. "That store clerk dies, you go down for felony murder. In Florida, that'll get you a ride on Old Sparky." He knew the electric chair had been discontinued, in favor of a method considered more humane, but Holder might not know that.

"Hold on," the lawyer said. "My client has already

stated that he didn't do this, and he has an alibi for the time of the robbery."

Dalton raised an eyebrow. "Who's the alibi?"

"The man who owns the place where Mr. Holder has been living for the past several weeks."

"Oh, yeah, I met that guy. Probably an ex-con just like your client. He'll make a great witness."

The lawyer turned to his client. "Is he an ex-convict?"

Holder gave him a look of disbelief, "Well, yeah, but he'll back up my story."

The lawyer rolled his eyes and glanced at the photos, a concerned expression on his face.

Dalton leaned forward, his elbows on the table. "Better hope that clerk doesn't die."

The suspected robber scowled. "Quit saying that. He ain't gonna die. I talked to the nurse."

Bailey jumped up from his chair and said to his client, "That's enough." He turned to Dalton. "I need a few minutes to confer with my client."

Shrugging, Dalton said, "I'll be at Morell's desk." He went out and stepped over to the deputy's workspace. "They're powwowing."

Morell offered him a chair and got him a cup of coffee. About twenty minutes later Morell's desk phone rang. He answered, and after a moment handed the handset to Dalton. "It's for you."

"This is Connie Duval in the DA's office. Mr. Holder has accepted a plea deal: twenty years with a chance for parole after ten. Lock him up to await court proceedings."

BACK IN HIS OFFICE, Dalton checked the time. He had a date with Robin, but it wasn't for another hour. Cobb stopped by on his way out, and Dalton updated him on the robbery case.

"Okay, good work." Cobb shrugged. "He'll probably serve only ten if he keeps his nose clean, but we did our job."

As he walked away, Dalton's phone chirped. Glancing at the display, he saw *Miami-Dade PD*, but waited until Cobb was out of earshot before answering.

"Detective Diaz, Miami-Dade PD. You left a message."

"Yes, thanks for calling back. I wondered if you would fax me the murder book on the Leonard Orlov case."

"You got a case going on with Orlov?" Diaz asked.

"Could be. I'm investigating four murders, and a possible abduction. Orlov is a person of interest."

"If his name came up, he's guilty. We were sure he killed the guy up here, but we couldn't get the DA to prosecute." The Miami detective sighed. "Man, I don't need to be reminded of that fiasco." After a long pause, he said, "You want the whole file? There's maybe twenty pages worth."

"If it isn't too much trouble. It'll save me a trip up there. And I don't need crime scene photos. I just want to get what information you dug up on him."

"Okay, I can do that."

Dalton gave him the fax number.

"Keep me posted. I'd like to know if he goes to jail for something."

"Will do."

A few minutes later the fax machine, only a cubicle away, beeped and whirred as it printed. He waited until the whirring stopped and went over and collected the pages. There were eighteen in all, including search warrants.

Orlov had produced an alibi for the time of the killing and was released. Dalton scanned further, wondering who had vouched for him. He found it toward the bottom of the detective's report buried under a lot of other details. A woman named Edna Lou Bates said he was with her at the time. Detectives had talked with her, and her story had some holes in it, but she didn't have a record, and the DA didn't want to risk taking it to court. The case went cold after that, and they never charged anybody else with the killing.

None of the information seemed to have any value to his murder cases, but provided good background. Several pages were notes on interviews with potential witnesses. People who knew Orlov or worked for him. Most just said what a great guy he was, and how they couldn't believe he was capable of killing anyone. That probably meant they were afraid. Dalton tired of going through the repetition after the first few, but kept scanning.

The last interviewee seemed a little bolder, saying, "…maybe he did it, and maybe he didn't. I don't know him all that well." The detective described the interviewee as flippant, and maybe too stupid to be afraid. Dalton went back to the top of the page and found the name he'd skimmed over. It was a familiar one. He'd worked for Orlov at the time as a courier for the Toole Parts Company. Probably ferrying cash, rather than parts. The boss must have gotten wind of what he'd said to the detectives and fired him. Or the guy regretted what he'd said and decided he'd better get out of town. In any event, he ended up working for Joe Pound's construction company.

Eldon Perl. Buster. *The link*.

THIRTEEN

AT EIGHT THE next morning, Dalton and Sam headed up the Overseas Highway toward Key Largo. They stopped for a fast food breakfast, and back in the car, while Sam checked messages on his phone, Dalton thought about his date the night before with Robin. They'd met at the restaurant she wanted to try. She didn't know about him getting the murder case back. When he told her, she seemed surprised about the ME's decision.

"Seems kind of thin," she said.

"Maybe, but he was convinced."

She frowned. "What a mess. Four dead bodies, and still no answers. You have any theories?"

"Yes, but nothing solid." He didn't want to talk about the Eldon Perl situation or Joe Pound's suspicious income until he had a chance to check things out, but he did ask her to check out Southpoint Progress when she had a chance.

"What's Southpoint Progress?"

"Could be nothing, maybe a charitable organization."

They rated the seafood as excellent, and he walked her to the car. Before getting in she put her arms around his waist and pulled him close. That, he'd enjoyed as well.

Sam brought him out of his reverie. "So you think

Joe Pound was doing something for this Southpoint group that connects to Toole Parts?"

He had told Sam about the revelations from the day before. "Maybe. Could've been bringing in drugs. Buster Perl worked for Pound, and before that he worked for Orlov at Toole Parts. Buster and Pound were murdered, so it sounds like somebody tied off the loose ends. And Pound's supposed suicide note wrapped up the other murders into a nice little bundle."

"All paths seem to lead to Orlov," Sam said.

Dalton nodded, and they rode on in silence. When they stopped at Toole Parts they found a For Rent sign out front. A look in the windows confirmed that the furniture had all been moved out. Dalton had thought about trying for a search warrant, but knew he probably wouldn't get it with such sketchy evidence.

A self-storage company occupied the space across the street. They rode into the parking lot, and Dalton peered up at the security camera on the eaves of the building. Pointed at the driveway, it probably captured the traffic in and out of the place. Toole Parts sat at a slight angle, but he thought the camera might also record activity there. He went inside, flashed his badge for the manager, and asked about the security video.

"It's motion activated, so it doesn't record unless a car enters the driveway."

"How about cars passing on the street?" He didn't want to mention Toole if he didn't need to.

"Yeah, it gets that, too. Why, what are you looking for?"

"I'm investigating an abduction case that might hinge on a vehicle passing on the street."

He wrote down the dates and the man agreed to make him a copy. Dalton said he would come back and pick it up later.

They headed to the residence where they had seen the moving van and found Lucinda Toole's Mercedes parked in the driveway. Dalton parked behind it so Sam, in the passenger side of his car, wouldn't be visible from the house.

"Wait here," Dalton said, "and watch for any visitors."

Sam nodded. He had his 9mm on the floor at his feet.

Dalton rang the doorbell. After waiting nearly a minute without a response, he knocked.

Lucinda opened the door a crack. "What do you want?"

He held up his badge. "Monroe County Sheriff. I need to speak with you."

"About what?"

"Rudy Banks. He's been missing for over a week, since he came to see you."

After a few silent seconds, she said, "You mean the accountant?"

"That's right, your CPA."

"I don't know anything about him being missing."

"I need to talk to you anyway."

She huffed a sigh. "I'm very busy. Can you come back later?"

"Sorry, this can't wait."

She rolled her eyes as she swung the door open and

stood there. "All right, I hope this won't take long." The view he'd gotten through the doorway didn't do her justice. Her dark hair framed a face that could grace the cover of a fashion magazine. He wondered how a man like Leonard Orlov, who probably had anything he wanted, would have let her go.

"I'd prefer to go inside and talk."

Pursing her full lips, she motioned for him to enter. "Okay, but the house is a mess, and there's no place to sit. I'm in the process of moving."

There was no furniture. A taped-up box sat near the entrance, maybe containing what she'd come to collect. Atop it sat a woman's purse.

Nodding, Dalton said, "Yes, I see. Where are you moving to?"

She ignored the question. "What do you want to ask me? I have a lot to do."

"Rudy Banks visited your office the day he disappeared. His receptionist, Barbara Spain, said he seemed disturbed when he returned. Did something happen at your office that day that would've upset him?"

"I have no idea what you're talking about."

"Are you saying he didn't visit you?"

"Yes, that's exactly what I'm saying. I only saw him one time, when I dropped off paperwork at his office."

Spain had no reason to lie about her conversation with her boss. "Banks said he needed to ask you something about your inventory. I saw your business location, and there was no warehouse there. Where do you stock your products?"

"I'm a pass-through distributor. I don't have inventories. Too expensive. When customers place orders, I have the manufacturers ship the products directly to them." It sounded rehearsed, as if a ready answer for anyone asking about her business.

"You handle this all by yourself?"

She seemed to mull this over before answering. "I have a couple of employees who help."

"Maybe Banks spoke with one of them when he visited."

Shrugging, she said, "Perhaps." She glanced at a watch on her wrist and picked up her purse. "Is there anything else? I have an appointment and have to get going."

"I'll need to talk with your employees. Can you give me their names and numbers?" He pulled his notepad and a pen from his pocket.

"I don't have that information with me. It's packed up with my office files. Give me your number and I'll call you with it later."

He handed her one of his cards. "You don't know their names?"

"My ex-husband hired them."

"You mean Leonard Orlov?"

Her face colored. "Yes, how could you know that?"

"He's well known in South Florida. So he handles some of your business?"

She headed to the door. "I'll call you with the information."

"I need your phone number, in case something comes up."

She turned, her lips tight as if trying to decide what

to do, and nodded. As she gave him the number he wrote it down, and then punched it into his phone. When he touched the Call button, he got a voice message saying the number wasn't in service. "Huh, maybe I wrote it down wrong." He held the phone up for her to see.

"Oh, sorry, that's the number of my other service I got rid of." She gave him another one and he tried it. Her phone chimed in her purse.

He smiled. "Yeah, that did it."

They exited and she locked the door behind her, leaving the box inside. An empty BMW sat on the street. It looked like the same one that had dropped the boat driver off at the old Toole Parts address the day before. Dalton didn't see Sam but heard a grunting noise to his left. He pulled his weapon and rounded the shrubbery. A man lay there, prone, a gun next to his hand. Sam stood over him holding his 9mm in one hand and an open wallet in the other, his foot pressed against the prone man's back.

"Get off me," the man said in accented English. "That hurts."

Sam grinned. "Yeah, I bet." Glancing at the wallet, he said to Dalton, "Boris here was waiting for you beside the door."

Lucinda stepped over to them. "Let him up. He works for me. He didn't know you were the police."

"Yeah, let me up. You're gonna lose your badge for this."

Picking up the gun from the ground, Dalton said to her, "Why's he packing? You need protection from something?"

Her face went blank for a moment. "We, uh, had some break-ins. He came by to check on me and must've seen the strange car."

Dalton nodded, guessing how the situation might have turned out if Sam hadn't been there. "Let him up. We'll take him to the sheriff's office so he can file a complaint about his mistreatment."

Sam withdrew his foot, pulled out his phone and snapped a photo of the man's driver's license.

Boris stood and brushed himself off. He was tall and swarthy and wore a blue guayabera and khakis. "It's okay, I can see you just made a mistake. Forget about it." He held out his hand and Sam returned the wallet.

"Yeah, I thought so. Before you leave, did you see Rudy Banks last week when he visited the Toole Parts office?"

Boris gave him a dramatic shrug. "Who?"

Dalton glanced at Lucinda, and she said, "He doesn't know him, and Banks didn't visit. He must have gone somewhere else." She said to Boris, "We need to go."

"Okay," Dalton said, "I'm keeping the gun unless you can show me a carry permit."

Boris thumbed through his wallet. "I must've left it at home."

"If you find it, you can claim the gun at the sheriff's office in Islamorada."

The thug's eyes narrowed. Looking as if he might protest, he glanced at Lucinda and she shook her head. He threw up his hands and headed toward his car.

Dalton watched as he drove away. He figured the guy would expect them to follow, and it would be a waste of time, but he did note the plate number he had missed the day before. As he walked past Lucinda's vehicle he said, "Don't forget to call me."

She gave him a scowl that did little to diminish her beauty.

As they left the neighborhood, Robin phoned. He put her on speaker and pulled over. Lucinda gave them a sidelong glance as her Mercedes passed by on the street.

"I got the information on that organization you asked me to check out." Robin's tone sounded sing-song-sweet. Dalton glanced at Sam and he grinned.

"Southpoint?"

"Yes, it's run by a wealthy woman named Dorothy Carlyle who lives in Key West. She's the eighty-six-year-old widow of Ezekiel Carlyle, who brought a steel fortune from Pennsylvania several decades ago. According to the story I read on the internet, she spends all her money and time on charitable endeavors in the Keys."

So Joe Pound might have been telling the truth about the money. It didn't seem to have anything to do with the murders.

"Before you go, how about checking out a guy I just ran into. He might've been involved in my missing person case."

"Sure, who is it?"

Sam handed him his phone with the image of the driver's license, and he relayed the information. He also gave her the plate number from Boris' car.

"Okay, I'll get on this. Things have settled down a little around here."

He thanked her and hung up.

"She sounds nice," Sam said.

"Yes, she is."

"And she likes you."

THEY WENT BACK to the self-storage place, collected the video footage the manager had promised, and headed south. Sam got out in Islamorada where he'd left his rental. Before continuing on, Dalton looked up the number of Joe Pound's residence and dialed. The widow answered, and he introduced himself and told her he needed to come by for some questions. She agreed, and a few minutes later she had the gate open and he drove through.

Inside, he took a chair in an expansive living room overlooking Florida Bay. A few minutes later she brought him a cup of coffee and sat down across from him. "The sheriff's office hasn't released my husband's body yet." She wore a housedress and no makeup, her hair in a ponytail, and her bloodshot eyes looked as if she'd been crying.

"That's one reason for my visit. The Medical Examiner has determined that your husband didn't take his own life." He watched her face as it contorted and tears slid down her face.

"That means…"

"He was murdered."

She stared for several beats. "But why?" Not waiting for an answer, she got up from her chair and went out of the room, returning a couple of minutes later with a box of tissues. After drying her eyes and blowing her nose, she apologized.

"I'm sorry to have to deliver this news. You asked why he was murdered. We think the murderer wanted to deflect the blame for killing those other men, but we don't know why your husband was the target."

After seeming to digest that for a moment, she said, "All right, what do you want to know? I'm eager to help any way I can."

He took out his notepad and laid it on the table next to his chair. "According to the police report, Carl Myron and the two men found murdered on your husband's boat worked for him. When I spoke with him, he said Myron was your cousin."

"Yes, that's right."

Nodding, Dalton said, "How is he related as your cousin?"

"What does that have to do with my husband's murder?" Alarm pinched at the corners of her eyes.

"Just trying to get a fix on the victims in this case, because their murders are all connected somehow, and you knew two of them personally."

She took a deep breath and let it out. "Okay, his mother and my father were siblings. They're both dead now."

He glanced at his notepad. "I see from a previous driver's license that you went by the name Heather Scott. Does that mean your father's last name was Scott?" He didn't think she would own up to using an alias, but wanted to give her an opening in case she had an innocent reason.

Leaning back in her chair, she crossed her arms and said. "Yes, it was."

Dalton just stared for a moment and then said, "All right. How about the other two men who were killed. Floyd Sparks and Eldon Perl. Did you know them?"

"No, I'd never heard of them before they were identified in the news." She seemed relieved to get away from discussion about her name.

He made a note in his pad. "Okay, let's get back to Carl Myron. Did you speak with him recently?"

"Yes, I tried to check up on him every week or so. He had a troubled past, and I wanted to help him all I could. I gave him money when he needed it. He could never seem to get by on his income." She paused, and her eyes narrowed. "I don't see how my contact with him could possibly relate to Carl or my husband's deaths."

"Yes, you're probably right. Can you think of anyone who might have wanted your husband dead?"

She shook her head. "No, everybody liked him. His employees always seemed so appreciative for their jobs."

"Do you know if he was involved in any kind of illegal activity?"

"No, of course not." Frowning, she added, "Why would you ask that?"

Dalton laid his notepad on the table. "The reasoning is this: Carl Myron took off in your husband's boat the day before he was found dead. Just a couple of days later, two more men were found dead on your husband's boat. About the same time as all this happened, a local man went missing. He did accounting work for a company in Key Largo named Toole Parts. The owner of Toole Parts is Lucinda Toole, who is the former wife of a man named Leonard Orlov, a known criminal figure in Miami. One of the murdered men, Eldon Perl, worked for Orlov a few months before going to work for your husband."

Her eyes grew large. "So you think Joe had dealings with this criminal you mentioned? Leonard something?"

"It crossed my mind."

"Well, he didn't. Joe built stores and homes and offices." Her voice rose in volume with each word. "He did very well at that and didn't need to do anything illegal."

"All right. I know you don't want to believe that, but there is some reason he was selected to take the blame for the other murders. Can you think of any reason that might be the case?"

"No, I can't, and I've had enough of your questions."

He stared for a moment, and then said, "Just a couple more, and then I'm done." Without waiting for her to protest, he continued. "Does your husband have an office here in the home?"

"Yes, of course. He handled some of his work here."

"I'll need to search it to try and find out why your husband was murdered."

"No, you just want to smear his good name, and I won't have it."

"Okay, I'll come back to that. I assume there's an insurance policy on your husband's life. Can you tell me how much will be paid on it?"

She sighed. "Yes, there is one. I haven't seen it in a long time, but I think it's for $5 million."

That would set the widow up for a long time.

When he didn't say anything, she filled the silence. "Surely you don't suspect me of shooting my husband?"

"Five million is a pretty good motive."

Tears streamed from her eyes. She stood and went to the door. "Please leave."

"Sorry, but I need to see the office before I leave."

"No, I already told you. Please go. Now."

He took out his phone and called Steve Chase. "Where are you?"

"Almost there."

Dalton asked her to open the gate for the deputy. She gave him a scowl, but stepped over to the wall and pressed a button. He had swung by the office that morning and asked Chase to get a judge's signature on a search warrant and bring it out. When the warrant arrived, he took it and showed it to Ms. Pound. She just shook her head, sat down on the sofa, and cupped her face in her hands. He asked Chase to keep her company while he located the office down the hall.

A search of the drawers in a mahogany desk yielded mostly ordinary office supplies. One drawer contained hotel receipts for two trips to Grand Cayman, the most recent just three weeks before. Both were for several days each.

Moving on to Pound's computer, he booted it up and checked emails. There were fifty-five unread messages, and virtually all of them appeared to be spam. One was from a realtor in Grand Cayman, from just that morning, responding to Pound's query about wiggle room on a house listed for $3.6 million. The realtor said he thought he could get the buyer down to an even three mil. Still, a lot of money. He wondered if Pound had a bank account in the Caymans.

An examination of the other computer applications, including social media accounts, yielded nothing else of value. He brought up browsing history and found it blank. Someone had erased it, which seemed suspicious in itself. If Pound had visited sites he didn't want discovered, he'd covered his tracks pretty well. A forensic examination of the machine might reveal his secrets, but they could just turn out to be embarrassing sites, which would be a waste of time.

Dalton checked the places where Pound might have written down information about a secret bank account. He searched underneath the keyboard and monitor stand, all surfaces of each of the desk drawers, and all the inside surfaces of the desk frame. By the time he finished, perspiration trickled down his brow. The search yielded nothing, so he went back through the drawers again, more thoroughly this time since he was looking for something specific. The information turned up on a small piece of paper in the bottom of one of the drawers, under a box of staples and a package of unopened writing pens. He had missed it when he'd thumbed through it the first time.

Two entries were written there that appeared to be an account name and password. He didn't know the name of the bank, so he brought up a mapping program and located the hotel where Pound had stayed in

Grand Cayman. There were two banks nearby. When he searched on one of them and entered the authentication information, he got a message saying no such account existed. So he tried the other one and Pound's account page popped up. It showed both husband and wife as owners. Their balance totaled nearly $8.5 million. A steady flow of deposits between $200 thousand and half a million per month had begun more than two years before. All were accomplished through electronic transfer, he assumed from an account belonging to Orlov. He didn't have any way to confirm that, though, at least not through legal channels.

Dalton printed a summary of the banking activity and turned off the computer. He continued down the hall to check out the rest of the house. When he didn't find anything else of significance, he made his way back to the living room and found Chase and the widow on the sofa speaking in hushed tones. They quieted when he entered and came over.

Standing before Ms. Pound, he said, "What can you tell me about the bank account in the Caymans?"

She appeared stunned for a moment and then recovered. "My husband set up an account when we visited there on vacation. That's all I know."

"It has your name on it, too." He held up the printout for her to see. "Can you tell me the source of the deposits?"

She took the sheet and studied it for several seconds, and then shrugged. "I assume it's money he earned in his business."

"I've seen his income statements for the past two

years, and his business isn't even remotely that lucrative."

Her eyes narrowed as she handed the paper back to him. "You're assuming he did something illegal for the money?"

Steve Chase stood and peered at the bank information, a frown on his face.

"I'm saying he had another source of income. If it's legal, you need to tell me what it is."

The tears flowed again, and she mopped her face with a tissue. "I don't know where that money came from. It must be a mistake."

They left, and outside Chase said, "You were pretty rough on her. You don't think she killed her husband, do you?"

"I don't know, but Pound was doing something risky that paid a lot of cash, probably moving drugs, and I think she knew about it."

Chase gave him a smirk. "I think you're barking up the wrong tree, but I'm just a flunky on this case. Don't be surprised if she complains to the sheriff, or Cobb."

Dalton shrugged. "Goes with the territory."

FOURTEEN

WHEN DALTON REACHED his office he went in to see the lieutenant and showed him the Cayman bank information.

"What did Ms. Pound say?" Cobb asked.

"She denied any knowledge of the deposits."

"But you don't believe her?"

"No. She may not have killed her husband, but she's far from innocent." He thought about mentioning her assumption of a dead woman's name, but decided that might bring up questions he didn't want to answer. "I could make a request from the bank for the source of the money, but they probably won't give it to me. If I had a warrant for Orlov's home in Miami, I might be able to trace the money back to him."

Cobb shook his head. "Good luck with that. You'd need more evidence. I heard he sued the Miami-Dade police for harassment last year."

The lieutenant's tone sounded as if speaking to a rookie investigator. It also seemed dismissive on the subject of going after Orlov, and Dalton wondered why. Maybe he could get the goods on the crime boss another way.

"Keep at it." The lieutenant picked up a piece of

paper from a file and appeared to be reading it. Interview over.

At his desk, Dalton went over his notes and updated the murder file to include his visit to Lucinda Toole, the interview with Heather Pound, and what he'd found at the Pound residence.

As he finished, Robin came by. "I got the information on Boris Ivashin. He arrived from Russia on a work visa ten years ago. It expired soon after and he never renewed it. No criminal record, other than being here illegally. You have his most recent address."

"I assume he doesn't have a carry permit for the gun."

"No, I checked that, too."

His desk phone rang and he answered.

"Can you drop back over?" Cobb asked.

"Sure, be right there."

Robin smiled. "That the boss?"

"Yep."

"Okay, see you later."

He headed to the lieutenant's office and Cobb waved him in. "I want you to meet somebody."

An attractive dark-haired woman in her mid-fifties sat in the guest chair. She wore civilian clothes, and Dalton recognized her from research he'd done prior to applying for his position.

"Sheriff Martinez, this is Detective Dalton." Cobb beamed, kissing up to the sheriff.

She stood and he stepped over and shook her hand. "Pleased to meet you, Sheriff."

"Likewise. I recognize you from your debut on the

local news." She stared for a moment, grinning, as if she'd just told an inside joke. "Have a seat." He took the chair a few feet from her. "Lieutenant Cobb brought me up to date on your investigation. It sounds like you're making progress, and I really need results. I'll be getting heat again once the word gets out that Mr. Pound's death wasn't suicide. In your TV interview, you said you could solve this case. I canceled your suspension because you have all this homicide experience and seemed confident. Are you still as certain as before?"

Dalton nodded. "Absolutely."

When he didn't say more, she said, "All right, I'm depending on you." Her smile drifted away. "On a different matter, I finally got a call back from the Cook County State Attorney's office. They still wouldn't say what their case is about, but they want you to return for a deposition. I told them I would allow it when you get your murder case wrapped up. So, you solve this thing and you get a free trip to Chicago."

"Oh, boy."

Lieutenant Cobb squirmed in his chair and Dalton glanced his way. His mouth hung open, maybe in surprise that the detective would make such a casual remark to the sheriff.

The sheriff didn't seem to mind. She reached out and patted his arm. "I knew you'd like that. Now, I'm up for reelection in a few months, so get out of here and do your thing."

He headed back to his desk. According to the sheriff's website, she had started her career as a traffic cop with the Miami-Dade PD and achieved lieutenant rank before running for office. While the sheriff had a solid background in law enforcement, public opinion and politics seemed to fuel her engines now. She would be ecstatic if he closed his case in a couple of days. If not, he would need to look for other work.

Remembering the video from the self-storage company, he pulled it out and plugged it into his computer. After a security scan he played the footage for the day Barbara Spain said Rudy Banks had visited Toole Parts. She said he'd returned to the office about 4:00 p.m., so that would have put him in Key Largo about an hour before.

When he viewed that window of time in the video, at first he just saw passing traffic and cars turning into the self-storage lot. The view of Toole Parts across the street was grainy, and facial identification would be impossible at that distance. No vehicles were visible in the lot out front, but a car sat at the far end of a driveway alongside the building.

At a few minutes past 3:00 p.m., a white van turned in and drove down the drive to the rear and parked behind the car. Two men got out, each carrying what appeared to be a brief case, and rounded the rear corner of the building.

At 3:10 a car turned into the lot, and a man got out and went to the front door. Dalton guessed this was Banks. After waiting a minute or so and getting no answer, the accountant ambled down the drive next to the building and disappeared around the rear corner. He didn't stay long before hurrying back to his car. A second man followed a few steps behind him with something in his hand, maybe a gun, and watched as the visitor sped into the street.

A few minutes later the two men with brief cases came back and got into the van and left. Apparently, they had either brought something or picked something up. Whatever the activity, Banks had stumbled into it and left in alarm.

About 3:40 another man came out from behind the building. He stood for a few minutes, maybe smoking, and then headed back around the corner. Fast-forwarding throughout the day Dalton saw no change, other than more smoke breaks.

The van returned after dark. Leaving the headlights on, two tall men got out and pulled a third man from the rear of the vehicle. His wrists appeared bound together. Another vehicle arrived and a small man got out. He and the other two led the bound man into the van's beams and disappeared in the distance, well past the building, Dalton assumed to the awaiting boat. One of the taller men returned a few minutes later. He turned off the headlamps and locked up, and then hurried back toward the shore. Other than their relative size, none of the men were identifiable. The video ended a few minutes later with no further activity.

THAT EVENING, shortly past dusk, Dalton and Sam turned into the lot of a shuttered business a few doors down from Toole Parts. They stretched on vinyl gloves and headed up the street on foot. Before entering the view of the camera at the self-storage facility, they donned ski masks.

Holding a penlight in his mouth, Sam worked his pick in the back door lock. Dalton ventured down to the water, but didn't find the boat he'd seen snuggled into the mangroves the day before. When he returned, Sam was entering the door and said, "I'll take the front offices."

Dalton took the stockroom and rear offices. A few minutes later they met in the hallway. "You find anything suspicious?" Dalton asked.

"Just empty office space. Looks like this place was originally built as a house and later converted to commercial use."

Dalton crossed the hall and went into another room. It looked like more of the same...until he saw the closet. The door had been removed. It stood against the wall, its hinges still attached. Inside the closet, holes large enough for lag bolts had been drilled into the corners of each of the walls, the floor, and the ceiling. More holes were in the jamb where a lock had been removed.

Sam said from the hall, "Nothing up front."

"Come in here."

Sam stepped in and peered inside. "Huh, what is it?"

"Looks like they had something bolted to all the surfaces, maybe steel, for reinforcement. And it had a big lock on it."

"Yeah, I see what you mean. They built a vault, and then dismantled it and took it with them when they left."

Nodding, Dalton said, "Probably had a steel door, too." His phone chimed, too loud, giving him a jerk. He checked the display. "It's Lucinda. I wonder if she knows we're here."

"I don't see how."

When he answered, she said, "Detective, this is Lucinda Toole. We need to talk. Soon."

"Okay. Can you meet me in Islamorada, an hour or so from now?"

"I can be there in two hours."

They agreed on the location and hung up. He and Sam left and retraced their steps to the car.

As they rode away, Sam said, "What do you think she wants to talk about?"

"Beats me. Could be a setup."

They were quiet until they reached the Overseas Highway and turned south. Dalton said, "I've been thinking about the video I got from across the street. It showed men arriving and leaving with brief cases. Probably dropping off cash. It also appeared that somebody stayed there around the clock guarding the place."

"I'm guessing it could be Leonard Orlov's stash from drug sales and extortion. From the size of that closet they could've had millions in it."

"The deposits to Pound's offshore account were electronic transfers. Those didn't involve cash, so maybe he arranged the drug purchases and paid for the product electronically, and Orlov paid him the same way."

Dalton glanced at him. "What do you think happened then, with the money, and Myron, and the other men who died?"

"Since Myron took the boat, the other two probably thought they'd get rid of him and hightail it to points unknown with all that cash. Split it two ways instead of three. Myron would catch the blame, and he wouldn't be around to squeal. Orlov probably caught up with the other two and took them out."

Slowing for traffic in Tavernier, Dalton said, "I think you're right about Myron, and the only problem I have with the other two is that Orlov or his thugs might've shot them in the face so they could see it coming. But they each got a bullet to the back of the head, making it appear they didn't expect it."

"Yeah, I see your point."

Spotting a coffee shop coming up on the right, Dalton suggested they stop for a cup. "We have some time to kill."

They used the drive-thru, and back on the road Sam said, "Have you forgotten about your friend Chase? He could've had a part in this, too."

Dalton took a sip from his cup and set it in the holder. "No, I haven't forgotten. He seemed pretty chummy with Heather Pound yesterday when I searched her husband's office. And you're right, he could have some involvement. It occurred to me that he could've engineered the robbery, killed those guys on the boat, and then Pound, so he could have the wife and the money. On the other hand, I don't think he has the brains to pull off something like that."

"How about the wife? She could be the brains."

"And she has a criminal past."

A few minutes later Sam said, "I'm picking up Simone at the airport in the morning about ten."

"Oh, yeah?" Dalton remembered the tall, raven beauty, a former CIA operative.

"She called today and sounded stressed over a job

she just finished. I told her to catch a flight and chill out for a few days in the Keys."

It didn't seem to ring true, those two chilling in the Keys. He glanced at Sam. "You two have a job planned?"

Shrugging, Sam said, "Maybe, but don't worry, we won't do anything that'll get you fired. Too bad you're a cop, I could use your help on it."

"Yeah, too bad."

On Big Pine Key Dalton turned into the parking lot of an old motel that appeared out of business and pulled over to the side under a streetlamp. "Maybe she just wants to talk. If not, we need to be ready." They got out with their weapons and waited on the far side of the car.

A few minutes later, a black Chrysler turned in and eased toward them. Dalton's pulse quickened. The car stopped, and Lucinda opened the driver's door and got out. "I'm alone," she said over the roof of the car. "Why don't you come over here."

Dalton let himself in and sat in her passenger seat while Sam stayed behind and watched for visitors.

"What's on your mind?" he asked.

She turned sideways to face him. Her skirt rode a few inches above the knee on her right leg. In the dim light, all he saw was eyes and lips, and she looked even more beautiful than the last time. "I'm not involved in my ex-husband's business. I want you to know that."

"You mean the parts company?"

"Yes."

"You're the official owner of record for that company."

"I know, but—"

"Hold on. I know you're laundering money for Leonard Orlov's racket and drug operations."

"No, no. That's what I'm trying to tell you. He put my name on the business license to throw off the police, but he runs everything. He makes me go to the office in case we have visitors or callers. Please, you must believe me."

She reached out and clasped his hand. He realized what she was doing. "Even if I believe you, somebody's going down for the laundering operation. I can't promise it won't be you."

Pulling her hand away, she sighed and said, "I understand, but I'm just a pawn, a victim in Leonard's criminal activity, and you need to arrest him. He controls everything. He even has a tracker on my Mercedes. That's why I rented this car, so he wouldn't know I came to meet you. He would kill me if he knew."

Dalton remained silent for a few beats and then said, "Is Lucinda Toole your real name?"

"Yes, Toole is my maiden name, and I went back to it when we divorced."

"The self-storage company across the street from your office has a security video. It recorded Rudy Banks' visit. He stayed only a few minutes and then hurried away. I think he saw your people bringing in a load of cash."

"I told you the truth before. Leonard got really angry with me. He said I caused him a lot of trouble because I wasn't in the office that day."

"The video also recorded two men bringing him back

that night. His hands were bound, and they took him off in a boat."

Shaking her head, she said, "I don't know anything about that."

Dalton thought he saw a tear on the side of her face. If she was lying, she was pretty good at it.

"Okay. After that, I believe some different men came and robbed your place, taking your ex-husband for a lot of cash."

Her breathing had become audible, and he knew he was touching on the truth, even if she wouldn't admit it. She remained silent for a moment too long, and then shook her head. "I don't know anything about that, either. If they took money from him, they'll be sorry."

"Oh, I think you're right. They were sorry for at least a millisecond before each got a bullet in the head. They were murdered, as was a man named Joe Pound. Then there's the question of what happened to Rudy Banks. I assume he's dead by now, too. All this happened in the span of a week, catalyzed, I think, by Banks seeing all that cash at Toole Parts."

Her hands went to her face, and she made sobbing sounds.

After a minute or so of that, he sighed and said, "Okay, you can cut the waterworks. I'm not all that interested in the money laundering. If you want me to believe you're innocent, you have to give me something that will connect your ex-husband to these murders."

FIFTEEN

AT A FEW minutes past midnight Dalton and Sam headed across the MacArthur Causeway in Miami toward the marina where Sam normally moored his boat. He had called ahead and asked the dock master about borrowing a skiff he'd used before. It had a large outboard and an electric motor. They parked and found the boat with the ignition key in a side compartment. A few minutes later they navigated out of the marina and under the causeway toward Palm Island. A manmade creation from dredging by the Army Corp of Engineers in the 1920s, Palm Island became the home of the wealthy and celebrated. Some were more notorious than famous, such as Al Capone, who had lived there toward the end of his life.

Lucinda had continued to deny any knowledge of her ex-husband's activities, but finally mentioned a boat he had at his Palm Island dock. She said he'd brought it in the day before and covered it with tarps. Dalton thought it could be the one stolen from Nathan Beam on Big Pine, and likely used to interrogate and dispose of Rudy Banks.

When they neared the island Sam shut down the motor and used the electric. It moved them along at a decent clip without sound. Several boats were docked along the waterfront properties. They zeroed in on the GPS coordinates for Orlov's address and found his dock. It lay in darkness and ran parallel to the shore. The stolen boat had white tarps stretched over its bow and stern. Dalton remembered that the registration number had appeared altered, but he wondered if they'd thought about the hull ID.

Nobody appeared to be standing guard, although someone could've been watching from the house about a hundred feet away. Sam eased the skiff up to the rear of the boat, which was uncovered. Dalton shone his penlight on the upper edge of the transom, starboard side, and illuminated the hull identification number. It appeared unaltered, with a light coating of mildew surrounding the digits. He pulled up the photo he had taken of the owner's registration certificate and compared the hull ID with the one on the transom. They matched. The letters and numbers, only a quarter-inch or so in size, had probably gone unnoticed.

"Let's ease away from here," he whispered to Sam. A few minutes later, about a hundred yards away, he dialed Detective Diaz's number.

When the policeman answered, Dalton identified himself and said, "Sorry if I woke you up."

"No, that's okay. I work nights since the Orlov fiasco. What's up?"

He told him about the stolen boat.

"You're sure about this?"

"Yes, I'm sure. It was stolen recently on Big Pine Key. I also think it was used last week in the abduction and murder of a man named Rudy Banks. It'd be great if you could arrest Orlov and impound the boat for crime scene examination."

"You bet I will."

He gave the detective the GPS coordinates.

"Give me an hour," Diaz said.

It took a few minutes longer than Diaz had predicted, but then a boat neared and spotlights crisscrossed the property. It had the emblem of the Miami-Dade Police on its hull. Dalton flashed his light on and off a couple of times, and the boat eased over and cut the engine. A man in uniform had the helm, and another officer handled the light. A third man, wearing civilian clothes, stood at the rail.

"You Dalton?" the man at the rail said.

"Yes."

"I'm Diaz. Is that the boat over there with the tarps?"

"It is. The hull ID number is visible on the transom."

Diaz nodded. "I'll check it out." He turned and asked the helmsman to take them over to the boat.

Sam punched up the electric motor and they glided behind them.

At the stolen boat stern, the uniformed officer shone the spotlight onto the transom. Diaz leaned close to read the numbers, and then turned and punched keys on a computer mounted on the dash. Within a few seconds he smiled. "Okay, I got a match. It belongs to a man named Beam, reported stolen about a week ago." He pulled a phone from his pocket, punched a couple of keys, and held it to his ear. After a pause, he said into the phone, "Okay, I've confirmed the stolen boat. Move in and take him." Returning the phone to his pocket, he said to Dalton, "I need you to come in and tell your side of the story."

"Roger that."

Diaz seemed to notice Sam for the first time. "Who's that with you?"

"Just the guy who brought me out here. He isn't part of this."

Nodding, Diaz said, "Whatever you say. See you at police headquarters." He turned to the officer with the light. "Get the covers off this boat. We're taking it in."

The officer turned the spotlight so it illuminated the boat, hopped onto the shore, and began untying the lines. A few minutes later a man ran out from the back of the house toward the dock. He had a gun in his hand. The officer pulled his weapon and yelled, "Halt and lay the piece on the ground!"

Still moving, the man pointed his gun. The officer fired, and the round appeared to hit the runner in the shoulder. He spun a half-turn and tumbled to the grass. His gun flew from his hand and slid a few feet away.

A man wearing a SWAT vest hurried out of the house to the downed man and picked up the weapon. "Good shooting," he said to the officer.

Sam started the outboard motor, and they headed to the marina. They drove to police headquarters, and Sam napped in the car while Dalton went inside. He gave his statement and said he wanted to be present when Diaz interrogated Orlov. The Miami detective agreed.

Dalton had never seen a photo of the career criminal. In his mind's eye he had pictured a stereotypically tall man with slicked dark hair and a manicured, three-day beard. But the real-life version sitting at the table probably weighed about one-twenty and would stand only five feet or so. To top it off, he had a clean-shaven face and thinning blond hair. He could have been the small man from the self-storage video who arrived at Toole Parts after Banks got pulled from the van.

"The boat tied to your dock was stolen," Diaz said. "How did it come into your possession?"

Orlov shrugged, his expression unreadable, and said in accented English, "One of my associates found it abandoned in Biscayne Bay, just yesterday. We planned to turn it in."

"So why did you paint over the registration number?"

The suspect smiled and shook his head. "No, we did not."

After several denials about how he'd acquired the boat, Dalton asked him what he knew about Rudy Banks' disappearance. He smirked. "Never heard of him."

"We have video of two men taking him out of a van at your place of business in Key Largo and putting him on that stolen boat."

Orlov leaned back and blinked a couple of times, maybe a little surprised, and then shook his head. "I don't have a business in Key Largo."

Dalton knew he wouldn't get anywhere with more questions, so he thought he would plant a seed. "Okay, you can stonewall all you want. We'll see what your friends have to say about it." Two others had been arrested along with Orlov. The associate with the gunshot wound had been taken to the hospital. Boris Ivashin, the man he knew from the visit to Lucinda's house, waited in a different interrogation room.

"They will tell you the truth." To Diaz he said, "I want my lawyer."

"Sure they will. We'll make them a sweet deal, and they'll serve you up quicker than you can say pierogi." He stood to leave.

Diaz followed him out, closing the door behind him. "I'll work on him a few more minutes and then talk to the other guy. If it's like the other times, they'll both be out on bail by noon, so I hope we get some good prints from that boat."

"I hope so, too. Better put a guard on it so it doesn't get firebombed tonight."

AFTER A FEW fitful hours of sleep, Dalton rose and showered. They had gotten back to the marina after 4:00 a.m., and Cupcake met him at the door, whining. Dalton fed him a can of tuna, just a snack for the big cat. Then he spent almost an hour updating his notes on the bust, and ate a piece of nuked pizza before getting to bed.

Eric had pastries and coffee on the deck for the guests, so Dalton grabbed one of each on his way out and drove north. He phoned Cobb and briefed him on the arrest. "I'm headed back to Miami now. We need our crime scene crew to scour that tub for prints and DNA. The sooner the better. If we can get a positive match for Banks and Orlov, or his men, we can charge them with the abduction."

"What makes you think he used that boat in an abduction?" Cobb asked.

Dalton had to be careful about explaining his knowledge of the boat. "I saw it at the Toole Parts property the day before. It sailed off before I could get anybody to look it over. The video I got from the business across the street showed a man being led to the shore. I believe it was Banks." He mentioned Lucinda Toole squealing on her ex about the boat.

"How come I'm just learning about all this?"

He felt his face flush, and after a couple of beats said, "Everything happened since I spoke with you and the sheriff yesterday."

The lieutenant gave a loud sigh. "All right, Detective, I've already warned you about keeping me updated." A silence lay on the line for several seconds, and then he said, "I'll send the crew to Miami." He hung up.

Dalton grinned. As he laid the phone on the console, Diaz called.

"You must be on overtime," Dalton said.

"Yeah, I gotta get home and catch some Z's before my shift starts again. I wanted to tell you, Orlov's attorney is here. He's trying to get a judge to let him bail on the stolen property charge. If our guys don't turn up something pretty soon this morning, he'll be gone. I'd hate for him to slip through our fingers again."

"You get a peek at the boat?"

"Yeah, it's a big mess."

"Good, maybe they didn't get a chance to clean it up. Before you hang up, what's the name of the guy that got shot last night?"

"Hold on. Here it is. Nolan Pierce. I checked him out. He's a three-time-loser on B-and-Es."

They ended the call. After mulling over the situation for a few miles, he called Lola Ann. "I'll give you a scoop if you promise not to quote me."

"You got it, cowboy," she said, enthusiasm in her tone.

He told her about the stolen boat and the arrest. "You should look for background on this guy. There's plenty of it."

"What's so special about him getting arrested for stealing a boat?"

"He used it to abduct and murder an Islamorada man."

"How do you know this?"

"I'm a detective. Just run the story. You'll be glad you got out ahead of it."

"Okay, but if I get burned—"

"You won't. Trust me."

"Hold on while I make some notes." After a minute or so she read them off to him.

"That's good. Go with it."

"I have a news slot at 10:30. I'll put it on then. You want to get a drink later and tell me more about it?"

"I'll have to get back to you."

Next, he phoned Lucinda Toole. "In case you haven't already heard, Miami-Dade PD arrested your ex-husband last night." He gave her the details. "You need to make yourself scarce in case he puts it together."

"Can't you keep him in jail?"

"Not long, unless we get him on something more incriminating."

She said she would keep in touch and hung up.

At 10:20 he entered Jackson Memorial Hospital and found Nolan Pierce's room. A police officer sat by the door. Dalton showed him his badge and went inside. Pierce lay gazing at the ceiling, an IV in his arm. He cut his eyes toward his visitor. "Who're you?"

Dalton identified himself and said, "Just checking on you to see if you're okay."

Pierce snorted. "Yeah, right."

"You comfortable, getting enough pain meds?"

"No, I'm not." He scowled and pressed the nurse button next to his bed. "I've been calling them for twenty minutes, and they haven't brought me anything yet."

The clock on the wall indicated 10:29. Dalton reached for the TV remote and pressed the power button. "Let's get the TV on for you. Maybe that'll get your mind off the pain." When the screen lit up, he switched to channel 6. Within a few seconds, Lola Ann's pretty face filled the screen. "Ah, good, it's the news. You like the news, don't you?" He glanced at Pierce, who still had the scowl, glancing from the TV to Dalton and back.

"You think I want to watch that? I'm in pain. That'll make it worse."

Lola Ann: *"Miami resident Leonard Orlov and two of his employees have been arrested for possession of a stolen boat. Miami-Dade Police seized the craft, worth in excess of $200,000 dollars, just after midnight last night at Mr. Orlov's estate on Palm Island. Mr. Orlov contends that one of his employees found the boat, and he'd planned to turn it in. However, an anonymous caller early this morning told a different story. This* *person said Mr. Orlov murdered an Islamorada man on the boat. We have no way of confirming whether this accusation is true or not, but we do know that police crime scene crews are currently examining the stolen boat for forensic evidence. As you may know, Leonard Orlov is no stranger to the Miami-Dade Police Department. Last year they accused him of murdering a Miami storekeeper. Those charges were eventually dropped and Mr. Orlov sued the Department for harassment. A Dade County judge later dismissed the suit. Now in other news—"*

Dalton punched the Mute button and turned to the patient, who had been glued to the report.

"Doesn't look too good for your boss."

Pierce stared at the soundless screen, his mouth agape. A nurse entered the room with a hypodermic. "I have your pain medication, Mr. Pierce. You won't be able to get any more for four hours." She injected the drug into the IV apparatus. "Do you need anything else right now?"

Shaking his head, Pierce said, "No, I'm okay." He seemed lost in thought.

"All right, press the Call button if you need anything." The nurse left the room.

"That news lady made that up." He'd had time to compose himself.

"Didn't sound like it to me. Somebody must've squealed. You know anything about the murder she mentioned?"

"Nobody got murdered. It's just like Leonard said.

We found that boat and was gonna turn it in. End of story."

"Well, if there is an informant, Leonard will be pretty angry with him."

"I told you, we didn't murder nobody."

Dalton stared for a moment, and then said, "He'll get bail in a few hours. You better hope he doesn't think you're the squealer. It doesn't matter whether you did it or not; He'll probably make a clean sweep. You'll be a sitting duck here in the hospital." He let that sink in, and then said, "You know, we could cut a deal if the informant was to give Leonard up to the police. He wouldn't get bail on a murder charge."

Pierce's eyes took on a dreamy quality, the drug doing its job. "What kind of deal?"

"If the informant didn't participate in the killing, we could get him off with a minimum sentence. That'd be better than a bullet to the back of the head."

Pierce blinked a couple of times, eyes getting droopy. "Well… I ain't worried. There's a cop outside my door."

"He'll be gone if somebody puts up bail for you." Dalton pulled a card from his pocket. "I'll let you know when your boss gets free, so you can be ready. Think about it. Give me a call if you change your mind." Pierce appeared about to doze off, so he laid the card on the table next to the bed and went out the door. Bad timing on the medication. It would be a shame if the guy didn't remember anything about their conversation when he woke up.

DALTON FOUND THE impound dock and met Robin as she exited the boat for more supplies.

"What've you found?"

"Plenty of fingerprints. We can run them against what we found at Banks' house. We also found some blood that could belong to him. The DNA from the spatters at his house came back from the lab, so we can do a comparison on that, too. I don't think anybody cleaned up any evidence, so we'll know if he was on this boat."

"Good work. How long do you think you'll be here?"

"Another couple of hours, at least. Then we'll get with the Miami investigators and share what we have. We should be back in Islamorada by late this afternoon."

He had hoped it would be sooner, before Orlov could get booted. "Okay, I'll see you there."

At Miami-Dade PD headquarters he checked in with Detective Ames, who had taken over for Diaz. Ames, a rotund man who looked at least ten years past retirement age, said, "We didn't get anything else out of them. Their lawyers came and shut everything down. There's a bail hearing at 1:00 p.m., so it's likely we'll have to release them."

"Too bad," Dalton said. "We should have some forensics this afternoon."

"Yeah, tell me about it. I was Diaz's partner when we tried to take this slime ball down before." Running fingers through his thinning hair, he added, "He'll probably sue again. I don't need this kind of aggravation." He gave Dalton a look that said, *You're the one who stirred this up.*

After a quick lunch from a street vendor, Dalton headed to the courthouse. The bail hearing went exactly as Ames had predicted: the lawyer made his case, and the judge set bail at $10,000 each for Orlov and Ivashin, without so much as a blink of an eye. They hit the streets before 2:00 p.m. Orlov gave Dalton a smirk as they strode out. He pointed at him with his index finger, his thumb turned up like a pistol hammer, and clicked his tongue.

As Dalton left the courthouse, Pierce called.

"Hey, man, I need to talk to you."

"Oh, yeah? Your boss just got bail."

"I know. The cop outside told me. Come down here. I want the deal you mentioned."

SIXTEEN

DALTON CALLED MIAMI police headquarters. Diaz answered, back on duty, and they agreed to meet at the hospital. When they got to the room, they found Pierce demanding pain meds from a nurse. She told him it was too soon and rolled her eyes as she left the room.

Pierce scowled at them. "I'm hurting, and they won't give me anything."

"You wanted to talk?" Dalton said.

Lowering his voice, Pierce said, "I think that cop out there is one of Leonard's friends. How about closing the door?"

Diaz did as he asked, and Pierce said, "What kind of deal can I get if I tell you what happened to Banks?" He looked from one to the other.

Dalton shrugged. "Depends on what part you took in it."

"I just drove the boat."

"Hold on," Diaz said as he set a video camera on the serving table and positioned it. "We need to record this." He punched the power button, identified the three of them, and then said to Pierce, "Tell us what happened, from the beginning."

"We hotwired the boat at a marina on Big Pine that night. I drove it up to Key Largo where we had a van, and we used it to pick up Banks at his house. When we got back to the boat, we took him out in the Gulf, and Leonard and Boris beat on him until he couldn't talk anymore. They never got anything out of him. He kept insisting he hadn't told anybody about what he saw at the place in Key Largo."

"What did he see?" Dalton asked.

"They were counting money in a back room at Toole Parts, and he surprised them. One of the guys pulled a gun and he ran."

Dalton nodded. "Okay, what happened after they beat him?"

"Leonard finally decided the guy was telling the truth, but by that time he knew he couldn't let him go." Pierce gulped a couple of times and turned away, maybe realizing he had reached the part that could send his boss to death row.

After a few beats, Dalton said, "Go on. What did Orlov do?"

The confessor turned back and stared for a moment before saying, "Leonard pulled his gun and shot Banks in the face. He died instantly. Then Leonard and Boris had a few drinks before Boris tied a cement block to the dead guy's feet. They dragged him out of there and threw him overboard." He remained quiet for what seemed like a long time and then said, "You got to protect me until Leonard goes down."

"Don't worry," Dalton said. "We'll protect you."

"What kind of deal can I get?"

"Did you have anything to do with the murder?"

Pierce's eyes widened. "No, I told you, they did it

all. I had to watch some of it, and it made me sick to my stomach, but I never touched the guy."

Diaz turned the camera off.

"We'll take this video to the DA's office and see what they can do," Dalton said. "You'll have to testify in court."

"That's okay, long as Leonard and Boris are in jail."

"You know they'll try to blame the killing on you."

"Yeah, but I volunteered this information. Won't that count more than what they say?"

Dalton nodded. "Maybe. Could you show us where the body went into the water?"

"I think so. It was about a hundred yards off a little island. I can probably go back to it. Tell them to bring my pain meds."

They left the room and stepped down the hall to the end.

Diaz said, "If word gets back to Orlov, he'll put out a hit on this guy." He called the watch commander and requested a second guard. After a couple of seconds he shook his head and sighed. "Okay I'll know who to blame if he dies."

Upon hearing Diaz's side of the conversation, Dalton stepped over to the nurses' station and asked if Pierce could be checked out of the hospital. The nurse said she would check with the doctor and let him know. He and Diaz got a cup of coffee and took a seat in the visitors' lounge.

The nurse found him about twenty minutes later and said it would be okay for the patient to leave, as long as he took it easy. "He didn't have any major damage. I don't know why he's complaining so much about pain."

"Maybe he had a dependency before he got shot," Dalton said. "Can you give him another dose before we leave?"

"That should be okay." She hustled away.

He turned to Diaz. "I want to take him down to the Keys and see if we can find that body."

Diaz nodded. "Okay, the officer and I can take him in the cruiser."

They went back to the room and waited. A few minutes later the nurse returned with a hypodermic. When the medicine had flowed through the IV, she unhooked it and wheeled it away. She brought back a prescription and handed it to Diaz. "This is for pain medication. You can get it filled downstairs."

Dalton retrieved Pierce's clothes from the closet. "Get dressed, we're leaving."

They checked him out of the hospital and got the pain meds. The officer went out and came back to the door with the car. A few minutes later they rode out of Miami toward US-1, Dalton's car in the lead. He called Cobb on the way and updated him. "I need some divers and a boat."

"Our divers are down in Marathon right now, searching for a drown victim."

"Okay, just launch the boat, and I'll get some gear from the dive shop. I keep my certification up to date."

Cobb said he would take care of it.

A couple of hours later they eased the patrol boat

away from the dock, leaving the uniformed officer behind.

"We went out about twenty miles, due west," Pierce said.

"You don't remember the coordinates?" Dalton said.

"No, but if you go to where we started, I can get you there."

Running the twin motors wide open, it took about ten minutes to reach the shore adjacent to Toole Parts. At that point, Dalton headed west. When they reached the twenty mile mark, he slowed. The boat cast a long shadow across the mirror of water. Probably only a couple more hours of good daylight. "Does this look familiar?"

Pierce's eyes skimmed the seascape. "Not yet, keep going." They passed several tiny islands, but at each Pierce told them the scene didn't look quite right.

Dalton wondered if the guy could remember the location, and if he might just be jerking them around so he could postpone going to jail as long as possible. But after a half hour of slow cruising, he said, "That's it, over there." He pointed to a chunk of land a hundred yards or so away. Two tall palms waved in the breeze.

"You're sure?"

"Yeah, pretty sure. Maybe ninety percent."

They slowed and cut a wide circle around the island until Pierce said, "Yeah, stop here." He turned to Diaz. "How about I take some of those pills?" The detective shrugged and opened the plastic bottle.

Dalton dropped anchor in almost thirty feet of water and suited up. He clipped on an Aqualite and flipped backward over the rail. Descending to the sea floor, he turned on the light and swam through patches of vegetation and coral. A silhouette several yards away resembled an erect body, but when he neared, it turned out to be just a thick stand of seaweed.

A three-foot barracuda stalked a school of colorful fish nearby. It seemed to spot him and glided his way, its fangs reflecting off the light. Dalton pulled a dagger from his pouch. Though no match for the teeth, it would have to do. He remained still as the fish slowed and eased to within a few feet of him. Then, with a jerk, it turned and resumed its hunt. Dalton could feel his heart thumping in his chest. After a half-hour of fruitless searching, covering a radius of at least thirty yards in every direction, Dalton gave up and surfaced.

"No luck?" Diaz said.

Dalton shook his head. "Maybe our friend here is leading us on a wild good chase."

Pierce scowled. "No, this is the place. I remember seeing the palms over on that island and wishing I could be there instead of on the boat listening to them drag that body up the ladder."

"Save the drama," Dalton said. "There's nothing down there but seaweed and fish."

"But it has to be here. I remember the palms." As Dalton removed his fins, Pierce said, "Wait, it was breezy that day, and the boat drifted. By the time they dropped him, we were maybe another hundred yards that way." He pointed. "Move over there and have a look."

Dalton sighed and said to Diaz, "We're here, we might as well check it out."

Diaz nodded and turned to Pierce. "Hey, pal, if we don't find anything down there, you're going back to Miami to a cell, and you won't be getting any more of those pain pills."

After weighing anchor, Dalton moved the boat to the place Pierce had indicated. He refastened the fins, checked his air supply—another thirty minutes left—and got back in the water.

Visibility had dimmed with the reclining sun, so he shone the Aqualite as he descended, illuminating several yards of murky water. Again he did a radial sweep, finding nothing more than he had on the previous dive, until the last quadrant. There it stood among tendrils of seaweed. The man's arms floated above his body, as if he might take flight, but the concrete block kept him tethered to the seafloor.

Dalton surfaced and climbed aboard. Diaz gave him a questioning look, and he said, "I found him." He retrieved a rope from one of the boat's compartments and went back in the water.

As THE SUN rested on the horizon, they headed back toward Islamorada with the body onboard. Diaz added to the footage on his video, making sure he got a good shot of the bullet hole in the dead man's forehead.

The trip seemed to take longer than it had going out. Nobody spoke. Diaz rode up front with Pierce, as far from the corpse as he could get, gazing into the cleansing vastness of the Gulf.

As they approached the dock in Islamorada, Diaz spoke on the phone with his partner in Miami. He told him to round up Orlov and Ivashin and hold them for pickup by Monroe County on a murder charge. "Take several blue suits with you. If he knows he's going down for murder, he won't have anything to lose."

The ME and his crew stood on shore at the marina. Dr. Lake stepped aboard and scanned the body. Then two men bagged it, transferred it to a gurney on the dock, and rolled it to a waiting van. Lake stepped off the boat and turned to Dalton. "We've had quite an uptick in murders since you arrived, Detective."

Dalton felt his face heat up. "Good to know, Doctor. I hoped it wasn't like this all the time."

Lake frowned, shook his head, and paced away.

Diaz debarked and told the waiting Miami-Dade officer to take Pierce to the patrol car and put him in the back seat. He turned to Dalton, who had stepped onto the dock. "I guess we need to talk about who takes Pierce. I'd planned to charge him with grand theft and assault on an officer, but the more serious charge is here in the Keys."

"Yeah, and he would be safer if he stays here, especially until you get Orlov and Ivashin into custody."

"Okay, it's settled, then. We'll hold our charges until you decide what to do with him."

"Can you give me a copy of the video? I thought I'd show it to the DA and see what he thinks about charges."

"Sure, you can burn a copy when we drop Pierce off."

Tavernier housed the nearest detention center, just

a few miles north. They caravanned to the location and put Pierce in one of the cells. Diaz left the pills at the jailer's desk. "He was shot, and I expect him to be squawking about pain pretty soon. Need to use these sparingly, though. He might not get any more."

They borrowed one of the center's computers and copied the memory card from the camera. After promising to keep in touch about the status of Orlov and Ivashin, Diaz left.

Dalton ambled back to Pierce's cell. "I'm going to give the video to the DA's office and see what they can do for you. I need to know something else, though. What do you know about the other murders?"

Pierce frowned. "What murders?"

"Those guys who stole the money from your boss. They were shot in the back of the head."

The prisoner shrugged. "Leonard got upset about something when we got back, but he didn't tell me what it was about. I heard on the news about them guys getting killed, but that contractor that committed suicide in Islamorada said he killed 'em all."

"It wasn't a suicide. He was murdered, too. You know those two dead guys had been hauling drugs for Leonard."

Turning his head, Pierce stared at the wall for a few beats, and then turned back. "Hey, you got all you're gonna get out of me. Let me talk to that DA."

Dalton pressed him for another few minutes, but Pierce didn't yield. Either he didn't know, or wasn't about to admit anything more. Though he seemed to have a lesser role in the Banks killing, his involvement with the others could be a lot worse.

As Dalton walked away, the jailed man said, "I need a pain pill."

Dalton ignored him and strode out the door to his car. Since he had to drive by the office on his way home to Little Torch, he stopped in to see if Robin had left. He found her at her desk.

"Burning the midnight oil?"

She narrowed her eyes in a mock frown. "Yeah, you should know. It's all your fault."

He grinned. "What've you found?"

"Banks was on that boat. He plastered his prints all over the deck of the forward compartment. Orlov did too, so you should have a good case against him. Where've you been so long?"

"We pulled Banks' body out of the Gulf." He told her about Pierce's confession.

"I'd say that seals it, then, long as he doesn't change his story."

"We have him on video, so he'll have a hard time squirming out of it. I don't know about the other murders, though. He wouldn't cough up anything on them." After a couple of moments of silence, he said, "It's late. Let's get something to eat."

She agreed and followed him to a nearby pub. They had a beer and sliders.

As they finished, Dalton's phone chimed: Detention Center in Tavernier. When he answered, the jailer said, "A couple of Miami cops are here to pick up Pierce."

SEVENTEEN

On his way to the jail, Dalton rang Diaz's number. He put the phone on speaker and laid it on the console. Nobody answered and he left a voicemail: "Call me. Two officers are here to pick up Pierce, and I need to know what's going on."

The jailer called again. "They're getting impatient. I don't know how much longer I can stall them."

"Tell them to chill. I'm almost there."

A tinny voice that sounded as if coming through a tunnel said, "Hey, you gonna let us in, or not?"

"You'll have to wait," the jailer said. "I'm holding for someone to authorize Pierce's removal."

"Yeah, well, make it snappy. I need to be back in Miami before the shift ends."

Within a couple of minutes, Dalton turned into the lot and parked next to the police cruiser. The two officers, standing at the door, turned as he got out. He showed them his badge. "Who asked you to take Pierce to Miami?"

One of the officers glanced at the other. "You remember the detective's name?"

"Yeah, it was Diaz," the partner said.

"Okay, let's see some ID."

"Hey, we're police officers."

"I need to see it." He eased closer.

One of them smirked. "We'll be sure and tell the chief how you treated us."

"You do that." Dalton snapped his fingers. "ID."

The smirking officer stepped forward and handed him a card. He glanced at the man's face and held the card up to the best light. Seeing that the photo resembled the man, a little, he gave it back and turned to the other officer, a tall dark man with thinning hair. The guy rolled his eyes, but pulled an ID from his pocket. As he reached to hand it over, it slipped from his fingers.

"Pick it up," Dalton said.

The man in uniform smiled, and Dalton glanced at the card on the ground. His pulse kicked into overdrive, and he and Slippery Fingers pulled their guns at the same time. Dalton shot him in the chest, sending him over backward to the concrete. He stepped over and kicked the man's weapon away. The guy groaned in pain, but there didn't seem to be any blood. *Probably wore a vest.*

The still-standing officer fumbled with his weapon and brought it up. Dalton aimed at him. "Next shot goes between your eyes. The vest won't help you a bit."

After a couple of seconds the man glanced at his disabled partner and nodded. "Okay, I'm putting it down." He stooped and laid the gun at his feet.

The door of the facility swung open, and a deputy who looked just old enough to shave stood there with a gun in his hand, his eyes wide.

"Pick up their guns," Dalton said.

The deputy stared for a moment. "Why'd you shoot him? He's a policeman."

"No, he isn't. Look at the ID." He nodded toward the dropped card, which displayed the photo of a man with red hair and a pasty face.

The deputy examined the photo for a moment. "Yeah, I see what you mean." He proceeded to collect the weapons and Dalton asked him to go inside and call the paramedics.

A tinny voice issued from the speaker next to the doorway: "They're on the way."

While they waited, Dalton and the deputy restrained the imposters' hands behind their backs, and took them inside to separate cells. Paramedics arrived within ten minutes and checked out the shot man. As suspected, he wore a vest, and the bullet had just popped a big bruise on his chest.

A search of the patrol car revealed two shoulder-mount rocket launchers in the trunk. Probably their backup plan: vaporize the place, and Pierce along with it. That would do the job, but their escape plan would suffer with only one road leading out of the keys.

As Dalton left the jail, Diaz called. "I don't know anything about anybody picking up Pierce."

"Yeah, those guys were phonies, and we locked them up. They probably work for Orlov, and two Miami cops are tied up somewhere or dead."

Back at the office, he sat down at his desk and wrote up the incident and the arrests while everything was fresh on his mind. He completed the paperwork after 2:00 a.m. and sent his boss an email telling him what happened. Everybody had turned in when he got home, and he saw where Eric had fed Cupcake, so he went straight to bed.

Waking at 9:00 the next morning, he showered and shaved and ambled out to the deck with a cup of coffee. Eric sat there with Sam and Simone. The big cat sat beside Simone's chair while she rubbed his ears. It surprised Dalton that she would be so comfortable around him.

Simone looked as beautiful as ever in exercise shorts and T-shirt. Both she and Sam had beads of perspiration on their faces and drank from frosty water bottles. They'd probably been out for a run.

Eric stood. "I'm gonna brew another pot of coffee while you three catch up." He smiled as he passed by, waggling his eyebrows, maybe a tad captivated by Simone.

She grinned when Dalton stepped over and took a seat. "Hey, my friend. How's it going?"

"Okay, I guess. I have my hands full right now."

"Yeah, Sam filled me in."

He told them about the previous day's events.

"You think Orlov killed those other guys, too?" Sam asked.

Dalton shook his head. "Hard to say. Pierce wouldn't admit anything, but he might have reasons of his own for not talking about those murders. I need to go over the forensics the crime scene crew collected from Joe Pound's boat."

"Well, let me know if you need anything from us,"

Sam said. "We're leaving tomorrow morning, but we'll be back in a couple of days."

Dalton didn't want to know any more, so he just nodded. He drained his coffee and stood. "Okay, maybe we can get together for dinner when you return. Great seeing you again, Simone."

"Likewise, Mick. Be safe." She gave him a smile that made him wish he could stay.

At the office, he found a skeleton crew. Most of the administrative staff didn't work on the weekend. He pulled the file on the two men murdered on Pound's boat, Eldon Perl and Floyd Sparks, and went back over the forensics. Nothing really telling. Just the two victims' blood and prints, Carl Myron's prints, and the prints of Joe Pound the owner. What if Pierce had told the truth, that he really didn't know anything about the murders? If Orlov or his men didn't kill them, who did? The killer had shot each of them in the back of the head, and Dalton had theorized that Orlov or one of his lieutenants would have looked them in the eye. It seemed they would also have killed them together in one spot, rather than one on the main deck and the other in the cabin below. That seemed as if they were friends with the killer. Could they have been friends with Steve Chase?

Joe Pound's suicide note claimed he had murdered them, but then he himself had been murdered, and that nullified the authenticity of the note. He looked back at the report Cobb had written and, as before, found nothing of value. As he reached to flip, he noticed something he'd skimmed over on his previous perusal. The list of items taken into evidence from Pound's office included two phones.

He checked the devices out of the evidence locker and went back to his desk. Each was enclosed inside a plastic bag. Unsure whether or not they had been dusted for prints, he stretched on vinyl gloves before handling them. The battery on each was nearly out of juice, but he was able to power them up. One appeared to be Pound's business phone. He had made recent calls to several people on his contact list—probably customers—and one or two each day to his wife. Dalton looked at the recent calls on the other phone, a basic flip unit and probably a burner. There were only a couple of numbers he had called and that had called back. Neither had been added to a contact list.

Dalton pulled out his notebook and found the information about the phones he and Sam had taken from Pound's boat the day they found the bodies. Eldon Perl had called a phone that J.T. hadn't been able to trace to an owner. It wasn't Pound's, but Pound had received a call from that same number the day he had been killed. Maybe the murderer?

He wondered if Robin had come in on a Saturday and headed over to her desk. Finding it vacant, he stepped into the break room. She sat talking with Steve Chase. They quieted when he entered the room.

"Hey, didn't know you were in today," she said as he poured a cup of coffee. "I heard you had a run-in with Miami police last night."

"Yeah, but not real policemen. They planned to blow

up the jail if they didn't get Pierce out of there." He stepped over to their table.

"You think they were going to kill him?" Chase asked.

"Probably. They knew he squealed about Orlov murdering the accountant."

Chase shook his head. "Bad business. The offer still stands, if you need any help on the case."

Dalton stared for a moment and nodded. Not a bad idea. A little conversation with the detective, just to clear the air. "I'm going up to Miami today to look for Orlov. He's still my best bet on the other murders. You want to tag along?"

"Sure. When are you leaving?"

"In a few. I'll let you know." He handed Robin the phones. "These belonged to Joe Pound. See what you can find out about the numbers he called and the ones that called him, especially the flip phone. It could've been the murderer calling him a little while before he died."

At his desk he called Detective Ames, Diaz's daytime counterpart, and hoped he would be at his desk on a Saturday. The detective answered and Dalton asked if they had arrested Orlov.

"No," Ames said, snorting a laugh. "He's probably back in Russia by now."

"Did you get a search warrant for his house?"

"We did, and we went through it but didn't find anything. You wanna have a looksee?"

"Yes, I'll be in town in a couple of hours. Can you meet me at the house?"

"Roger that." He sounded excited. "Get me out of here for a while."

Dalton pictured the oversized man who had overstayed his time on the job, maybe waiting for his pension to grow another dollar each month.

"I'll call when I reach Miami."

He and Chase left a few minutes later, Dalton driving.

After twenty-or-so minutes of quiet, Chase said, "I want to apologize about the way I acted when you first came here."

Glancing at him, Dalton said, "Sure, I understand." He understood that Chase had wanted him off the case for some reason, and he hadn't forgotten the cocaine someone had planted at his cottage.

"I thought the LT should've tossed that case to me. But I see now it was over my head, especially the way it's turned out with those other murders."

Although Dalton agreed, he made no comment. A few minutes later he said, "Somebody planted a bag of cocaine at my place my first day on the job. Deputies came out looking for drugs. They said an anonymous caller tipped them off. You know anything about that?"

Chase's eyes grew large, but he shook his head. "No, I hadn't heard about that. I guess they didn't find anything."

Dalton gave him a smirk. "No, they didn't find the cocaine. I discovered it before they got there."

No comment.

Dalton continued. "I heard you had a cocaine bust a couple of weeks ago."

Looking straight ahead, Chase said, "Yeah, I did."

"Who was it?"

"Some small-time distributor. A uniform called me in on it. Caught him peddling out of a bar."

"You've never been down to my place in Little Torch, have you?"

Chase turned and stared for a moment. "No, I haven't."

"Too bad. It's really my uncle's marina. You'll have to come by sometime. I have a rescued cougar as a pet. His name is Cupcake. Wouldn't hurt a flea."

If he planted the drugs, he had first-hand knowledge of the cougar.

The deputy said, "You trying to accuse me of planting the cocaine?"

Dalton shrugged. "The cougar drew blood from the intruder's leg. I can have it analyzed for DNA and find out who did it."

Chase just stared for a few beats and then turned and looked straight ahead, his breathing audible over the hiss of the air conditioner. He didn't say anything else for the remainder of the trip.

Dalton dialed up Lucinda Toole and asked her if she knew where her ex-husband might have gone.

"I have no idea. When you called about him getting arrested, I left town."

"Where are you?"

She hesitated, and then said, "I'd rather not say. Leonard could've tapped my phone."

He didn't like her answer, but didn't think it made

much difference. "Does he have any properties in the vicinity, other than his home, where he could've gone?"

"I don't know of any. We were married only a couple of years, and I don't remember him buying any property during that time."

"Okay, let me know if you hear from him."

"I will. You need to arrest him before he kills me." She hung up.

On the outskirts of Miami, Dalton spoke with Ames. They met at Orlov's waterfront home a half-hour later. Chase hung back, maybe pouting, as Ames introduced his partner, a tall, thin man who had also probably stayed on the job a good decade past his prime. They made for quite a pair of detectives. The two probably hadn't run down a suspect on foot in years. The partner appeared disinterested in helping search the place and got back in the car with the air running.

At the door, Ames cut his eyes back toward the vehicle. "He's addicted to gambling on his phone. According to him, he wins lots of money, but he never seems to have any of it on him when it's time to pay for lunch." He chuckled and pulled out a key. "We had the lock changed and posted a patrol car up the block in case Orlov tries to come back here."

They stretched on vinyl gloves and entered.

"How good a search did your guys do of this place?" Dalton asked.

Ames shook his head. "Not too much. We've had other priorities."

After a quick walkthrough of the home, Dalton said

to Chase, "Why don't you take the bedrooms and I'll take the office."

"What're we looking for?" the deputy asked, his eyes narrowed.

Dalton stared for a moment. "Something that'll tell us where he's hiding."

Chase nodded and headed down the hall.

The office contained a desk and a spot where a portable computer had sat. Drawers in the desk appeared to have been rifled. There were no little black books with names and protection payments. No records of any kind. Apparently, Orlov had taken anything he didn't want the police to see, but Dalton hoped he hadn't thought of everything.

A search underneath the drawers and on the surfaces inside the desk, where the crime boss might have hidden secrets, produced nothing. The man had made a clean sweep. After Dalton had been at it for a half-hour, Chase stopped by.

"You find anything?" Dalton asked.

The deputy shook his head.

Stepping down the hall, Dalton noticed an alcove with a closed door inside. It didn't seem a large enough space for a bedroom or bathroom. "What's this?"

"There's a spiral staircase in there, maybe going to the attic."

They entered and climbed the steps. The single-story house had a steep roof, and a finished attic ran the length of the structure. Like most people, Orlov had utilized the space to store a lot of innocuous articles he probably didn't care to look at anymore, but didn't want to put in the trash. There were lamps, tables, book ends, golf clubs, and a couple of pop art paintings, all of it covered in a thick layer of dust. A box sat in one corner, its top flaps crisscrossed to close it up. Upon opening it they found old letters written in Russian, all from the same person, a woman, maybe a girlfriend. And in the bottom lay a yellowed document, an income statement dating back eleven years from a business named Spot-On Towing.

"It has a Miami address," Dalton said. "See if you can find it on your phone."

Chase brought up a search-engine, and after a couple of minutes said, "I don't see a business by that name in Miami."

"That's okay, we can check it out when we finish here."

They scanned through the remainder of the papers without finding anything of significance and left. Dalton entered the address of the towing company into his navigation system and drove out of Palm Island. With steady traffic it took them almost thirty minutes to get there, even though only a few miles away. A faded sign stood out front. Rather than turn in, he drove on to a convenience store a few doors down where he could observe the place from a distance.

He retrieved his field glasses from the back floorboard and put them to his eyes. The building, constructed of painted cement blocks, resembled a defunct auto garage. It had four closed bays and an empty parking lot.

"Looks vacant," Chase said.

"Call Robin and ask her to research the ownership of that address."

Chase dialed her number and spoke for a couple of minutes before hanging up. "She said she'll call back as soon as she finds something on it."

They sat in silence until Chase's phone chimed twenty minutes later. He repeated the details as Robin gave them to him, and Dalton recorded them in his notepad. A man named Harry Kohler had owned the business and sold it eleven years before to a man who died the same year. The date of the sale was near that found on the document in Orlov's attic. Robin had also researched Harry Kohler and found telephone numbers under that name in Virginia, Georgia, and Arizona. Dalton dialed them all and hit pay dirt on the one in Virginia.

"Are you the Harry Kohler who owned a towing company in Florida?" Dalton asked.

"Who's calling?" His tone sounded wary.

Dalton identified himself and said he was trying to locate a man who might have purchased the business from him.

Kohler hesitated for a few beats before answering. "Well, I did own a towing company. Built it from the ground up. Why are you looking for the person who owns it now?"

"We found records on your business in the attic of a suspect in a murder case. I need to know who bought the place from you."

"Uh, that might not be in my best interests."

"Are you afraid of the man who bought it?"

"You bet I am, and he didn't exactly buy it. He just came in one day and said he wanted to partner with me. I didn't want a partner, but he threatened to hurt my family if I didn't go along. I finally gave in, and he brought in men who took over. My part of the profits got less each month after that. I gave it about a year before I told him he could have it, and I left town. I always figured he was doing something illegal, but didn't have any proof of it."

"Why didn't you go to the police?"

"That's a laugh. The guy had a cop friend who stopped in every now and then. I knew calling the cops would be a mistake."

"Okay, you going to tell me who edged you out?"

"Sorry, I've already said too much. If you arrest the guy, please don't tell him you spoke to me." He hung up.

Dalton sighed as he laid down his phone. "He wouldn't say, but I'd bet a year's salary it was Orlov, and he could be inside that place."

Noticing movement at the building, he peered through the glasses and saw a man exit a side door and light up a cigarette. It reminded Dalton of the man who came out for a smoke while guarding the money at Toole Parts. Maybe Orlov had recovered his cash and moved it to that location. He called Detective Ames and told him about the place. "Can you get a search warrant?"

"Maybe," Ames said. "Might take a while, though. Judges don't like to get calls on Saturday."

"Okay, do your best. Can you send some uniforms out to watch the place while you're working it?"

Ames sighed. "Why can't you just stay there?"

"I will, but if somebody leaves the building, I want to be able to follow them."

"Yeah, good point. I'll ask a patrol car to meet you there."

They hung up, and a few minutes later a police cruiser showed up. One of the officers came over to his car and Dalton briefed him on the situation. The officer said they would stay until shift-change at five and another car would relieve them.

Dalton said, "If anybody leaves that building, I'm going to follow them." The officer nodded acknowledgement and they exchanged phone numbers.

After watching the building for a couple of hours without any activity, Chase went inside the store and brought back sandwiches and drinks. They ate and waited. The new police crew came in as expected, and then about 6:30, one of the bays on the building opened and a van drove out. Tinted glass on the vehicle prevented identifying anybody inside. The door rolled down behind the vehicle as it headed to the street. Dalton started the car and wedged into the traffic.

The van got onto I-95 South and drove for a couple of miles before taking the off-ramp to US-1. After a few blocks, it turned into a strip mall and parked in front of a grocery store. Two men got out and went inside. Dalton drove down the access road and turned at the row where the guy had stopped. As he eased by the rear of the vehicle, he lowered his window and could hear the exhaust from the van's running engine.

"You recognize them?" Chase asked.

Dalton shook his head as he pulled into a spot where

he could watch the van. "No, but they left the motor running, so somebody else is still inside."

The two from the van exited the store a few minutes later carrying bags and put them in the vehicle. Instead of getting in, they hurried to a liquor store next to the grocery. One came out with his arms wrapped around two cases of beer, and the other carried two large paper sacks. They loaded their purchases into the van and headed back to US-1 going south. When they neared Dadeland Mall, they turned east. Traffic thinned as dusk descended, and Dalton dropped back a quarter mile or so and disabled his automatic headlamps.

As they neared the coast, faded sale signs dotted lots on a failed waterfront development. The developer probably had big ideas for the place, and purchased the land at a premium prior to the real estate crash a decade before. Even though the market had healed, few homes had been built. Most of the lots were overgrown with weeds and scrub, rendering a ghost-town eeriness.

There were no streetlamps, and the van's taillights lit up as darkness enveloped the would-be mecca. The target vehicle wound through several streets before slowing and climbing over the curb of a treeless lot. It rolled across the grass and weeds toward the water's edge.

Dalton stopped the car before reaching the spot where the van had turned in. They got out and hurried down alongside the street, weapons drawn. When they reached the lot adjacent to the van's entry point, they spread out and made their way through the brush toward a light source at the coast. A cruiser of about forty feet sat in the water near a seawall, its engine running, a floodlight illuminating the gangway. The two men they had seen before walked across it carrying armloads of supplies. They made a trip back to the van and came back with four large suitcases. A minute later, Orlov got out of the vehicle and ambled down, glancing both ways.

Dalton checked GPS coordinates on his phone and called Diaz, who was at home on his off day. He asked for backup, speaking in low tones, hoping noise from the boat's engine would prevent the men from hearing.

"Orlov's there?" Diaz said, doubt in his tone. "You're sure it's him?"

"Yes, I'm sure. There's a boat, and I think he's leaving the country." He relayed the coordinates and hung up.

Something moved to Dalton's left. He turned with a jerk, and an object struck the side of his head. White light buzzed behind his eyes as he descended to the warm and embracing ground, and then the pain flooded in and switched everything off.

EIGHTEEN

REVERBERATING PAIN WOKE Dalton as they dragged him across the gang plank. Ivashin had one ankle, and another of the men had the other. His head bounced on the rough boards, and he fell unconscious for a time. When he opened his eyes again, he lay next to the bulkhead in the boat's salon, the running engine droning to the pulsing throbs inside his skull.

Footsteps clomped nearby and Ivashin said, "He's conscious, Boss," his accent seemingly more pronounced than before at Lucinda's house. Pushing up against the wall to a sitting position, he wondered what had happened to Chase. He had been several yards to his right, and the blow had come from the left. Maybe they didn't see him. Or maybe they shot him.

Orlov stepped over and squatted a couple of feet away. "So, what did you think you were doing out there?"

Dalton focused on the man's face, which bore an expression of amusement. "Watching you run like a coward." He reached to his holster, but found it empty.

Ivashin pulled what appeared to be the missing service weapon from his waistband. "Looking for this?"

"We saw you following," Orlov said. "Did you call the police?"

"No, I didn't have a chance to call anybody."

Orlov pursed his lips, eyed him for a moment, and stood. "He is lying, of course. Tie him up, and we will dispose of him in the deep water."

"Hey, now, wait," an approaching man said. "I didn't sign on to kill anybody. Just take you to Cuba, that's all you said."

The crime boss turned to face him, a rangy man with a week's growth of beard wearing a dingy ball cap. "Plans change, Captain. You will be well compensated."

One of Orlov's men stepped into the salon. "Lines are free. Ready to go."

"Get us out of here," Orlov said to the captain.

Sighing, the man took off the cap and ran his fingers through his greasy hair, staring down at Dalton.

"He means now," Ivashin said, pointing the gun.

Dalton felt a shift in the boat, and Steve Chase stepped inside pointing his weapon at the standing men. "Lay down the gun," he said to Ivashin. Then the man who had untied the lines came up behind Chase and stuck the business end of a gun to his head. Chase cut his eyes to one side and then glanced at Dalton. He opened his mouth, as if to speak, but seemed to freeze and nothing came out.

Dalton knew they would die if he didn't do something. He thrust out his leg and kicked the side of Ivashin's knee, producing a muffled popping sound similar to breaking an ear of corn. Ivashin screamed and fell sideways to the deck, grabbing his leg, Dalton lunged for the gun and tore it from his hand.

The man behind Chase let go of him and swung the

gun around. Dalton shot him twice in the chest. He turned to see Orlov bring up a weapon and shot him in the face. The crime boss stared for a moment, a look of surprise in his eyes, before falling over backward.

The boat's engine revved, and Dalton said to Chase, "Go up and tell that guy to shut it down." Chase nodded, his eyes wide as if in shock, and hurried toward the wheelhouse.

Dalton checked Ivashin for a weapon and collected a handgun from his pocket. After cuffing him he went looking for the fourth man. He headed down the ladder to the cabins and didn't see anyone in the passageway. "Give it up, and you'll be okay," he called out. "Your boss is dead, but you don't have to die."

No answer. He stepped to the forward cabin where upper and lower bunks hugged each side of the boat, but didn't find anybody. Turning around, he eased to the entrance of the main cabin. "Okay, last chance. You're about two seconds away from a bullet in your brain."

After another step, a man in the cabin said, "Wait, I give up. Don't shoot me."

"If you have a weapon, leave it in there and come out with your hands in the air."

The man did as instructed, and Dalton put the gun to his back and followed him up the ladder, binding his hands at the top.

The boat's engine had died, and Chase had the captain in the salon. Dalton thought about the mysterious phone number that had been in contact with Eldon Perl and Joe Pound before they were murdered. He checked the phones from Ivashin and Orlov's pockets. Neither of the numbers matched. That didn't mean they hadn't made the calls; it just meant they didn't make them with those phones.

Blue lights flashed outside. Dalton holstered his weapon, put his hands up, and stepped onto the gangway to the shore. Two police cruisers sat about twenty feet away. Four officers had their weapons pointed at him. Diaz stood in the center. He held up his hand. "Stand down. He's one of us." He said to Dalton, "You okay?"

Dalton nodded. "Yeah, I'm okay. Orlov and one other are dead, and Ivashin is on the floor with a broken knee."

"Sorry we didn't get here sooner."

While the officers went aboard to collect the prisoners, Dalton told him what had happened.

DALTON AND CHASE spent the next four hours at police headquarters giving statements and going over what they'd found on the boat. One of the suitcases contained a little over $200 thousand in cash.

Diaz came in as they stood to leave. "I wanted to let you know, those two guys impersonating cops at your jail killed the officers and left them in an alley. So we need to pick them up."

"I thought as much," Dalton said. "We tagged them with a number of felonies, but we'll be glad for you to take them off our hands. What about the warrant on the towing company? Was Ames able to get that through?"

"Yeah, they searched the place, but it was a bust. They found an apartment upstairs, and it looked like somebody had slept there, but they didn't find anything of significance. I guess it doesn't matter now, since Orlov is dead."

"No cash?" Dalton said.

"Nah. They must've taken all they had when they fled." As Dalton turned to leave, Diaz pulled him to the side, out of earshot of the other detectives and Chase. "Don't give a second thought to taking that scumbag out of commission. He deserved what he got, and you did the citizens of Miami a big favor. You ever need a recommendation, let me know."

ON THE TRIP back to the Keys, Chase told him he was too far away when Dalton got slugged, and didn't realize what had happened until he saw Ivashin and the other guy carrying him to the boat.

"I'm glad you came in when you did. If you hadn't, I'd be a dead duck."

"I just wish I'd seen that guy with the gun when I boarded the boat. Maybe we could've avoided the bloodshed."

"Don't worry about it. Things worked out. They're dead or locked up, and we're not." The distraction had given Dalton an opportunity to take control of the situation. Had that not happened, they would both be feeding the fishes at the bottom of the Caribbean.

Chase just nodded and remained silent after that, maybe replaying the scene in his head and wishing he could go back for a redo. Back at the office, Dalton went through the same motions as the night before, writing up the events and updating Cobb on email. He arrived at his cottage after 3:00 a.m. again, and fell into bed. Sleep proved fitful, with a throbbing headache waking him every hour or so. His dreams consisted of a video loop of the action on the boat that played over and over.

At 7:00 a.m. he dragged himself out and had a quick shower and a cup of coffee before heading north to the office. He hoped there wouldn't be anyone there, and he would have a chance to catch up on some paperwork.

A note from Cobb lay on his desk. It read: *SEE ME! LT.* Dalton drew a deep breath and let it out. *Why was he here on Sunday?* His head still ached, and he really didn't feel like talking to the lieutenant. The email he had sent explained everything, but he thought he knew what Cobb wanted. He decided to bite the bullet, went by the break room for a second cup of coffee, and took it in with him.

The lieutenant had the phone to his ear, but motioned for him to enter. He said into the receiver, "Okay, I'll let you know," and hung up.

Dalton took a seat, and Cobb gave him a rare smile. "So, you and Steve had a good night in Miami."

Shrugging, Dalton said, "A couple of guys died, and I might have a concussion, but other than that…"

Cobb frowned. "You need to get that checked out." The frown dissipated. "We'll have to investigate your shootings, but based on what you've told me, everything should come out fine. What I need to know, though, and I was just on the phone with the sheriff, is if this closes out your murder case."

Hesitating, Dalton took a sip of coffee and shook his head. "It isn't that simple."

"Don't give me that. You rode all over South Florida to catch this guy, and now he's dead. Tell me he's the guy that killed Joe Pound and those two thugs on his boat."

"Those guys stole a ton of cash from Orlov. If he killed them, he would've recovered that money, but we didn't find it. Not on the boat last night and not in the place he'd been holing up."

"He could've hidden it somewhere else."

"Maybe, but I think he would've taken it with him if he was leaving the country."

Cobb stared for a couple of beats and narrowed his eyes. "Okay, this is what we're going to do: we're going to tell the sheriff we got our man."

"Your call." Dalton stood to leave.

"Yes, it is, and I'm calling it." He picked up the handset and pressed a speed dial button.

Back at his desk, Dalton lay his head back on the tallback chair and closed his eyes. He understood the pressure the guy was under. Five homicides and only one resolved. The sheriff would be up for reelection soon, and she needed closure. She was a big fish in a little pond, and everybody in Florida knew about the murders. If they wanted to close the cases, why should he care? The victims stole money and transported drugs. Bottom feeders. Except the accountant, and they had Orlov and Ivashin cold on that one.

He perused the files to ensure he had included all the pertinent facts, readying them for closure. When he finished, he returned them to his desk drawer and headed out for an early lunch. On his way to the restaurant, Connie Duval called from the DA's office.

"I met with Mr. Pierce on the Rudy Banks murder. We offered him ten years in prison if he stands by his testimony against Orlov and Ivashin. He didn't like it, but he agreed."

"You only have to worry about Ivashin, now." He told her what had happened the night before in Miami.

Duval paused for a few beats, maybe digesting the ramifications, then said, "Okay, that makes it simpler, and less likely Pierce will recant."

They hung up as he pulled into the restaurant. He had the fish sandwich again. The detention center was only a mile or so away, so Dalton swung by and went in to speak with Pierce. "I heard you got a deal," he said.

"Yeah, if you can call it that. I still gotta do time."

"Could be worse. You could be on the hook for murder. I have some news for you: Orlov is dead and Ivashin is locked up. They were on their way to Cuba."

Pierce gave him a smirk. "Figures. Couple a cowards."

Silence filled the next few moments, and Dalton said, "Now that he's dead, you have anything to add about the murder of those two guys who stole his money?"

The jailed man shook his head. "I told you, I don't know anything about that."

"Okay, tell me this: do you know how much cash Orlov kept in that closet at Toole Parts?"

"I know what I heard. Somebody told me he had five million in there at one point."

"Who guarded the money?"

"A guy named Vigo, but I heard he disappeared after the money got taken."

"Disappeared? You mean ran away, or disappeared to the bottom of the Gulf?"

Pierce grinned. "That last part. Leonard pitched a fit when we got back and his money and Vigo was gone. Leonard found him at his cousin's house and slapped him around. Then him and Ivashin left with Vigo in the van."

"Did you hear what Vigo had to say about the robbery?"

"Yeah, he swore three guys came in with guns and masks and made him open that closet safe. He said they made him lie face down on the floor while they took the cash."

"So he couldn't identify them?"

"No. He might've lived a little longer if he could've done that."

Dalton headed back to the office. The missing cash bothered him. It appeared that Orlov hadn't recovered it, which meant he probably didn't kill the guys on Joe Pound's boat.

At his desk he wondered if he already had some speck of the truth, but had yet to recognize its significance. If such a nugget existed, it could be in the files, so he pulled them out and lined them up, Banks first.

He summarized the events in his notepad. Lucinda Toole asked the CPA to work on something for her, and he had a question about inventory. When he couldn't contact her, he went to her business location and stumbled upon men counting cash. A guy pulled a gun and chased him away. Orlov, Ivashin, and Pierce abducted him at his home and took him out in the Gulf.

Carl Myron had washed up on the shore of Little Basin. Shot in the head. He'd taken Joe Pound's boat out the day before, the same day Orlov went after Banks. Though not in the files, Dalton and Sam had found the bodies of Perl and Sparks, the other two men who had gone out in the boat with Myron. The three had robbed the cash at Toole Parts while Orlov and Ivashin were busy torturing Banks. Dalton believed Perl and Sparks killed Myron to reduce the split of the cash.

About a week passed before Joe Pound turned up dead. Somebody had shot him in the head and left a suicide note. It claimed he had murdered Myron, Perl, and Sparks, to wrap up everything in a neat bundle.

Someone using Myron's phone had made calls to a mystery number. A phone found at Joe Pound's office after his death had called the same number. It probably belonged to the killer.

Dalton put the files back in the drawer and wondered if Robin was putting in overtime. He found her at her desk. "Hey, did you learn anything from those phones I gave you?"

She gave him a scowl. "No 'hello' or 'did you hear about my big night last night?'"

"Sorry. Yeah, we got Orlov and his crew. About those phones…"

Sighing, she said, "I looked them over. Most of the calls on one phone were with businesses that were probably his clients, and several were with his wife. On the flip phone, though, I couldn't trace those numbers to anybody. It's probably a burner from a retail store."

"Yeah, I was afraid of that."

"I thought your case was closed. That's what Cobb is telling everybody."

"You're right. I just need to tie up some loose ends. Can you find out the location of the call made to Joe Pound's flip phone the night he died?"

With a sidelong glance and narrowed eyes, she said, "You're lucky I like you."

"Okay, I'll leave you to it."

He hadn't seen Steve Chase and assumed he'd stayed home. The night before had probably traumatized him to a certain extent, especially if he'd never been present to see a man killed. Even though he'd been instrumental in saving their lives, Dalton still wasn't sure about his trustworthiness. That brought to mind an idea. He returned to his desk and brought up arrest reports on his computer. It took a few minutes to find the one he wanted. About two weeks before, a man named Rollo Tan had been arrested for possession of cocaine with intent to distribute. The report named Steve Chase as the arresting officer, and the charges were dropped the day after Tan's arrest. How could that be true? The man had more than twenty bags of cocaine on him.

Rollo Tan. The name seemed familiar, for some reason. He noted the home address from the arrest report and left. His navigation system led him to a seedy motel. A sign out front advertised weekly rates.

The office clerk said Tan hadn't been in for a few

days. "Maybe he found another place to live. Can't imagine why; it's so nice here." He grinned.

"You know where he hangs out?"

"Yeah, I've seen him a few times at the bar around the corner. Bilko's."

Dalton had seen the sign. He drove to it and parked under the shade of a banyan tree. Only three other vehicles present. Inside, he went to the bar and ordered club soda with lime. Two men sat near the end, engaged in a conversation about which rock group had the best greatest-hits album. They appeared twenty-somethings, and threw around names of bands unfamiliar to Dalton. Neither resembled the mug shot of Rollo Tan.

The bartender brought over the soda and set it down. Another man came around the corner at the end of the bar, maybe from the restroom, and took a seat between Dalton and the other two patrons. He glanced in the mirror at Dalton and turned the other way. Rollo Tan. He resembled a beach bum, with longish, dirty-blond hair and a sun-bronzed face.

Dalton asked the bartender to bring Tan another of whatever he was drinking. When he did as requested, Dalton paid for the drinks and stepped over, his drink in one hand, badge in the other. "Hey, Rollo, how about joining me in the corner." He nodded toward a table with a dim light hanging over it.

Tan glanced at the others, and then nodded and picked up his beer. He walked with a slight limp.

When they sat down, Dalton said, "I saw the report on your arrest a couple of weeks ago."

"What do you want?"

"Just some information. Why'd they drop the charges?"

Beach Bum narrowed his eyes. "What's it to you?"

"Just curious."

With a shrug, Tan said, "I guess they decided I was innocent." He grinned, displaying a set of white teeth. After a pause, he said, "Listen, I don't want to be seen talking to you. People could get the wrong idea, if you know what I mean."

"The coke, how much did they bust you with?"

Tan eyed him for a moment. "You're the law, you should know that."

"There's a discrepancy in the amount."

"I don't remember, okay?"

"Maybe you could remember if I took you over to the sheriff's office."

"Hey, I don't have to put up with this. We had a deal." He opened his mouth to say more, but then appeared to change his mind.

"What kind of deal?"

The silence lay there between them, and Tan turned toward the bar, as if someone there might help him. The two on the stools were still talking rock bands, and the bartender had his face pasted to a TV screen, the sound too low to hear from their table.

"What kind of deal?" Dalton repeated, a little louder.

"I gotta go." Tan stood and limped toward the bar. He wore sandals. His right foot appeared swollen and scabby. Dalton realized he'd been looking at the situation from the wrong angle, and he remembered something else: the email address found on Steve Chase's computer. *RollT*. Rollo Tan.

"Come back and talk, or I'm running you in."

Tan turned and stared for a few beats, then shook his head. "You guys are killing me." He took a deep breath and returned to the table.

"You broke into my place and planted a bag of cocaine, but the big cat tore up your ankle when you tried to leave. I have the DNA, so I can prove it was you. You'll take the rap."

Beach Bum's eyes grew large, his breathing labored. He put his head in his hands and kneaded his temples. "I was just doing what I was told. He said the charges would go away if I did it."

"Who told you that?"

"That cop. The one that arrested me."

NINETEEN

MONDAY MORNING, Dalton asked Robin, "Have you seen Steve?"

She shook her head. "He must've called in sick."

"Okay, thanks." Maybe a visit to his condo would be better for confronting him with Rollo Tan's admission.

Tan had hurried off after their discussion the night before. Dalton didn't see any future in bringing him in for planting the cocaine. He would have to accuse Chase, which would stir up a messy corruption scandal for the sheriff's office. That wouldn't do anybody any good.

At his desk he found an email from the sheriff asking him to call. He got her on the phone a few minutes later, and she congratulated him on closing the murder case.

"I knew you could do it. That's the reason I told Cobb to assign the case to you in the first place. The other guy there is too green. He needs guidance. Maybe you can bring him along."

When Dalton didn't comment, she told him the other reason she wanted to speak with him. "I promised the State Attorney's office in Chicago that I'd let you go for the deposition when you closed your case, so my assistant booked you on a flight at two o'clock."

Dalton glanced at the time. "That's just a few hours from now."

"Yeah, sorry about that. They need you there first thing in the morning. You can pick up your tickets at the airport." Her tone didn't indicate any room for argument.

HE CAUGHT THE FLIGHT, which connected in Orlando with a two hour layover. While he waited, he dialed up an FBI contact in Chicago and asked about a counterpart in the Upper Keys. The agent steered him to Special Agent in Charge Marvin Spatz in the Key Largo office. When he got Spatz on the line, he gave him a rundown on Leonard Orlov.

"Yeah, I heard about it," Spatz said. "Congrats on nailing that guy."

"I'm pretty sure they were laundering money at the Toole Parts business in Key Largo. They moved out recently, but I thought you would want to check it out. Orlov's ex-wife ran it, along with several of Orlov's guys. She says she was just the name on the business license, but I think her involvement might be more."

After a short pause, Spatz sighed. "I appreciate the call, but if he was laundering money in Key Largo, he isn't anymore, and we have our hands full with other stuff going on down here."

"So you're not interested?"

"Sorry, no. It's a matter of priorities, but like I said, I appreciate the call, Detective." He hung up.

Dalton made an entry in his notepad. Though he didn't particularly care if they went after Lucinda or not, he had done his due diligence. He certainly wasn't going to pursue the laundering angle himself.

His flight arrived in Chicago after 6:00 p.m. The hotel accommodations were as expected: clean, but on the cheap and threadbare side. He had a decent steak at a restaurant across the street and headed back to his room. Sleep overtook him within seconds after lying down on the saggy bed, and unlike the previous night, he didn't move until the alarm sounded at 6:00 a.m.

After a shower and a shave, he repacked his bag and had a quick breakfast at a deli next door. The lawyers had already assembled in the meeting room when he arrived a few minutes early. He remembered Alecia Grant, the Assistant State's Attorney who sat at the head of the table. Three others, also employees of the State's Attorney's Office, were strangers. All of them, including Grant, gave him cool stares, as if he might be on trial. Grant turned on a video recorder and proceeded with the formalities of establishing the date and time, parties present, and introducing Dalton as a former detective with Chicago PD homicide.

Grant: "Mr. Dalton, please tell us about your dealings with Cook County Commissioner Harry Combs prior to the night of October 17th of last year."

Dalton: "I was investigating the murder of a man who did business with the county. In an interview at police headquarters, an eyewitness named Mr. Combs as the killer. The witness died of gunshot wounds later that day. After failed attempts to locate Mr. Combs, he called me late in the day on October 17th and suggested we meet. He insisted I come alone."

Grant: "Where was this meeting to take place?"

Dalton: "In a parking garage on Clark Street, level 4."

Grant: "What happened when you arrived at the meeting?"

Dalton: "Combs got out of a car and offered me $10,000 to back off the investigation. I refused and he turned and waved to two men in a vehicle behind us. They got out and I recognized them as detectives from vice, but I didn't know their names. They walked over and Combs said, 'Kill him and get rid of the body.' They drew their service weapons, but I got mine out first and shot them both. When Combs saw what happened, he pulled a gun, and I shot him, too. The detectives died, and Combs survived. I charged him with multiple counts of murder."

Grant: "So you killed two detectives and wounded the commissioner, but got cleared of wrongdoing. Why is that?"

Dalton: "I had a bug in my pocket that picked up everything. He missed it when he checked me for wires. The police department has the original recording, and my lawyer has a copy for safekeeping."

Grant: "If you were cleared, why did you feel the need to retain a copy of the recording?"

Dalton: "Just a precaution, in case others in the department are involved."

Grant: "Can you name others who were involved?"

Dalton: "No."

Grant: "If you can't give us names, why do you think there were others?"

Dalton: "I didn't say that. You're twisting my words."

Grant: All right. We'll come back to that. You left your position with the Chicago PD. Were you forced out?"

Dalton: "No. My uncle needed me in Florida."

In actuality, Captain David Greer had told him to resign or be fired.

They spent another thirty minutes on clarifications and more questions about police corruption, but the story remained the same. Finally, Grant told him they were finished and he could leave. It sounded more like *Get out before I throw you out.* In the hallway outside, Captain Greer sat waiting to go in.

"I heard you would be here today," Greer said. "I hope you did the right thing."

Dalton ignored him and kept walking. He caught the first flight out and got home at 6:00 p.m. After putting away his bag, he joined Eric and a couple of marina guests on the deck for cold beers. They made small talk about Chicago and the weather. Then the two guests downed their drinks and said they were going to get dinner. When they left, Eric asked him about his deposition.

"It went fine."

When he didn't say more, his uncle said, "You see any of your former coworkers?"

Shaking his head, Dalton said, "No, I didn't go by the department. The captain was outside the room waiting to be deposed. I think they'll nail him in their investigation, but it won't be because of anything I told them. Dirty cops eventually hang themselves."

Eric remained quiet for a minute or so, maybe pon-

dering the ethics of the code of silence concerning fel-
low officers' indiscretions. Dalton had done it himself
a time or two. "I suppose all the old timers I knew are
gone, and I'm glad I got out of there when I did."

Dalton smiled and cracked open another beer. "Yeah,
glad I did, too."

"Maybe you won't run into that sort of thing down
here."

That comment brought him back to the conversation
with Rollo Tan. "We'll see."

AT WORK THE next morning he got a cup of coffee from
the break room and stopped by Robin's desk.

"I heard you went to Chicago. Must've been a quick
trip."

"Yeah, and quick was the best part."

Although she gave him a questioning look, he didn't
provide any of the details. "Did you get that information
on Joe Pound's flip phone I asked about?"

She shook her head. "Cobb put me on another case,
and I haven't been able to get back to it."

"What case?"

"He said to keep it under wraps."

He took a sip of coffee and stared for a moment, wondering what was so secret she couldn't tell him. Shrugging, he said, "That's okay, just give me the phones." It
came out snappier than he intended. She frowned and
handed them over.

"You're such a grump today."

"Yeah, guess I am," he said over his shoulder as he
paced away.

Back at his desk he called the wireless company. After switches to several different staff members, he found a technician and gave her the call time and the associated phone numbers. "All I need is the location of the cell tower where the call originated and terminated. No privacy information." After complaining about the difficulty of the request, she said if her supervisor approved she would try to get the information to him by email in the next day or so. The response didn't instill confidence that he would get anything.

Steve Chase still hadn't shown up for work. Dalton wanted to lower the boom on him about the Rollo Tan information, but wondered if that might bring an unpredictable outcome. Chase would deny it, and it would be his word against a drug dealer. Chase might go to Cobb, and that would be bad for everybody.

His cell phone sounded, and he glanced at the display. Lola Ann. He answered and asked her to hold while he stepped outside to a table in the shade of a cluster of palms.

"I thought I would've heard from you by now," she said.

"Oh, yeah?"

"I ran that segment just for you about Leonard Orlov and the anonymous squealer. After you pulled that body out of the Gulf and killed the crime boss, the Miami guys ran with the story. I should've been the one covering it. The way this works is, I do something for you, and you return the favor."

"Yeah, well, I got hit on the head pretty hard. I wasn't exactly thinking about the news."

"Aww, poor thing. You think that lets you off the hook?" She sounded sarcastic, but her voice turned flirty when she followed up with, "Don't worry, I'm kidding. I was just thinking about you and wanted to hear your voice."

He suspected she could turn on the sultry words as needed, but an idea came to mind. "I have something that might interest you."

"Okay, I'd love to see you."

They agreed to meet at a restaurant after work.

Lola Ann looked dazzling in a tight floral dress. It displayed her curves and accented her long auburn hair. She ordered a margarita, Dalton a beer.

When the waiter left the table, she gave him a wan smile. "So, what do you have?"

"Right down to business, huh? What happened to that 'I'd love to see you' comment?"

The wattage on the smile spiked, and she reached across the table and patted his hand. "Oh, we'll get to that, but you said you had something that might interest me."

"You already know most of the story, but I bet you don't know what started the ball rolling."

The smile leaked away, and she raised a perfect eyebrow. "Okay, what started it rolling?"

The drinks arrived and they ordered burgers. It surprised him that she didn't get a salad. They swigged their respective beverages as the waiter hustled away.

Dalton set his beer down and said, "Orlov ran a money laundering business in Key Largo. CPA Banks stumbled onto his men counting cash at that site, and they killed him to keep him from talking."

"Money laundering. That's interesting, but Orlov is dead, and that sort of deflates the story."

"There's more. But I have some conditions. You can't mention anything about the sheriff's office or me. You'll have to develop your own sources."

She leaned back in her chair and eyed him for a few beats, and then said, "You got it. Tell me."

"His ex-wife is Lucinda Toole, and the business was in her name: Toole Parts. She says she's a victim and did what Orlov ordered her to do."

"You don't believe her?"

"No. I spoke with her early on, and she seemed anything but innocent."

Nodding, she said, "What about the Feds? Won't they be looking into it?"

"They aren't interested, so I don't expect you'll get any blowback from them."

When the waiter brought the meal, Lola Ann dug into the burger and ate half of it before stopping. "Wow. That is good. I don't remember the last time I had one of these."

When they finished, she patted her lips with a napkin and said, "So, where do I find this Lucinda Toole?"

"I don't know, but I have her phone number, and I'll deny it if you tell her I gave it to you. She might spill her story now that her ex is dead. But watch out digging too deep on any of those guys who worked for her. They won't like TV coverage, and they're dangerous."

"Sounds exciting," she said, her green eyes aglow.

They left the restaurant, and he walked her to her car in a dark end of the lot. At her door, she said, "Thanks for the tip. I'll let you know if I decide to run it down." No more romantic innuendo after getting what she wanted. He stood there watching her drive away. *If I decide to run it down.* For some reason, roadkill came to mind.

Dalton remembered his harsh tone when he'd spoken to Robin earlier and decided to go by her place and apologize. As he pulled into a parking spot, he saw a man leaving her door and heading to a vehicle. A streetlight at the edge of the lot illuminated his face, and he recognized him: Cobb. The lieutenant drank from a beer bottle and then dropped it into a waste container. Before getting into an SUV, he lit a cigarette.

Could they be having an affair? It seemed unlikely, from what he knew about Robin, but he obviously didn't know everything. She wouldn't tell him about the mystery case Cobb had asked her to research. And he knew next to nothing about Cobb. Early research he had done when applying for the position indicated that the man had been the commander for about a year and a half. Before that he had worked in Miami-Dade as a homicide detective. Robin had also transferred from Miami, and she had never said anything about knowing him there. As a CSI, it seemed likely she would have, and it also seemed likely she would mention it. Unless she didn't want Dalton to know, but for what reason? Maybe spying on him for Cobb?

Dalton's face felt heated, and he turned up the AC. He pulled out, caught up to the SUV, and fell back a block or so behind until it turned into a neighbor-hood. The homes would cost a half-million or so, which seemed expensive for a policeman. Dalton drove on past as the SUV pulled into the garage, and he noticed another car there beside it before the door came down. So the lieutenant probably had a wife, and maybe a second income.

Diaz called and asked what he wanted done with Ivashin. "I figured you'd call about transferring him."

"Yeah, sorry. I had to go to Chicago, but I'm back. I'll send a couple of uniforms up to get him tomorrow, if that's okay."

"Sure, whatever works."

Dalton thought about Cobb and asked if Diaz knew him.

"Kevin Cobb? Oh, yeah. I worked with him on a couple of cases. I think he got a supervisory job down your way."

"Yeah, he did. He's my boss."

"Huh, don't know how he would be as a boss. As I remember, he had a thing for one of the CSIs. She moved down there, too, soon after he left. I think her name was Robin."

TWENTY

SAM AND SIMONE were outside with Eric when Dalton arrived at the marina. Tiki torches cast a warm glow over the deck. The full moon shone across the mirror of water beyond the mangroves. A cooler held iced beer, probably courtesy of Sam. Eric didn't usually spring for beer.

"Hey, come join us," Simone said.

Dalton sauntered over and nodded at the three. He twisted the cap off a bottle of beer and drank down a third of it.

"Rough day?" Eric said.

He sighed and settled into a chair. "I've had better."

Simone looked as if she had just showered, with her hair up and no makeup. The flickering torches accentuated her natural beauty.

"We're celebrating Sam and Simone's treasure haul," Eric said.

"You dive a shipwreck?" Dalton asked Sam.

Sam nodded. "A friend found an old galleon about ten miles off the coast of Key West. A recent storm exposed part of the mast and stem on the sea bottom. He figures it was headed back to Spain after stealing from the Aztecs. We brought up some gold bars and art objects. There's probably a lot more down there."

It sounded like a lot more fun to Dalton than chasing criminals and giving depositions. "You going back down?"

"Sure," Sam said. "Probably several more times. It would be great if you could come along."

"We could've used another experienced diver," Simone said. "I just got in the way."

Sam gave her a smile. "You're never in the way, and you did great."

They had several more rounds before Eric called it a night. Dalton stood, as well. "Yeah, me, too. I have to get up early and get back to the grind." Sam and Simone wished him a good night. Their faces seemed to say, *Poor fool*, but it could have been his own disposition bouncing back at him.

As he reached his cottage, he saw the two ambling down the dock toward Sam's boat, arm in arm. *Lucky guy.* Cupcake greeted him inside with a big *Rowww* and a sad expression that made him feel guilty for not bringing him outside with the others. He opened a pack of ground meat, and the big cat's mood seemed to improve.

DALTON'S HEAD THUMPED from too much drink as he shut down the alarm. After a quick shower and shave, he made a cup of coffee and took it with him out the door. At the office, a perusal through his email yielded little of importance. No response from the phone carrier yet. One message from Cobb said he had a couple of new cases he wanted Dalton to take on and asked if he had closed the files on the murders. That could wait. He noticed Steve's empty chair again, and thought maybe he should pay him a visit.

Draining his coffee cup, he swung by the break room on his way out and got a refill. As he resealed the lid, Robin entered. "Hey, good morning. You still mad at me?"

He drew a blank for a few seconds, wondering how she would know he'd seen Cobb at her place the night before. Then he remembered the phone research she had sidelined. Trying for a smile, he said, "Oh, no. Sorry if I sounded angry."

"I'm sorry I couldn't get the information for you."

"No worries. I should have what I need today." He had forgotten the headache, but it started up again.

"You want to get a drink after work?" she asked.

"I'll have to get back to you on that."

Dalton got in the car, drove to Chase's condo, and rang the doorbell. No answer, so he pushed the button again. After a minute or so, he turned to leave and the door cracked open. Steve Chase peeked out. "I called in sick. What do you want?"

"Can I come in for a few minutes?"

Chase sighed and swung the door open. "I was asleep." He looked as if he'd been asleep for days, hair tangled and unwashed, stubble on his face. He shuffled to the kitchen in slippers, wearing wrinkled pajama bottoms and an undershirt. "You want coffee?"

"No thanks. I already had plenty." Dalton took a seat in the living room and waited.

When Chase returned and sat down, he sipped the brew and drew a deep breath. "Cobb send you out here?"

"No, I just thought I'd check on you."

The deputy nodded and took another drink before setting his cup down. "I'm fine. Thought I'd use up my sick leave. Don't tell LT, though."

Dalton stared for a moment and said, "I don't buy it."

Chase sipped his coffee. "What are you getting at?"

"Maybe you had a bad night and can't get the guns and blood out of your mind. Or maybe I hit a nerve when I mentioned somebody planting cocaine at my place."

"So, Mr. Perfect Detective, are you a psychologist, too?"

"Save it. I talked with Rollo Tan."

"Rollo Tan?" Chase said, furrowing his brow.

"Yeah, the guy you busted with the cocaine."

"What's that got to do with anything?"

"He told me what happened. You promised to drop the charges if he sneaked into my cottage and planted the drugs."

Chase's eyes grew wide, and he stood. "You've lost your mind. Get out of here."

"It came directly from Tan. Why would he lie?"

The deputy shook his head and turned toward the hallway. "I'm gonna get dressed. Don't be here when I come back."

Dalton drove down the block and waited. A few minutes later Chase's car tore out of the condo driveway and sped up the street. A couple of vehicles came by right after, making it easy to follow. Within a few miles the deputy turned into Bilko's, Rollo Tan's hangout. Dalton eased in a few seconds later and parked in a shady spot as Chase entered the bar. Within a couple of minutes, Tan came out with Chase right behind, shoving him. They got inside Chase's car and he started the engine. They sat there for several minutes with the windows up. The deputy appeared to be doing all the talking as he gestured with his hands and poked Tan on the shoulder. After a while, things seemed to settle down and Tan got out. As the beach bum hurried back inside, Chase got on the phone. When he finished the conversation, he backed out and left the lot. Dalton decided to let the situation simmer for a while, rather than tail him again.

Back at the office, Dalton checked email again. Still nothing on the flip phone, so he decided to bite the bullet and go to Cobb's office.

"You wanted to see me?"

The lieutenant looked up from his computer screen. "Yeah, come in and shut the door."

He did as asked and took a seat in front of the desk.

"You close out the murders?"

"Getting close."

Cobb made a face. "What's the holdup?"

"Just a few loose ends to put in the files."

That seemed to satisfy him. "Okay, I've got a couple of cases I want you to look into. I would give one to Steve, but he's still out." He stared for a moment, then said, "He called and said you'd been by to check on him."

"Yes."

"He seem all right to you?"

"Don't know. He said I woke him, and he looked as if he hadn't shaved or showered in a few days." Dalton wondered if Chase had mentioned the subject of their conversation.

"He might be having some repercussions from the shoot-out you had with those guys."

"Could be. Something is bothering him."

The lieutenant said, "Okay, I want you to get busy on these. When he comes back, I'll get him to help with the legwork." He handed over two file folders. "One's a burglary. Electronics store. They cleaned out the backroom during the night and took some cash from the safe. The other is a theft of a vintage vehicle worth about a hundred grand."

Dalton nodded. "Anything else?"

"No that's all." After a pause, he said, "Oh, yeah, the sheriff said she's putting you in for a commendation on the Orlov murder case."

"That's nice. Tell her thanks for me."

Cobb gave him a wan smile. "I thought you'd be more excited about it."

"Yeah? Well, you can tell her I'm excited." He had a boxful of commendations from the military and the Chicago PD. It sat on a shelf in his uncle's storage shed.

When he got to his desk, he perused the new case files. CSIs had been to both crime scenes and dusted for prints, but had yet to forward the results.

It would be pleasant to investigate something that didn't involve murder, for a change. He headed to the car, the files under his arm. Maybe check out the electronics store first, about fifteen miles north, and then swing by the rare car owner's home on the way back.

According to the report, about twenty thousand had

been stolen from a safe at the electronics store. Getting into a safe sounded like an inside job, unless they blew the door off with explosives. Why would the store have twenty grand in cash on hand? Most purchases would likely be made with credit and debit cards. He supposed the owner could be laundering money, like Toole Parts, though the amounts were vastly different.

It still nagged him that he hadn't located Orlov's missing cash. Although it made sense that the crime boss had killed Perl and Sparks and recovered his money, the dots didn't quite connect without that money.

He still had a few minutes of driving and dialed up Lucinda Toole. When she answered, he said, "I guess you heard about your ex."

"Yes, I saw it on the news. You're the one who shot him, right?"

"That's right. He tried to kill me, and I got him first."

"The news speculated that he was trying to escape to Cuba."

"He was, but he didn't have nearly as much cash with him as I would have expected. I wondered if you knew about any places he might have stashed it for access later. Maybe friend's houses, other businesses he might've owned, or self-storage."

"I told you before, I didn't have anything to do with his money. I'm so glad I won't have to deal with him anymore."

Silence stretched across several seconds, and then she said, "I appreciate what you've done, keeping me out of this trouble, but I hope you won't contact me again."

It seemed a little abrupt, but he said, "Okay. I can't

think of anything else I need right now." He supposed she wanted to put it all behind her, and she got lucky that the FBI didn't want to go after her. Rudy Banks had died because of something she put into motion, but she couldn't have predicted Banks would insert himself as he had. "Can I ask you one more question?"

Sighing, she said, "All right, but then I have to go. I need to find a job. Leonard cut me out of his will a long time ago, so I don't have anything."

"This is just out of curiosity, but what did you ask Rudy Banks to do for you? Surely Orlov had financial people who could do the work."

She remained silent for a long time, and Dalton wondered if his connection had dropped. "You still there?"

"Yes. I needed a financial statement for a loan application, but I didn't want Leonard to know about it."

"What did you want with the money?"

"I needed to get away from him and start a business of my own. He had me over a barrel because I didn't have any income, and he paid me just enough to get by."

Just enough to get by? She had lived in a nice home in Key Largo and drove a Mercedes, so money probably wasn't the biggest issue. "Okay, then, good luck finding a job."

She had already hung up.

He arrived at the electronics store and a clerk took him to the owner, Bert Land, in the storeroom. They talked about the fact that the back door and safe hadn't been damaged. "Who has a key and knew how to get into your safe?" Dalton asked.

"My former assistant manager, Troy Decker. He left

for a better job, but I heard he got fired from it." He shook his head and sighed. "I should've changed the locks and the combination, but it never occurred to me that he would come back and rob me."

"Why'd you have so much cash in the safe?"

The owner shrugged. "It's just built up over time, and I don't trust the banks."

"You insured?"

"Oh, yeah. I hope they'll cover it."

Dalton got Decker's address and left. According to his navigation system, he lived a few miles away in a mobile home. He answered the door and Dalton flashed his badge. "I need to talk to you about a burglary at the store where you worked."

Decker, a middle-aged balding man, gave him a scowl, but let him in and pointed to the sofa in the small living room. His left hand was missing two fingers, and he had scarring on the side of his face. The place looked neat and clean. A row of diving magazines covered the surface of the coffee table.

"You a diver?" Dalton asked.

Decker smiled. "Yeah, whenever I get the chance. I got into it when I was in the Navy."

"Oh, yeah? You were a SEAL?"

The man nodded. "Long time ago."

An attractive woman entered the room, appearing surprised to have a visitor. Decker introduced her as his wife. "This is Detective Dalton. He wants to ask some questions about a robbery at one of the stores I worked at."

She smiled and said she'd be in the back if he needed her.

When she had gone, Decker said, "So, what's this about a robbery?"

"Actually, a burglary, at Bert's Electronics. Mr. Land said you were a former employee who had a key to the place."

Decker leaned back in his chair, his eyes narrowed. "He said I did this? I didn't have a key. I gave it to him when I left."

Dalton stared for a moment. "He said you had the combination to his safe, too."

The suspect shook his head. "That's a lie. Bert never let anybody have the combination. Anyway, I'd be surprised if he had anything of value in it."

"You know why he would've singled you out?"

Shrugging, Decker said, "Sure, he owed me two month's back pay. That's the reason I left. He ran his store into the ground, taking money out and not replenishing inventory."

"He said you're out of a job."

"Well, yeah, that's true. It was just temporary. I have an interview in an hour for another one." He smiled. "I also get a disability check from the Navy." Holding up his right hand, he said, "Low-bid explosives."

"You have an alibi for last night?"

Decker grinned. "My wife and I bowled until around ten. You can check with the bowling alley. After that we came home and went to bed."

Dalton thanked him and went to his car. It sounded as if Bert Land might be trying to cure his financial situation with a fat insurance payment. He called the store owner and asked the name and telephone number of his insurance agent. Land left the phone and came back a couple of minutes later with the information. When he phoned the insurance company, the agent told him Land had already filed a claim.

"I need a police report to back it up, though," the agent said.

"You should have your investigator grill Mr. Land about his financial situation before paying," Dalton said. He told the agent he would complete his report in a day or two, and they hung up.

Deciding to postpone the interview with the owner of the stolen car, he headed back to the office. When he got there, Steve Chase pulled in a few seconds later and caught up with him at the door. He had cleaned up and wore a button-down shirt and pressed khakis. "I need to talk to you," he said to Dalton.

"Okay."

"Let's go over to the picnic table in the shade."

Dalton followed him and they sat.

The deputy arched an eyebrow. "What are you planning to do about what you said at my place earlier?"

Shrugging, Dalton said, "Nothing."

"You're not going to Cobb with it?"

"No, I wanted you to know I figured it out, and now I just wonder why you did it."

Chase shook his head. "Yeah, but you have it all wrong. I didn't get Rollo to plant that cocaine."

"You saying he's lying?"

"No, he didn't lie. I talked to him a couple of hours

ago. He said he told you the guy who arrested him is the one who put him up to doing the deed."

"Yeah, and you arrested him."

"I was there, but he wasn't talking about me. See, Rollo and I go way back. We used to hang together in high school, and I been trying to keep him out of trouble ever since. The night he got caught with the blow, he asked the uniform to call me. The deputy tried, but I was out of range, so he got Cobb on the phone. In the meantime, I called the officer back and he told me what was going down. I got to the bar about the same time Cobb did, and I told the uniform we would handle it. We got Rollo in the cruiser and were going to take the drugs and give him a scare, then let him go. Only thing, he gave Cobb some lip, so he got mad and hauled him in. He put me down as the arresting officer, said I needed the credit."

"You're saying Cobb put him up to it?"

"Yeah, I didn't know anything about it at the time, but when you mentioned it the other night on the way to Miami, I thought about something Lobo, the nightshift evidence custodian, told me. He said Cobb came down there and told him if he would get them a coffee from down the street he would cover for him. Lobo thought it was a little strange, but he didn't argue. That was the day you started your job here. So, I put that together with what you said, and thought Cobb planted the stuff at your place."

"That why you haven't been to work?"

Chase, shrugged. "Yeah, I knew you would figure it out, sooner or later, and he would find a way to leave me holding the bag. I planned on quitting, but it makes me mad that he dragged Rollo into it. He didn't deserve that."

Dalton didn't know whether to believe him or not, but it made sense, except for one thing. "Why would Cobb try to set me up like that?"

"I don't know. I've been trying to figure that out myself."

"Okay," Dalton said. "If you're telling the truth, nobody's going to leave you holding the bag. I have some experience with corrupt bosses."

TWENTY-ONE

DALTON FOLLOWED CHASE to his desk and handed him the new case files. "The LT gave me these today. How about taking them over?"

"Okay, sure."

"I think the guy at the electronics store made up the burglary for the insurance." He briefed him on what he'd done so far and about calling the insurance agent. "I haven't even started on the other one."

Chase seemed appreciative and said he would get right on them.

The conversation about Cobb slipped back into Dalton's thoughts. The LT wanted him canned, but why? Could he be involved in the murders? The sheriff had said she wanted Dalton on the case. So maybe the LT didn't have a choice on assigning him, but thought he could get him sacked with the cocaine bust. There was also another potential motivation: Robin. She might have mentioned that she planned to go out with Dalton for a drink, and he decided to put a stop to that before it started. Jealousy often caused people to do much worse things.

An email response on the flip phone waited on his computer. He opened it and saw the GPS coordinates of the cell tower where the call had originated the night Joe

Pound had been murdered. Dalton accessed a mapping program and punched in the coordinates. The program highlighted a place in South Miami near Coral Gables.

Any person in Orlov's crew could have made the call from that location. Ivashin, or Orlov could have done it, but Dalton didn't think so. Since the same gun was used on the three robbers and Pound, that would mean Orlov or Ivashin also killed Perl and Sparks. If they had done that, they would have recovered the money, and they didn't appear to have it. Dalton wondered if another of Orlov's associates might have done it. One whose name hadn't even surfaced in the investigation. Investigating all the crime boss's cronies would require a lot more legwork, which wouldn't fly, since Cobb and the sheriff wanted the case closed.

Dalton sighed. Lots of possibilities, but he didn't seem any closer to solving the case than he had before getting the phone information. He had been naïve to think the location of the caller would point to the killer.

Dreading the task of going over the files again, he pulled them out and began ticking off items from a checklist needed to close the cases. The Carl Myron file contained reports from the CSIs and the ME, and Dalton had included his own notes, which he had read and reread.

The Eldon Perl and Floyd Sparks file also contained the CSI findings and those from the ME. The file didn't indicate that anybody had investigated the personal lives of Perl and Sparks. That was probably a mistake. Dalton had gotten so wound up on other things that he hadn't done it, either. Someone close to one of the two goons might have shed some light on who killed them.

The checklist for the Joe Pound case appeared complete. He made a note to send the information about the offshore bank account to the local DEA office in case they wanted to pursue Heather Pound's involvement in her husband's drug trafficking business. Could she have been involved with Perl or Sparks? She probably knew them since they worked for her husband, and could have been intimate with one of them. But all four victims were killed with the same gun, and Dalton didn't think she would have killed her cousin, Carl Myron.

He went back over the chronology of presumed events. Rudy Banks witnessed something at Toole Parts. Orlov, Ivashin, and Pierce took him out in the stolen boat and killed him. In the meantime, Carl Myron commandeered Joe Pound's boat and picked up Perl and Sparks, and maybe a fourth person. They robbed Orlov's stockpile of cash. One of the robbers killed Myron and tossed him overboard. And then the mysterious fourth person killed Perl and Sparks and left with the money.

Dalton's head throbbed from all the detail, as well as the prospect that the killer might be an unknown person who had worked for Orlov. Someone who knew about the heist, and could avoid Orlov's radar when the crime boss went searching for the stolen cash. He stuck the files back in his desk and returned Joe Pound's phones to the evidence locker. The two phones he and Sam had removed from Pound's boat would stay with him, since he couldn't explain how he had gotten them.

Lola Ann called, and he told her to hold while he went outside.

"No luck on your tip," she said. "Lucinda Toole won't answer the phone."

"She's probably wary of numbers she doesn't recognize. Why don't you send her a text?"

"I had a better idea. I'll just go with what you gave me. It'll still make a good story, and I won't have to get her onboard. If she has any gripes, she can call me."

"I told you I don't want to be quoted."

"Yeah, I remember that, but it'd be great if you'd back off that requirement. I mean, you've solved the case, haven't you? So what's the problem?"

A germ of an idea took shape in his head. "Yeah, you're right. You up for another TV interview?"

Lola Ann had the camera set up when Dalton arrived at the outdoor restaurant. She looked as beautiful as ever and greeted him with a smile. He handed her a piece of paper.

"What's this?" she asked, glancing down at the sheet.

"Those are my questions."

She gave him a smirk. "Sorry, Charlie, I do my own questions."

He smiled. "Yeah, I understand your normal procedure, but you have to use these this time."

"Come on, you're killing me. I don't do this for anybody."

Shrugging, he said, "How many detectives do you get to interview?"

With a pout, she laid the questions on the outdoor

table. "Okay, we'll do it your way. Just don't get up and leave in the middle if I make a mistake."

"Better stick to the questions."

They sat down and the cameraman made his adjustments. "Okay, on three we're rolling," he said, and counted off.

"We're here in Islamorada with Sheriff's Detective Mick Dalton, the lead investigator on the recent murders of five local men. Detective Dalton has graciously agreed to bring us up to date on the murder cases with new information that hasn't been aired on the news by anyone."

She turned to Dalton, and he laid out the chronology he had gone over so many times in his head.

"So you think Leonard Orlov killed Rudy Banks and also the men who stole his cash?"

"Yes, he killed Banks because Banks witnessed his men delivering a load of cash. Then, when the three men robbed his place, Orlov found them and shot them all."

Lola Ann nodded. "And did Mr. Orlov also kill Joseph Pound, the local building contractor?"

"Yes. We believe Mr. Pound and the murdered men on the boat were running drugs for Orlov, and he knew the investigation would lead back to him if Joseph Pound talked. He killed Mr. Pound and tried to lay all the blame on Pound for the other killings. After we got the goods on him for a separate murder, Orlov tried to leave the country and died in a firefight."

"So that closes your case, for one of the worst murder binges we've ever experienced in the Keys." She glanced down at the sheet. "I assume you found the cash that caused all this mayhem?"

Dalton arched an eyebrow. "No, that actually remains a mystery. It isn't part of our murder investigation, so we're not looking for it, per se."

"How much cash are you talking about?"

"One of my sources says it's more than $5 million."

Part of what he had said was true, and he hoped the killer was watching. He didn't mention the money laundering angle, since it would be a distraction from what he wanted to cover.

They wound up the interview and he got up to leave. "When will you put it on the air?"

"It'll be on the evening news. We'll have to edit it a little to fit the time slot."

"Okay, but make sure the part at the end about the missing money stays in."

She gave him a quizzical smile, but said, "Will do."

Although he didn't really believe much of what he had said on camera, it would serve his purpose in finding the real killer.

WHEN HE GOT HOME, he relaxed with a cool drink and waited for the Lola Ann show. She came on at six and introduced the clip, looking even more glamorous than she had in person. The edited interview lasted less than two minutes, but she had retained the exchange between them about the missing money. He hoped the killer had watched.

Needing a fresh phone with no history, Dalton drove to the nearest big box store and purchased a burner.

Back in the car, he activated the phone and disabled GPS, in case the killer had a way to track the device. He composed a text on the new phone: *Buster gave me this number. He told me you might double-cross him. The news said you got 5 million. Give me half or I'll rat you out to the cops.*

When satisfied with the wording, he fired it off to the mystery number. As he got behind the wheel, Lola Ann called on his personal phone. "You see the interview?" she asked.

Backing into the street, he said "Yes, it was perfect."

"My boss liked it, too. You're making me look good at the station."

In his mind's eye, Dalton saw her in front of the camera: beautiful hair and eyes, full lips, sultry smile. "You'd be a star no matter who you interviewed." The words tumbled out before he realized he'd said them out loud.

"Aww, that's sweet of you to say. You want to go for a drink?"

He sighed, wondering if he would get a reply to the text he'd sent. "I might work late today. How about tomorrow night?"

"Okay, it's a date." They agreed on a time and place and hung up.

Though he watched the phone the rest of the day and into the evening, the reply he hoped for never came.

THE NEXT MORNING, Lieutenant Cobb stopped by Dalton's desk with a scowl on his face. "My office, right now." He stomped away.

Dalton took his time, perused his email, and then stopped by the break room for coffee to carry into the office.

"Shut the door," Cobb said from his seat behind the desk.

He complied and took a chair.

"What did I say about TV interviews?"

Dalton took a sip of coffee. "You don't remember?"

"Okay, that does it. I'm putting you on suspension. Hand over your badge and weapon."

"I don't think so."

"Pardon me?" he arched an eyebrow. "You don't have any choice in the matter."

"I had a talk with Rollo Tan. He told me what you ordered him to do."

The lieutenant's eyes widened. "What are you talking about?"

"You know what I'm talking about: you told him to break into my place and plant drugs."

Cobb glanced at the door, maybe hoping no one stood outside listening. He stared for a few seconds then seemed to recover. "Whatever he told you is a lie. Nobody will believe him."

"Oh, they'll believe him. He said you would drop the charges if he did it, and you made good on that promise. What I wonder is: why? I can think of some reasons, a couple of which would land you in prison, or worse."

After a pause, Cobb said, "Sure, I dropped the charges. He's a confidential informant. I needed him back out there getting us information."

"Nice try. Tan left DNA when he escaped through my gate, so I can prove he did it."

The lieutenant drew labored breaths, and leaned back in his chair. He attempted a smile, but didn't quite make it. "So, you gonna try to get me fired? Is that your angle?"

Dalton shook his head. "No. Dirty cops eventually hang themselves." He stood to leave. "In the meantime, you'd be wise to stay out of my way."

On his way to his desk, Robin passed by heading toward Cobbs office. "You have a minute?" she asked.

"Sure."

"I'll be right back. Maybe we can talk outside."

"Okay, I'll see you there." He went out and took a seat at one of the picnic tables in the shade. She came along a minute or so later.

"What's up?" he asked.

She glanced around. A couple of uniformed deputies sat at another table about twenty feet away, catching a smoke.

"I saw Cobb when he went to see you. He looked pretty angry. Was it about the TV interview?"

"Huh, you don't miss much. Yeah, it was."

"Did he lower the boom?"

Smiling, he said, "No, he's okay with it."

She furrowed her brow, as if surprised. "Oh, good. I was worried he might fire you or something."

"You were concerned for me?" he said, the smile dissipating.

"Sure, of course I was. Why would you ask me that?"

He remained silent for a few beats, and then said, "I dropped by your place a couple of nights ago."

"Huh, I must've been out."

"I think you were home. As I parked, Cobb came out with a beer in his hand. He looked like he'd had a few."

A frown crept onto her face when he mentioned the lieutenant, and she turned her gaze to the table with the other men, maybe so she wouldn't have to look him in the eye. She turned back. "Yeah, he came by, but he didn't stay long. He'd already been drinking when he got there and had the beer with him."

"So you two are tight?"

Shrugging, she said, "He has problems at home and wanted to unload them on me."

He nodded. "I heard you knew him before you transferred down here."

Shifting in her seat, she drew an audible breath and let it out. "Yeah, I did. He was a detective in Miami, and he asked me out a couple of times. I turned him down, because he was married. After he transferred, he offered me a job, and I took it on the condition that there were no strings attached. So, no, we are not tight, but he still calls every now and then when he's drunk."

"He ever ask you to spy on me?"

Her eyes popped wide. "What? Are you kidding?"

"I got the impression he wanted to keep tabs on me, and I thought he might've given you the assignment." She just stared, and he continued, "It's okay if you did it. I just want to know what's getting back to him."

"I can't believe you would think that." She stood and took a few steps away, but returned and said, "Okay, he did ask about our conversations a couple of times. I didn't see any harm in telling him."

Well, that was interesting.

DALTON MET LOLA ANN for the Friday-night drink they had agreed on. The conversation with Robin kept creeping back and commandeering his attention. It wasn't that he was completely smitten with her, but he liked her a lot, and had considered her a friend. After their conversation, all he felt was betrayed. He didn't remember saying anything that would have compromised his position or the murder case, but what he told her probably got back to Lt. Cobb. A man who wanted him fired bad enough to plant drugs in his home.

Lola Ann said, "Is something wrong? You seem distracted."

"Yeah, sorry. I had a weird day. Is it okay if we call it a night and I make it up to you next week?" They agreed to go out again the following week.

SATURDAY CREPT BY without event. He helped Eric with some chores and went shopping for supplies. That evening, Sam and Simone joined him and Eric on the deck for drinks. Cupcake pestered them, nuzzling their elbows until they scratched his ears, and finally lay down at Simone's feet for a snooze. When everyone retired, he put the cat up and checked the burner phone. No response to his text.

Dalton spent the next day replacing gnarled boards on the dock. He quit about an hour before sundown and took a shower. When he sat down for a beer, he checked the phone again. This time the message notification light blinked.

Message: *Who are you?*

He replied: *Forget it. I know you. You don't play ball you'll be sorry.*

A few minutes passed, and then a reply popped up: *Ok, I'll give you the money. Meet me tomorrow night in Miami at Spot On. 9:00*

Dalton keyed: *No way. I pick the place.*

Spot-On Towing was known by Orlov's cronies and too risky. He phoned Sam and told him the setup. After thinking about it for a minute, Sam came up with a Miami restaurant near Southland Mall. They hung up, and he sent a text describing the location. He added: *Put the money in a duffle. Drop it in the trash bin behind the place at 9:00. Do anything cute and you'll die.*

TWENTY-TWO

SAM HAD PICKED a good place for the proposed drop. The trash bin in the rear of the restaurant could be viewed only from one side. A building and a tall fence obscured the view on the other side and the rear. The place had recently gone out of business, so innocent bystanders getting hurt would be unlikely if the scheme resulted in gunfire. Dalton had phoned Diaz an hour or so earlier, but got voicemail and left a message for a callback.

Dalton reasoned that the killer would station himself at a point where he could see the bin, so he could identify or shoot whoever visited it. Having only one viewing side meant he would need to position himself in the parking lot across a small street from the side of the restaurant. A large parking lot beyond the street increased Dalton's ability to cover the area and identify the killer.

Arriving at 8 p.m., Dalton eased his uncle's pickup along the far side of the adjacent parking lot looking onto the designated pickup point. The shooter would be watching the bin, and he would be watching for the shooter. He found a spot in the far end of the lot, about a hundred feet away. A car next to him shielded most of his truck from view from the direction of the restaurant but allowed him to peer over its roof. Wearing sunglasses, he sat and waited. For an assist, he utilized a camcorder with zoom to watch the activity.

As the sun winked out behind him he removed the shades. Dusk blanketed the area, and street lamps started up with a buzz, casting a warm glow over the lot. The driver of the car next to him came out of a store nearby and ambled over with a shopping bag in his hand. He gave Dalton a wary glance before getting in and driving away.

Without the cover of the car, he sank low in the cab and rested the camera on the bottom edge of the open window. He twisted the LCD screen so he could use it like a periscope. A half-hour later, he had a stiff neck and had observed no suspicious vehicles. Some could have passed more than once without him noticing, since many looked similar in the dim light. A few minutes later, two cars pulled up to a spot near his target area and parked. Several teens poured out and stood around for a while. He wished they would get out of there, and finally, a few minutes before 9 p.m., they jumped back in the cars and drove away.

The phone chimed and Dalton answered.

"An SUV is inching toward your truck from behind," Sam said. "I can't see the driver with the tinted glass." He had followed Dalton up from the Keys and stationed himself to watch his back.

Dalton lay down on the seat and pulled the camera in. "How close?"

"Closing on fifty feet, still going slow. Might be just killing time before a movie. Stay down."

As the vehicle neared, Dalton heard the hum of a large engine, and then it revved and the SUV went on past.

Raising the camcorder, he recorded the rear of the vehicle, a Lexus, as the image retreated into a darkened part of the lot. He refocused on the target area to see if it reappeared there. Sure enough, it pulled up near where the teens had congregated, and stopped.

"He's in place," Dalton said. "Gotta be him. I don't want to risk a shoot-out here, though. Too many cars. Let's wait until he leaves and follow."

"Roger that. When he moves, I'll head that way."

The Lexus remained in place until 9:45 and then eased away. Dalton waited until he saw Sam's rental going after it and proceeded to follow. The street they took fed onto South Dixie Highway and they drove north about twelve miles before the SUV exited. A half-mile later it turned into a high-rise condominium complex and entered a gated garage underneath. Probably the origination point of the call to Joe Pound the night he had been murdered.

Sam turned into a shopping center across the street that offered a view of the condo entrance. Dalton followed.

"You get the tag number?" Sam asked, getting into Dalton's car.

"Yeah, I got it, but I'm hesitant about calling it in. I'd just as soon not expose my plan if I don't have to. Maybe I can get him to come back out." He composed a message on the burner phone: *I just left the pickup point. The money wasn't there. You playing games with me?*

A few minutes passed before a reply appeared: *I didn't see anybody, so I didn't want to leave the money.*

Dalton texted: *One more chance. Bring it now, same place. Face to face. If I don't see you, I'm calling the cops.*

Reply: *Ok, thirty minutes.*

They had some time, so Dalton tried Diaz again and he answered. After listening to the details of the situation, Diaz said, "So you think this guy killed those men on the boat instead of Orlov?"

"I'm pretty certain of it. The phone I've used is clean except for the texts, and I think it'll hold up in court, especially if we find the stolen cash."

"Okay, I'll bring uniforms for the arrest."

"Tell them to suit up with body armor. This guy is deadly."

"Will do."

As they hung up, the Lexus exited the condo and turned toward South Dixie. Sam followed, and Dalton brought up the rear. When they neared the Southland Mall, Sam entered a gas station and pulled up to a pump. The Lexus headed back to the spot where it had previously parked and stopped, probably waiting for a car to enter the restaurant lot. Hanging back, Dalton kept going past and turned onto the street on the far side of the restaurant. With light traffic, he pulled over to the edge of the street and stopped. Idling there, he had a partial view of the Lexus. He phoned Diaz.

"The cruiser is here with me," Diaz said. "We're in the corner of the lot, and I see a Lexus SUV close to the restaurant. Is that the vehicle?"

"Yeah, let's take him."

Dalton turned in and headed toward the Lexus. At the same time, the police cruiser sped across the near-empty lot at an angle. It turned in front of the SUV and slammed on brakes, blocking forward movement. Two officers exited the car on the side opposite the killer's vehicle. Using the cruiser as a shield, they pointed their service weapons over the roof at their target.

Diaz drove up behind the Lexus and stopped, blocking it in. Before he could exit the vehicle, the Lexus slammed into his car with its rear end and pushed him back. It then cut an arc to its left. Tires screamed on the black top as the SUV lurched forward, missing the fender of the cruiser by inches.

Dalton punched the pickup's accelerator and followed the vehicle into the street. The Lexus sped away, its engine more powerful than that of the pickup. The cruiser passed by in pursuit. Giving up, Dalton slowed, turned around, and drove back. On the way, he called Sam. "The Miami PD has control of the situation, so you can head back to the marina."

"Roger that," Sam said.

The passenger side of Diaz's car was caved in, and the Miami detective stood outside with a phone to his ear. When he finished his conversation, Dalton asked if he was okay.

"Yeah, no big deal. The car is trashed, but I think it'll run. I just called for other cars in the area to join the chase. We'll get him."

"I have the plate number," Dalton said. He'd found it on the camcorder earlier, while they waited, and written it down. Diaz got back on the phone and relayed the information. Dalton drove them to a coffee shop outside the mall. They bought a couple of cups and took seats in a booth.

After a few minutes, Diaz's phone chimed. He answered, spoke for a minute or so with a scowl on his face, and hung up. "He got away. They found the Lexus in an alley, but it was empty, the driver's door swung open. We ran the plate and found out it's a rental. I've got somebody calling the agency for a name."

"I know where he lives. It's a high rise condo north of here. He'll probably go back to get his cash, and we can catch him if we know the unit number."

Diaz nodded. "Maybe their security guys can ID him from the vehicle or plate number. Lead the way and I'll follow, assuming my car still works."

When they got back to the mall, Diaz's car seemed to run okay. Dalton led him to the condominium complex, and they parked and went in through a visitor entrance. A security guard eyed them with skepticism when Diaz told her what they wanted. "I think you need a warrant to look at resident information."

"We just want the name of a resident who drives a certain vehicle, and we want his unit number."

"There's some pretty well off people living here who would give us a hard time if we did that. You can't get a warrant?"

"Sure, we can, but like I told you, this is an urgent matter."

She shook her head. "I don't know—"

"Is there anybody else we can talk to?" Diaz said, his face reddening.

The guard shrugged and picked up the phone. They took a seat and waited.

About ten minutes passed before a man came through a door next to the security counter. He looked about fifty, balding with a beer gut. His nametag read Roy Hurd.

"You look familiar," Hurd said to Diaz when he introduced himself.

"You were on the force," Diaz said. "I remember you."

"Yeah, traffic. Retired first chance I got. This pays just as good, and it's a lot less stress."

After a quick chit-chat about the department, Diaz told him what they needed.

Hurd gave them a grin. "Corporate has some pretty rigid rules, but I guess I could make an exception for an old comrade." He led them down a long hall to an office. Several security monitors hung from the wall, each with the screen split into six frames. They crowded around Hurd's computer, and he accessed a resident database. Diaz gave him the plate number and he ran a search. The system returned the name of a property management company.

"Looks like this company owns the unit, and they rent it out," Hurd said. "There's a realtor's name here, but he ain't the resident."

"So you don't have a name anywhere for the person living there?" Dalton asked.

The security man pulled up several more screens and shook his head. "Guess not. Maybe this person didn't want to be found. Looks like that vehicle has only been on the database for a couple of weeks." He leaned back in his seat. "You can check with the realtor, but they're probably closed right now."

Diaz shook his head. "Yeah, we can't wait until morning."

They eyed each other for a couple of beats, and Dalton said, "Can we look at video of the garage entrance from about an hour ago?"

Hurd shrugged. "I don't see why not."

Dalton gave him the time they had followed the Lexus to the complex, and he accessed the footage beginning a few minutes prior. "Okay, I'll run it slow-mo," Hurd said. "Tell me if you spot the car."

Activity exceeded what Dalton expected for that time of night, maybe residents returning from dinner. The Lexus entered at exactly the time Dalton had given the man, but the image didn't help. The camera, from several feet up on the wall, didn't get a recognizable shot of the driver's face because of the tinted glass.

"Try the garage exit," Dalton said. "Start about ten minutes past that time." He feared they might have the same issue with that camera image, but thought it worth a try.

The security man brought up another view that peered directly at the side of the vehicles. Only a couple of cars exited before the Lexus came up again. "Stop it there," Dalton said. Hurd did as requested, having to back it up a couple of frames for the best vantage point. The driver had lowered the window and glanced left checking for traffic before pulling out. A clear image of a face stared back at them.

LUCINDA PACED IN the alley, wishing she could go back three weeks and start again. She remembered it like yesterday. Leonard arrived at the office a few minutes after she sat down at her desk.

"How long you been here?" he asked.

"About an hour."

The little Russian eyed her as if she might be lying. "You need to launder the cash faster. We have about five million now."

"You want us to get caught? We move too much at once and the banks will get wise and call the Feds."

He backed down, but said he was going to look around for a more efficient operation. She could only be so lucky. Toole Parts hung around her neck like an albatross.

A few minutes after Leonard walked out, the phone chimed. She glanced at the display and answered. "Hey, Sis."

"Hey yourself. What're you up to?"

"The usual," Lucinda said. "Just arguing with Leonard."

"You oughtta ditch him."

"I wish I could. You know he didn't give me anything when we split, so I need a source of income."

"Yeah, tell me about it. I'd leave my husband if I could afford it."

"He hit you again?"

Her sister paused for a couple of beats. "Just some bruises. Nothing makeup won't cover."

Lucinda shook her head. "I wish we both had a way out of this life. I can't see myself punching a clock, but I had an idea about getting a start-up loan for a business."

"Go for it. You can do it."

She had no way of knowing how it would turn out. All she did was ask that accountant to fix up a financial statement. He was young and probably needed the business. And she thought he wouldn't ask too many questions. A couple of days later, Leonard came storming in the door of the office and said, "A guy went in the back door a little while ago while they were counting. He was looking for you, said his name was Banks. Boris pulled his gun, and he ran off." His face glowed crimson, as if on fire. "I know you had something to do with this. Now I've got to take care of this guy. I'll deal with you when I get back."

Lucinda thought her heart might explode. After a frantic few hours, she went into the back room where Vigo sat and asked about Leonard.

Vigo gave her a smirk. "Boris called, said they had something to do that might take all night. He said he wouldn't be back to relieve me. That ain't fair, you know? I hope I can stay awake."

Although she felt bad for Rudy Banks, there was nothing she could do about it. Leonard would probably kill him. And then he would come back and kill her. She had to get away, but she needed money to do that. All that money in the back room, and she couldn't get her hands on any of it.

Sis had called again. "Too bad you can't knock out that guy guarding the cash and take it."

"Leonard would find me," Lucinda said.

"Get somebody else to do it for you."

Chuckling, she said, "Yeah, right," but that was when she thought about Buster.

They'd had a fling when he worked for Leonard, and she knew he still carried a torch.

Buster answered when she called, and after a couple of minutes of flirty talk, she asked if he would be interested in a heist. He got excited, said, "Sure, anything for you babe." Next, she called Carl and got him on board. She hated to bring him in on it, too, but he had access to the boat.

It didn't do any good to hash it over now. All this was her fault, but she couldn't snap her fingers and change anything. She just needed to get that cash and make herself scarce.

Her sister picked her up at the mouth of the alley, and they rode away, heading south out of town.

"It took you long enough," Lucinda said.

"I told you I should go with you. Why didn't you listen?"

Lucinda sighed. "I just wanted to get a glimpse of the guy. He said he knew me, so he had to be one of Leonard's thugs. And Buster knew him well enough to tell him they were stealing the money."

"I wonder how Miami's finest got onto you."

"Yeah, me too," Lucinda said. "I didn't stay around to see what they wanted. They pulled guns, so I knew it was bad." She remained silent for a couple of minutes and thought about the money. "You check on the cash today?"

"It's still there. Quit worrying. Nobody knows about it."

"Yeah, nobody but this guy texting me, saying he's going to the cops. He'll do it for sure, now."

Sis glanced at her. "I told you to stop worrying. Nobody's gonna do anything. What's this guy got to gain by going to the cops? If they got you, they'd get the cash, too, and he would be out of luck. We just need to lay low and find out who he is."

"We were stupid to do what we did." Lucinda leaned back in the seat, closed her eyes, and listened to the whispering drone of the highway. The scene replayed in her head, like the loop of a horror film she couldn't turn off.

They took a twenty-foot skiff out to meet Carl and Buster, and the other guy named Floyd. She didn't know him, but Sis did, said he had a thing for her. When they got close, they threw Buster a rope. He pulled them over to the bigger boat and helped them climb aboard.

Lucinda looked around and said, "Where's Carl?"

"Uh, that's something we need to talk about. Carl got greedy, telling us he wanted half the take 'cause he got us the boat and the cops would come after him first." Buster hesitated and glanced at the bulkhead.

Lucinda's face turned red hot. "What did you do?"

Sis stepped over. "Yeah, Buster, what did you do?"

Buster shook his head. "Things kinda got out of hand, and..."

When he didn't say more, Sis' eyes narrowed. "You killed him?"

Nodding, Buster, said, "Yeah, we had to do it. He was spouting off about turning us in if we didn't give him what he deserved."

TWENTY-THREE

A SEARCH OF Lucinda's Lexus yielded nothing. No cash, no guns, only a rental agreement in the glovebox. At a few minutes past 2:00 in the morning, Diaz obtained a search warrant for her condo unit. That search disappointed as well. Dalton didn't think she would've put the money in a bank box, because of the bulk, so she probably had another place. The police never found her after the chase, so maybe someone had picked her up. Nothing else could be done until they figured out where she had gone. He headed south toward home.

The next morning at the office, Cobb's door was closed, and his lights were off. Dalton hadn't planned on updating him on Lucinda Toole anyway, since the case was considered closed in the LT's mind.

Dalton began an online search on Lucinda, but found nothing. He wondered if the Miami PD had fingerprinted the Lexus. Diaz would be off duty, so he called Detective Ames.

"Yeah, we ran the prints. Hold on." Noises over the phone sounded like papers shuffling, and then Ames came back on the line. "The woman's name is Linda Nash. Her prints were in the database, and I also found a news story on her. She was arrested in Ohio on suspicion of murdering her husband. Apparently, she had accused him of beating her up a couple of times, so she seemed like a likely candidate. But a few days after the arrest, she got alibied by her sister and released. I didn't see where the police ever found the killer."

Dalton thanked him and said he would check out the story. The name sounded familiar, and he pulled out his notes. After a few minutes, going back to the first week of the investigation, he found where he'd written that Heather Pound's real name was Wendy Nash. She and Linda had to be related. Maybe sisters? Wendy could have been the sister who gave her the alibi when her husband got murdered. He accessed the DMV database and pulled up the driver's license photo for each. Though both were drop dead gorgeous, the only thing he saw as resemblance was their eyes. Both had blue eyes. The color of their hair, one blonde and the other brunette, could have been altered. Wendy, AKA Heather, was thirty, almost two years older than Linda.

Wendy had to be the person who picked up Linda/ Lucinda after the car chase. Maybe they went to the Pound residence, and maybe they had the cash there as well. He and Steve Chase had searched the home, but not the boathouse. Maybe they had the cash stowed there. The Nash women could have already left Florida, but if they didn't suspect the law knew about them, they could still be at the house.

He needed somebody to tag along in case there were problems. Although still on the fence about trusting Chase, he decided to risk it and found him at his desk.

"There's been a new development," Dalton said, "and

I need to go back to Joe Pound's house. You have time to go along?"

Chase shrugged. "Sure, if you need me."

On the way, Dalton told him about the texts and Linda Nash, AKA Lucinda, and her sister.

"You're kidding?" Chase said. "I thought all that was finished and the Russian guy did it."

"I'm pretty sure he only killed Rudy Banks. Nash wouldn't have responded to the texts unless she was guilty."

"Yeah, guess so."

They reached the neighborhood of the Pound residence and parked at the edge of a vacant lot nearby. As they eased into the street, Dalton spotted an SUV parked in front of the property. "Isn't that Cobb's vehicle?" He asked.

Chase stopped walking. "Yeah, it is. Are we gonna get in trouble for this?"

"Don't worry about it. Cobb is dirty." They walked the rest of the way and scaled the fence, which stood only about five feet. Dalton drew his service weapon and advised Chase to do the same. Rounding the house, they headed toward the back yard. As they approached the far corner, the sound of Cobb's voice stopped them.

"I knew you had it," Cobb said, "and I want my part."

Dalton chanced a peek. The yard sloped down to the boathouse and dock. The LT and the two sisters stood there among several large suitcases, one of which lay open. Stacks of cash were visible inside.

The brunette, Linda, got in his face. "You don't have a part."

Dalton pulled out his phone and started up a video. He held the phone around the edge so it would capture the images and the conversation.

"You two ruined a sweet operation," Cobb said. "If it wasn't for you, we'd still have cash rolling in. So you owe me."

"Joe paid you on every load," Wendy said. "Not sure what you did for it, though."

"Are you kidding? I kept him informed of the DEA's activities. Without that he would've been caught."

Linda thrust her palms against his chest, pushing him back. "Get lost. You didn't have anything to do with this heist. We did it all on our own."

"Yeah, along with the three guys you killed so you wouldn't have to split with them."

"That's not how it was," Wendy chimed in from behind her sister. "Floyd and Buster killed Carl. He was our cousin, so we had to kill them. For family, you know."

"So you would've split the money five ways if they hadn't killed Carl? I don't think so. You planned to kill them all along." Cobb stepped back and pulled his weapon. "I've changed my mind. I'm taking it all. Get in the boathouse."

The sisters protested, but he repeated his order, this time louder as he shook the gun tip at them. Scowling, they turned and shuffled across the dock.

"We need to get down there," Dalton said. "He's going to kill them."

They ran down the slope. As they neared, a shot rang out inside the boathouse. Dalton reached the dock and bound across it to the doorway the three had entered. Cobb lay at the edge of a boat slip, blood pooling around his head, his fingers still wrapped around the stock of his handgun. Linda stood over him with a pistol in her hand. Wendy, Joe Pound's widow, held an oar with blood on its tip.

Linda turned the gun on Dalton, and he sidestepped around the corner as she fired. The round blew out a chunk of wood from the doorway. A boat motor started up and he risked a peek. Wendy throttled a skiff's outboard as Linda leapt aboard and fell into a seat. They sped out of the slip and cut right. No chance to get off a shot. He hurried to the doorway, bumping past Chase, and stepped out in time to record the boat registration number on video.

Another boat, about fifty feet long, lay in the other slip. It would never catch up with the smaller craft. "Call it in, officer down." Dalton said as he rushed to Cobb and knelt. The lieutenant's eyes stood wide open, staring at the ceiling. No pulse. "Tell them to send the CSI team and the ME, too."

When Chase got off the phone, he said, "You think all these bags are full of cash?"

"Probably. It belonged to Leonard Orlov."

Dalton told him to go inside the house and get the gate open. He then called the watch commander. "We need an APB on two women going by the names Lucinda Toole and Heather Pound. They're in a small boat headed northeast on Florida Bay, and they're armed and dangerous. One of them killed a deputy," he said, deliberately being vague. He gave the man the boat number.

"Alert marine patrols in the area and the Coast Guard. They could be heading out to open water north of here."

"You said a deputy got killed. Anybody I know?"

Dalton hung up and punched in the sheriff's number.

When she answered, he told her the situation, including the part about Cobb threatening the sisters for the cash and getting shot.

"Lt. Cobb is dead?" she said, disbelief in her tone.

"No pulse, but EMTs are on the way, and so is the ME. I spoke with the watch commander. He's putting out an APB."

"Oh, man. This is worse than bad. Are you sure about what Cobb said?"

"Yes. Steve Chase is here with me, and he heard it all, too." He glanced at Chase, who nodded in agreement. Though Dalton had the video, he didn't want to mention it unless he had to.

"So you think these women murdered those men on the boat and Joseph Pound?"

"Yes."

"I thought Leonard Orlov was our guy."

"That's what everybody wanted to believe."

"But you didn't?"

"No."

A sigh whispered across the line. "Why didn't I know about this before now?"

"I told Cobb about my reservations, but he wanted to close the case."

She paused, and then said, "It looks as if he had a good reason, at least for him."

"Guess so."

Another sigh and a pause, maybe giving her space to figure out a way forward. "Okay, don't talk to anybody else about this. I'll put out a statement for the media." She hung up.

EMTs arrived first. "Nothing we can do for him," one of the techs said.

Dalton nodded. "Yeah, I thought so. The medical examiner is on his way."

When the CSIs arrived, Robin gave him a smile. He told the team about the downed deputy and asked them to dust the luggage bags when they finished in the boat-house. He hoped they would find prints of the dead men from the boat and both women, thinking the combination would help convict the two women.

Intercepting Robin before she could enter, he said, "The dead man is Cobb."

Her smile faded as the news sank in, and a moment later tears filled her eyes. She wiped them away with her fingers. "How did it happen?"

"Heather Pound and Lucinda Toole are sisters. It looked as if one of them hit him with an oar and the other shot him. I'm sorry."

She nodded and staggered over to the luggage, seemingly in a daze.

Dr. Lake showed up later with a couple of assistants and a gurney. Dalton told him the identity of the victim and what had happened. The doctor just stared for a few seconds, and then shook his head. No wisecracks. He trudged inside the boathouse to examine the body. An hour later, his staff had Cobb on the gurney, dragging the wheels through the grass toward the front drive.

The CSI team began counting the cash, and Dalton hung around until they finished. It totaled $5.2 million, mostly in twenties and tens. He asked Chase to follow them to the evidence cage. "I'm going inside and see what they left behind."

Chase agreed so he stretched on vinyl gloves and entered the house. In the living room he found a purse containing a driver's license, a debit card and several credit cards belonging to Lucinda Toole. Another purse with similar contents for Heather Pound sat on a dresser in the master bedroom. The two obviously had planned on bringing the cash into the house or taking it to their vehicles, but surely hadn't planned on leaving their purses behind. That meant they probably had no access to funds, unless they grabbed some of the cash as they left. It also meant there would be no electronic trail of expenditures from credit cards, unless they had them on their person when they fled.

He didn't find any phones, so they probably had them. Thinking the phones might contain apps they could use for purchasing, or obtaining cash, he went to Joe Pound's desk down the hall and found documents on Wendy's bank and wireless accounts.

When he got back to the office, he logged the purses into evidence and asked Robin to contact the bank and get them to track Wendy's activity. "Sure, I'll be glad to," she said with a smile. "What do you think will happen to all that money?"

Dalton shrugged and headed toward his own workspace, saying over his shoulder, "The state can worry about that."

An hour or so later, Chase came and got him. "It's on the news in the break room."

Dalton followed him to a TV hanging on the wall. A Miami news alert played, and Chase ran the DVR back to the beginning of the segment. A male talking head said, "Two women fled the Keys in a small boat a little more than an hour ago after shooting a Monroe County deputy. They were last seen heading north in Florida Bay." Images of the two flashed onto the corner of the screen. The newsman gave their names and a physical description, probably straight off copies of their driver's licenses provided by the sheriff's office. "What we know now is that deputies went to the address of Joseph and Heather Pound to arrest the two women. The reason for the arrest has not been provided. Joseph Pound, the husband of one of the women was murdered a couple of weeks ago, and investigators here at channel four speculate that the attempted arrest today might be related to that crime. If you have any information about the whereabouts of either of them, please contact the Monroe County Sheriff's Office." The telephone number and email address displayed on the screen. "In other news here in Miami—"

Chase froze the screen. "Did you give the information to the TV station?"

Dalton shook his head. "I told everything to the sheriff. She said she would handle the media release."

Chase frowned. "Yeah, but they didn't even identify the LT."

"I noticed that," Dalton said. The sheriff would eat some crow after going on the tube and naming Orlov as the murderer, so she probably wanted to stretch out the media feeds, hoping to dilute the effect over time. She would also want to minimize the negative press on the sheriff's office, and needed a good explanation of why Cobb was on the scene. The easiest answer would be to gloss over his involvement altogether. It would be up to her if she wanted to do that. Dalton didn't care one way or the other. He turned to leave and added, "He was dirty and did himself in."

"That's cold, man."

TWENTY-FOUR

LOLA ANN CALLED. "It's all over the news about those two women killing a deputy. Why didn't you come to me with it? I thought we had a good thing going."

Dalton smiled. "Yeah, sorry. The sheriff gave me a gag order. She handled the release herself."

"Why would she do that?"

"Just being careful. Everybody thought this case was all over."

She huffed into the phone. "Yeah, but you and other deputies went after the women, so I guess you were holding something out on me. I'm hurt."

He knew she was just grandstanding, but thought there could be a hint of truth to it. "Can I make it up to you with dinner?"

"I don't know. I get the feeling I'm being used."

"You're kidding? Just a few days ago you said I made you look good at the station."

"Yeah, well, that's true. But my manager thought I had an 'in' with the sheriff's office. Then, today, we got the press release about the same time Miami ran it, so we only had old news to report."

An 'in' with the sheriff's office? "So, you want to get dinner, or not?"

Lola Ann paused for a couple of beats and sighed. "Well, I guess you owe me that."

They agreed to meet at a restaurant at 7:00 p.m. and hung up.

Dalton thought back about the conversation between Cobb and the sisters and didn't recall anything being said about Joe Pound's murder. Apparently, he hadn't been involved with the heist of Orlov's cash, but somebody had killed him with the same gun used in killing the others. It had to be one of the two women, and he assumed Linda probably did it, since the CSIs didn't find gunshot residue on Pound's wife. The widow had a motive, though: the deposits in the offshore account and the insurance policy on his life. The two women seemed to be operating together, and having her sister deliver the kill-shot made it more likely they would get away with it. No one had known they were sisters, and there was no reason to suspect Leonard Orlov's ex-wife of killing Joe Pound. The missing cash brought them down.

Robin dropped by his desk and said, "According to the bank, Heather Pound withdrew $500 from an ATM in Key Largo."

"You have the address of the machine?"

She gave it to him and he found it on the computer's map: only a couple of blocks from the Toole Parts address where they could have landed the boat. Probably nobody noticed, and they could have walked to the ATM from there. After that they would need transportation, and could get a taxi or a bus, or hire a private car. A rental would be difficult without a driver's license.

Robin said, "You need anything else right now?"

"No, but this is good work. Stay on it. If we don't get them today, they'll probably get another $500 tomorrow, and that'll tell us the direction they're traveling."

Dalton and Chase headed to the Key Largo bank branch where the sisters had accessed the ATM. The manager allowed them to view the camera footage. It showed Wendy Nash punching in a code from her phone and retrieving cash. She smiled directly into the camera and winked.

"I'll take this side of the street and you take the other," Dalton said to Chase.

They canvassed businesses in the immediate area and flashed photos of the women. After going into a gas station, a convenience store, a doughnut shop, a couple of fast food restaurants, and an insurance office, Dalton hadn't found anyone who had seen the two. As he exited the last place, Chase hurried across the street. "Hey, one of the sisters went in the drugstore over there. The lady at the counter said she bought a bunch of stuff: hair color, makeup, a couple of cheap purses, and sunglasses. She said the woman waited outside for a few minutes and then left in a taxi. I got the name of the company."

They got into the car and headed north on US-1, Chase behind the wheel. Dalton called the taxi company. After identifying himself, he asked about the fare. The dispatcher checked the records and said the cab took them to Miami, but he didn't have an address.

"Give me the driver's phone number," Dalton said.

"I don't hand out the drivers' personal numbers. Besides, how do I know you're who you say you are? You could be the woman's jealous husband, or boyfriend."

"This is important. These women murdered a sheriff's deputy in Islamorada a few hours ago. I'll give you the sheriff's number, and you can call about my identity."

After a brief hesitation, the dispatcher said, "That's okay, I believe you," and relinquished the number.

He got the driver on the phone and said, "This is Michael Dalton with the Monroe County Sheriff's Office. I'm calling about the two women you took to Miami."

"Oh, yeah, the beauties. What do you want with them?"

Dalton told him, and he remained silent for a few seconds. "Huh, I wondered why they wanted me to pick them up at the drugstore."

"Can you give me the address where you left them?"

"Uh, no, but I can tell you the name of the place."

It turned out to be an old motel off Dixie Highway near Cutler Bay. They took the turnpike when they reached Florida City and arrived a few minutes later. In the office Dalton flashed his badge to the clerk and laid the photos on the counter. "Did these women get a room here?"

The clerk, a young man with acne, studied the images and said, "One of them did, just a few hours ago. After she went out the door, I saw through the window there was another woman with her. Could've been the other one in the picture."

"What room number?"

"It was room twelve." He shrugged. "But they're gone now. A car picked them up about twenty minutes ago."

Two security monitors sat next to the wall behind the counter. Dalton nodded toward them. "How about checking your security system and see if it picked up the vehicle."

Acne Face scratched his head. "Okay, I think I can do that." He took a seat at the computer and punched some keys. "Here you go." The image of a green minivan appeared on the screen. It sat in front of one of the rooms.

"Can you run it forward and see if we can get the plate number?"

The clerk complied, and the video moved forward in slow motion. It displayed the two women coming out of the room and getting into the rear seats.

"Back that up and print it for me," Dalton said.

Acne Face printed the screen and handed it over. The copy had low resolution, the distance making it worse, and no color. Dalton couldn't say for sure he could tell the two women apart, but was pretty certain it was them. He asked the guy to roll the video forward again, and when the vehicle backed around, the plate number came into view. "Okay, stop there where we can see the plate and print that, too." Dalton gave the pages to Chase and asked the clerk if he could let them into the room.

"Yeah, I guess. You're the law."

They went out the door and the young man opened up unit twelve. Except for indentations in the bedspreads where it appeared someone had sat, the room appeared unused. In the bathroom, empty hair color boxes lay in the bottom of the waste basket next to the sink. Water spatters dotted the sink top and the surrounding floor. Dalton took the boxes and they left.

In the car, they headed in the same direction as the minivan. Dalton called Robin and asked her to run the plate. He waited on the phone and she came back with the name of the owner. "It's registered to a Chad Renko." She gave him the phone number and address and they hung up.

Chase turned into a shopping center so Dalton could enter the location into the navigation system. It indicated they were about ten miles away. "Get us there as fast as you can," Dalton said. He estimated that the women were thirty minutes or so ahead of them.

Chase shrugged, sped out into the street, and floored the accelerator. Dalton gripped the armrest as the deputy passed several cars and weaved in and out of traffic.

The stucco cottage sat on a side street nestled behind a couple of Royal Poinciana trees. It looked a century old with no garage. Chase slowed the car as they approached. A minivan sat out front. It wasn't the one from the motel, and this vehicle didn't have a plate. He checked the address Robin had given him and verified it was the same as on the mailbox.

They kept going and made a trip around the block. As they approached the residence again, a man about thirty years old and balding came out the front door. He went to the vehicle, popped the rear hatch, and pulled out two suitcases. Dalton sighed. "I don't think this is our guy."

"You want to talk to him?"

"Yeah, pull over."

Chase did as he asked, and they got out. The man

didn't appear to be armed, and he turned around as they approached.

"Sheriff's detectives," Dalton said, flashing his badge. "Can we ask you a couple of questions?"

"Sure, I guess. What's this about?"

"Are you Chad Renko?"

The guy's eyes widened. "Yeah, that's me."

"You have another vehicle?"

"Nope, just this one."

"Okay, we're looking for a minivan with a license number that's registered to you." Dalton read off the number.

"Right. That's my tag number," Renko said as he turned and glanced at the rear of his vehicle. "Hey, my tag is missing."

"You just return from a trip?"

"Yeah, I did." The guy stared at the vacant spot for a couple of seconds. "I parked at the airport for three weeks. Somebody stole it while I was gone."

"You remember your location in the lot?" Dalton asked.

Renko pulled a note from his pocket and handed it to him. "Here, I wrote it down. I knew I wouldn't remember it."

Dalton thanked the man, told him to report his stolen tag to Miami Dade PD, and they headed to the airport. When they arrived, Chase parked in the drop-off lane. He flashed his badge for a security guard approaching them as they got out.

"Okay," the guard said, "but you can't stay there long."

They located the security office, and after an explanation to two officers as to what they wanted, they were taken into a room full of video monitors. An officer sat them down at a computer and accessed video from three weeks before, zooming in on Renko's parking location. Running the footage in slow motion, they spotted him entering the spot and getting out with the suitcases. After a few more minutes of viewing, the minivan from the motel pulled into a space a few cars away and a man got out and eased over to the rear of Renko's vehicle. He stood there for a few seconds, looking around, and then stooped over. Though they couldn't see what he was doing, Dalton assumed he was taking the plate. When he returned to his vehicle and pulled out, his tag number was in view.

"Get us the best images you can of the guy's face and of his license plate," Dalton said.

The officer reversed the video and played it again for the screen shots. "You want hard copy or digital?"

"Both," Dalton said, giving the officer his phone number.

Dalton thanked him and they left. On their way out of the airport, he phoned Robin and asked her to check out the new license number. A minute later, she said, "Sorry, that plate was stolen a month ago."

He relayed the news to Chase, who said. "So, I guess we're out of luck."

"Yeah, maybe. The guy was stealing tags, probably trying to stay ahead of the police. He picked a good one this time, removing the plate just a few minutes after the car got parked. And Renko was away a long time, during which he didn't know it was missing."

They remained silent for a few seconds, and then Chase said, "You saying the thief knew Renko would be gone for three weeks?"

"I think that's a possibility." He sent the photo to Chad Renko asking if he recognized the man. Within a couple of minutes, his phone vibrated with a reply from Renko.

Renko: *Is he going to get in trouble for stealing it?*

Dalton: *Probably.*

Renko: *What if I don't press charges?*

Dalton punched in his number for a voice call. "Are you saying you recognize this guy?"

"Yeah, maybe, but I don't want him to get in trouble for it."

"Well, it isn't that simple. He gave a ride to two women wanted for murdering a sheriff's deputy in Islamorada."

"Oh, man, that can't be true."

Dalton said, "Tell me who he is, Chad."

After a protracted silence, Renko sighed and said, "I thought he was my friend."

TWENTY-FIVE

RENKO TOLD DALTON the man's name was Spiro Metz. "He works for a pawn broker in Little Havana."

Upon getting the name of the shop, Dalton hung up and located the place on his navigation system. Just a few miles away. He called Robin and asked her to check for a police record.

"A man by that name is wanted in Miami for grand theft auto. Apparently, he skipped bond on his way to trial a few weeks ago. Is that your guy?"

"Probably." Dalton thanked her and hung up. He thought Metz could be one of Leonard Orlov's men, and decided he should check in with the Miami PD before visiting the pawn shop. Diaz would be on duty, so he phoned him and described the situation. "These women are dangerous, and if the guys at the pawn shop are part of Orlov's operation, they are, too."

"Okay, I'll come and bring a couple of squad cars."

Twenty minutes later, Dalton and Chase sat parked on a side street near the shop's location. Diaz and the cruisers arrived and pulled up behind him. They agreed that Dalton, Chase, and Diaz would enter and ask about the women, and the officers would watch the back door.

Diaz got a folded newspaper from his car and stuck his weapon inside. The three ambled down the block to the shop entrance. When they pushed through, a bell rang, and then a young man still in his teens came out from a back room to the counter. Dalton stepped over, flashed his badge. "We're looking for one of your employees: Spiro Metz."

"Spiro? I think he left a little while ago."

Dalton took out the photos of the women and laid them on the counter. "We have a witness who saw him bring these two women to your shop within the last hour or so." A lie, but worth a try. "Do you recognize them?" The kid glanced at the images and his eyes grew large. He shook his head. "Don't think so."

Dalton waited a beat, staring. "Is there anybody else we can talk to?"

Frowning, the teen said, "Uh, hold on. I'll get my uncle." He turned and went through the door to the back. They waited a couple of minutes before a man came out. He appeared in his fifties, balding and overweight, and wore thick glasses. Before the man could speak, Dalton heard a popping noise that seemed to come from the back room or the alley beyond.

Diaz's radio squawked, and a tinny voice said, "The women ran out the back, and one of them shot Ponder in the neck."

The man with the thick specs turned and headed through the door, and Dalton rounded the counter after him. He ran through a back room with a desk and computer equipment toward a door that stood open to the outside. The proprietor stopped at the doorway, and Dalton pushed by him to see one of the officers kneeling over another on the ground, pressing his hands over the wound. Blood pooled around the downed man's shoulders. Sirens blared in the distance.

"Which way did they go?" Dalton asked.

The kneeling man pointed toward the corner of the alley. "Rivera and Carson went after them."

Chase and Diaz came out the door and Dalton asked Chase to stay with the shopkeeper and see what he could find out. He and Diaz ran toward the corner the officer had indicated and down the alleyway. They passed employee parking for a string of stores and offices on their left as they headed toward an opening on the other end. The alley ran across a street and behind another long row of businesses.

An officer came out of one of the buildings across the street and yelled, "I think they went in one of these stores!"

When they caught up, Diaz said, "Where's your partner?"

"Rivera went around front, in case they came out that way."

"I'm going around to help him," Diaz said to Dalton. "You and Carson search the rear."

Dalton nodded, and he and the officer continued down the alley. They passed a shoe store and a phone store, and found the back door ajar on the third place, a Chinese restaurant.

"I'm gonna check in here," the officer said.

Dalton followed him over as an Asian man pushed through the door coming out. He wore a long apron and stuck a cigarette in his mouth, as if ready to light up.

"Did anybody come in your door from out here?" the officer asked.

"No, nobody come in." He stared at Dalton, cutting his eyes back toward the door a couple of times, as if to signal.

Nodding, Dalton glanced at Carson. "Let's move on." They hurried around a wood fence toward the next place, and he stopped and said to the officer, "Hold on." He pulled out his phone and called Diaz. "I think they're in the Chinese restaurant, third place down. Flush them out and we'll be waiting."

"Roger that," Diaz said.

They stood out of sight behind the fence, and Dalton peered around the edge. The Asian man had gone back inside. A minute or so later the door flew open and the sisters ran out. Lucinda/Linda had a pistol in her hand.

Dalton rounded the fence with his service weapon aimed at them. "Stop right there, and drop the gun!"

The two slowed, but Linda raised the barrel tip and pointed his way.

"Don't do it, Linda! You'll die! Drop it!"

Calling her name seemed to throw her off balance, and she just stood there for a long moment, and then nodded. As she began to lower the gun, a weapon discharged from behind Dalton. The shot hit her in the shoulder, whipping her to one side, and she stumbled to the ground.

Wendy ran toward her sister. "You shot her! She was gonna give up!"

Dalton beat her there and wrested the weapon from

the downed woman's hand. Diaz came out the door and grabbed Wendy.

"Get the paramedics down here," Dalton said to Carson, his tone sharp. The officer just stared for a moment, as if in shock. "Get going, now!"

"Okay, I'm on my way." Carson ran toward the pawn shop shouting into his radio.

Kneeling, Dalton checked Linda's wound, which was bleeding more than expected. He pressed on the entry point hoping to stem the flow.

"Am I going to die?" she asked, her eyes pleading.

"EMT's are taking care of the officer you shot. They should be here soon."

"You shoot her?" Diaz asked, standing with Wendy, her hands in cuffs.

Dalton shook his head. Though he believed the officer had fired prematurely, he didn't want to pass judgement. She had already shot two cops, and might have gotten the drop on him, too. He didn't think so, but there was no way to be certain.

"That cop shot her," Wendy said. "She was giving up."

Linda squirmed, probably from the pain. "I don't want to die."

"Just stay still. Paramedics will be here soon." He wanted to tell her she should've thought about that before going on a killing rampage, but didn't see anything to be gained by saying it.

A NEWS TEAM arrived as the officers hauled Wendy away. One of the cruisers followed the ambulance carrying the downed officer and Linda. Both were still alive when they left. If the officer died, Linda would be booked on a murder charge, that is, if she survived, too.

As Dalton and Chase headed toward their vehicle, a newsman in a suit and a photographer approached. The suit said, "Hey, are you cops? Can you tell us what happened?"

Dalton waved him away, and he and Chase got into the car and pointed it at police headquarters. On the way, Dalton got the sheriff on the phone and updated her on the situation.

She didn't respond for a few seconds, and then in a chilly tone said, "So, you think this does it? It's over?"

"Yes, it's over. I'll get with the prosecutor and work out the charges."

"Okay, call me when you get the details." She hung up.

Dalton and Chase spent the next few hours giving their statements. When they finished, Dalton called the hospital. After a couple of transfers he got the ER, identified himself, and learned that Linda and the officer were both in stable condition and were expected to recover.

As they were about to leave, Diaz asked to speak with Dalton. When the two were alone in an interview room, the Miami detective said, "How did the shooting go down? Was she giving up, like the sister said?"

"She appeared to be. After I told her a second time to drop the gun, she nodded and I thought she began to lower it when the officer fired. I guess it was a judgment call."

"You think he needs more training?"

"Couldn't hurt."

DALTON ARRIVED BACK in Islamorada in time for his dinner date with Lola Ann. After agreeing they were off the record, he told her about arresting the sisters.

"You think they'll be convicted?"

"I think so. Steve and I were there when Linda shot the deputy, and an officer saw her shoot the Miami cop."

"What about the other murders?"

"We might get them on those, too. The problem is, we don't have any hard evidence that they killed those men on that boat or Joe Pound. They ended up with that cash, but the origin of the cash is just supposition, including the notion that it was stolen and was on that boat where the men got murdered. Unless we get something else, our evidence is all circumstantial. We have a witness who says Leonard Orlov's money got stolen, but it's just his testimony, and a defense attorney might argue that the witness is unreliable, because he's getting a lesser sentence for his crimes." He left out the part about hearing Wendy say they killed the men on the boat, and didn't mention anything about the slain deputy being Lt. Cobb. Though they had the off-the-record agreement, he felt the information could still find its way to the airwaves.

Lola Ann's brow furrowed. "This is all good press. Too bad I can't use it."

Dalton smiled. "Yes, too bad."

After dinner, they had coffee and Dalton paid the check. They strolled out and he walked her to her car. Before opening her door, she leaned into him and they kissed. It lasted longer than a simple good-night gesture, kicking his pulse into overdrive. When she broke away, she said, "Would you like to come by my place for a nightcap?"

A nearby lamppost shone behind her. In the radiant glow, her eyes and lips glistened. His pulse swished in his ears. He wanted to say *Yes*, but knew getting in too deep with a member of the media could cause him grief with his cases. "I'd love to, but how about a raincheck?"

THE NEXT MORNING, Dalton checked out a video camera from the equipment locker, and he and Chase headed back to Miami. Robin called on the way and Dalton put her on speaker. "We found fingerprints and blood on the luggage that held the money," she said, excitement in her voice. "The prints belong to the two men on the boat and to the sisters, and both the women's prints were fixed in wet blood."

"Hey, that's good work," Dalton said. "Hopefully, the blood is from the dead men."

She told him it matched the types from the two men, and she had sent it off for DNA confirmation. He thanked her and they hung up.

"Sounds like we have them cold," Chase said.

"Yeah, maybe. Keep your fingers crossed."

A police officer stood guard outside Linda Nash's hospital room. They entered as she pushed a food tray out of the way. The light meal appeared untouched. Chase hung back, near the door, as Dalton approached the bed. "So, how do you feel?"

She gave him a scowl. "How do you think I feel? I have a fractured collar bone, and they dug a bullet out of my shoulder. What do you want?"

He shrugged. "I thought you might want to come clean about the murders."

"I didn't murder anybody. I was just protecting myself from policemen trying to kill me."

The memory of Cobb getting shot after forcing the sisters into the boathouse at gunpoint flashed behind his eyes. He knew her lawyers might mount a successful defense on that killing. He had checked on the Miami officer before coming to the room, and learned that he was out of danger and would be fine within a couple of weeks. A heavy charge there, but not murder.

"I was thinking more in terms of Eldon Perl and Floyd Sparks."

Shaking her head, she said, "I didn't have anything to do with their deaths."

He waited a few beats before saying, "That isn't what the evidence shows."

"What evidence?" Her eyes seemed to widen a fraction.

"We found lots of prints on that luggage containing the cash. They belonged to you, your sister and the dead men."

"They worked for Leonard, so they would've handled that luggage way before we got it. Doesn't mean we had anything to do with them dying. Leonard found those guys and killed them. He got his money back, and I just recovered it after he got killed. Face it, you don't have anything on us."

The two had been pretty careful, but they didn't expect the police to ever get their hands on those bags of money. "Oh, yeah," he added, "I forgot to mention that you and your sister's prints were set in the dead men's wet blood. That could happen only when they were murdered, not days later."

She glared at him. "I don't believe you."

He let that settle in before going on. "One thing has me puzzled, though. Why kill Joe Pound? At that point, nobody suspected you two of killing those men. We thought your ex did it. So you didn't need Pound to take the blame. He was your sister's husband."

"Yeah, and he beat her up every chance he got."

"So you shot him?"

When she didn't reply, he said, "You might have a chance for a deal with the District Attorney, if you're willing to tell your story. If not, you and your sister will be charged with first-degree murder. It'll be up to a judge or jury, and both of you could end up on death row."

"Get out!" She grabbed the bedside alert and pressed a button.

"Can I help you?" a nurse said over the speaker.

"I need my medication!"

Dalton laid a card on the table beside her bed, said, "Think about it," and he and Chase left.

Next, he took a run at Wendy Nash at the jail. Her lawyer arrived a few minutes after they did, and they went to an interview room. The room was small, so Chase said he would wait outside. Wendy seemed relieved to get out of her holding cell for a little while, but she didn't budge on the murders, either. Dalton assumed both women had consulted with the lawyer beforehand, because she said about the same thing her sister had.

The only difference happened when Dalton mentioned the fingerprints in the wet blood. The lawyer, a man named Phillip Geiger, seemed to sit up a little straighter. He glanced at Wendy, uncertainty in his eyes, maybe thinking things were a little more serious than she'd led him to believe.

"If you want to talk about a deal," Dalton said, "now's the time, but we'll need the whole story."

Wendy huffed a chuckle and shook her head. Geiger frowned. "Could you leave us for a few minutes? We need to talk." The last part seemed to be directed at Wendy more than him.

Dalton nodded, got up from his chair and headed to the door. "Ask the guard to call me when you're ready." He went outside to a break area and joined Chase for a cup of coffee. After updating him on the conversation inside the room, the guard signaled for him to return. When he entered, he noticed that Wendy's eyes were red, her cheeks moist with tears.

"Okay," Geiger said. "She's agreed to tell you what happened, but we'll need your prosecutor here and an assurance of no death penalty."

"Let me make a call." Dalton stepped outside and phoned Connie Duval in the Monroe County DA's office. It took some coaxing, but she agreed to drive up and could be there in a couple of hours. He went back into the room and gave them the news. The lawyer handed him a card and they agreed to meet back when she arrived.

Dalton and Chase left and got lunch at a restaurant near the Miami River. After paying the bill, they walked around the area, killing time until Duval phoned. She said she would be there in twenty minutes, so he called Geiger and headed back. While he waited for the prosecutor to arrive, he arranged for a video recording of the interview. Duval got there first, and he told her about the evidence.

"Not bad," she said, nodding, "but a good defense still might poke holes in it. Hopefully, she'll give us a clean confession."

Geiger and Nash shuffled in and sat down. Dalton told them the interview would be recorded. He turned on the video and stated the date and time and the attendees present. "Please proceed," he said to Geiger.

"Ms. Nash will tell her story," Geiger said, "but first we need an assurance that the death penalty is off the table."

Duval said, "We can do that, but it has to be truthful. If we find out she's lying, all bets are off."

Geiger stared for a moment, but nodded and said to Wendy, "Go ahead."

Wendy had composed herself since she'd left the room earlier. She swept her hair over one ear and clasped her hands together on the surface of the table. "I want to start by saying I haven't killed anybody. My sister did all the shooting."

TWENTY-SIX

WENDY'S STORY WOULD lead a person to believe her involvement amounted to that of an innocent bystander, simply along for the ride. According to her, Linda cooked up the plan to get the guys to rob Orlov's five million, and she went alone to the boat and killed Perl and Sparks. She had borrowed Joe Pound's boat from Wendy, and when she showed up at her house with the money, Wendy didn't know where it came from, but helped her unload it and store it in a locker in the boathouse. And that's how her prints got on the money bags.

She stopped for a breather, and Connie Duval said, "Tell us about the murder of your husband, Joseph Pound."

"Linda did that, too," Wendy said, her eyes glistening with new tears. "We'd planned to go away with the money, which I assumed came from her ex-husband, Leonard Orlov. But I told her my husband would come after us. Joe abused me the entire time we were married, so I knew he would kill me if he caught up with us. The next thing I knew, Linda called and said she'd solved the problem, and Joe wouldn't be able to hurt us. I didn't know she'd killed him until I heard on the news that he was found dead at his office."

They took a break and Dalton and Duval joined

Chase in the break area and sat down with a cup of coffee. Dalton gave Chase the gist of what Nash had said.

"What do you think?" the prosecutor asked Dalton.

He shook his head. "I don't buy it. Right before she and her sister escaped in the boat, Steve and I heard her admit to killing the men on the boat. She said: 'Floyd and Buster killed Carl. He was our cousin, so we had to kill them.'"

Duval's eyes narrowed and she turned to Chase. "You heard it, too?"

Chase nodded. "Yeah, just like he said."

"Would both of you testify to that in court?"

They assured her they would.

"The Carl you mentioned," Duval said. "Was that Carl Myron, the floater from a few weeks ago?"

"Yes. I thought the two men had killed him, and her statement confirmed that."

"Okay, let's back up. To whom did Wendy make the statement that they had killed the two men."

Dalton knew the news would be out soon enough, so he told her. "Lieutenant Cobb. He was with the sisters in the dock area at Wendy's house. Joe Pound had been moving drugs for Leonard Orlov, and Cobb told the women he had been tipping Pound off on DEA plans so they wouldn't get caught. Since the operation had gone belly up, he said he deserved a share of the loot."

Duval's eyes grew large and she leaned back in her chair. "Huh, that's the first I've heard about Lieutenant Cobb's involvement. Who else knows this?"

"Just me, Steve, and the sheriff."

"Okay, I've heard enough. Let's get back in there."

Dalton called Geiger and told him they were ready to reconvene. They went in, and Wendy and the lawyer returned right behind them.

When they were settled, the prosecutor turned on the video, said for the record that they were continuing the interview, and turned to Wendy. "We believe you lied to us about your involvement. The evidence suggests that your part in killing the men on the boat was that of an active partner. So, I want to give you a chance to correct anything you've told us."

Geiger stared for a moment, his eyes narrowed. "Is there additional evidence? Ms. Nash explained how her prints got on the luggage."

Duval's eyes narrowed. "Detective Dalton and one other person heard her tell Lieutenant Cobb of the Monroe County Sheriff's Office that she and her sister killed the two men on the boat. She said they did it because the men had killed their cousin, Carl Myron. This happened right before Wendy and Linda killed the lieutenant."

Geiger turned to Wendy, his face flush. "Is that true?"

"I don't remember saying that. He must've misunderstood."

"All, right," Geiger said, nodding, "Do you want to amend any part of your account of what happened?"

She shook her head. Tears welled in her eyes. "No, I'm innocent. I didn't kill anybody."

"Then this interview is over," Duval said. "We will proceed with a murder-one charge and let a jury decide what's true and what isn't."

On the way out of the complex, the prosecutor said, "Let's pay a visit to her sister and see what she has to say."

THEY WOKE LINDA NASH when they entered the hospital room. She didn't seem as cranky as before. Duval introduced herself and asked if they could talk with her for a few minutes.

"I guess so," she said, sitting up in bed. She eyed Dalton and gave him a sneer. "The only people I shot were cops trying to kill me."

Duval told her about Dalton and another deputy hearing Wendy admit that the two had killed the men on the boat. "That's tantamount to a confession, and you don't stand a chance in court."

Linda shrugged. "Their word against mine."

"We just had a long talk with your sister, and she squealed on you, said you killed everybody, and she was just an innocent bystander."

Linda's eyes grew large. "I don't believe you. She wouldn't rat me out on a phony charge."

The prosecutor just nodded and pulled her phone from her purse. She had downloaded a copy of the interview. "Let me show you."

The video started up, and Linda's face twisted into a scowl when Wendy said her sister had done all the shooting. The expression remained there for the duration of the interview, a little over ten minutes in all. At its conclusion, she shook her head. "She's lying. She isn't so innocent."

"What do you mean?"

Linda looked out the window. The sun shone through, its rays hitting the fingers of her left hand. She drew a deep breath and let it out with a sigh.

"Tell us," Duval said. "What did Wendy do?"

"She started it all. I didn't go on that boat to hurt anybody." Tears welled in her eyes. "I can't believe she turned on me like that."

Duval shook her head. "She thinks she can blame everything on you, but she's wrong. We have enough hard evidence and testimony to get a guilty verdict on both of you, even without a confession."

Linda just stared at her and wiped the tears.

"If you're willing to give us a complete and truthful confession, I'm pretty sure I can arrange mercy on the death penalty."

After a silence of several seconds, Linda said, "What will happen to her?"

"Depends on which way she goes. If she wants to fight it out in court, she'll lose, and the judge might not be inclined to just give her prison time."

Linda nodded, but didn't say anything. Duval worked on her another few minutes before she gave in, still wiping tears. "All right. I don't want to die."

Dalton set up the video camera and started it rolling. Duval stated the date and time, the purpose of the interview, and who was present in the room. She asked Linda to begin.

"After what happened with Rudy Banks, I knew Leonard was going to kill me. I wanted to get away, but I needed money. So I arranged for Carl Myron, Buster Perl, and Floyd Sparks to rob the Toole Parts stash. I'd heard there was over five million in that closet. Me and Wendy planned to meet the men on the boat and sail away with the loot. But when we got aboard, Buster and Floyd said they had killed Carl. Carl was our cousin, and we couldn't stomach the idea of sharing the money and going away with them. We made a snap decision. Wendy went below and shot Floyd, and then I shot Buster. Served them right for killing Carl. We took the money and went back to Wendy's house to regroup."

"Tell us about Joseph Pound," Duval asked. "Who killed him?"

"Killing him was an afterthought. He found the money in the boathouse and knew Wendy was leaving him. He told her he would kill her before letting her go, so I arranged to meet him at his office. When I got there and sat down in front of his desk, I sent a text to Wendy, signaling her to call him. He answered the phone and turned away, and I shot him in the head. I wrote the note on his computer, doused his mouth with booze, and put the gun in his hand. Wendy said nobody would suspect me, so I did it for her. And she repays me by trying to lay all the blame on me."

Dalton thought Linda had told the truth. Perl and Sparks had started the killing, and probably thought themselves clever by getting rid of Myron. One less to share in the haul. Then the same thing happened to them, and each ended up with a dead man's take. All the victims, including Pound, were criminals, but did they deserve to die? Dalton would leave that question to the court.

DALTON AND CHASE headed back to Islamorada. On the way, Dalton called the sheriff and updated her on the confession.

"That's good news," she said. "Are you on your way to the office?"

"Yes. Should be there in about twenty minutes."

"Okay, can you come on down to Key West? There's something I want to discuss with you."

"Will do."

They hung up and Dalton wondered what she wanted. The drive didn't bother him, because he would be closer to home, and would head that way when they finished talking.

Chase glanced at him when he laid his phone on the console. If he'd heard her side of the conversation, he didn't say anything about it. "Bet you're glad this case is over."

"Yeah, you got that right." After a few beats, Dalton said, "With so much happening, I haven't asked about the cases I gave you."

Shrugging, Chase said, "They're going okay. I'm waiting on information. I should close them out in a day or two. I'm pretty sure you were right about the electronics store guy trying to scam the insurance company. The investigator said he's holding up the payment." He remained silent for a minute, and then said, "I appreciate you having faith in me. Cobb never did. Anything of any substance, he did himself."

Feeling a little guilty about his past suspicions, Dalton hesitated before saying, "I was sure glad you were there when we took down Leonard Orlov. They would've killed me if you hadn't stepped in when you did."

The deputy seemed to blush at the praise. "Yeah, well, I'm glad, too, even though I botched it."

"You did fine."

Dalton dropped Chase off and said he had to go for a face-to-face with the sheriff. "Probably a dress-down for all the missteps."

"I don't see where there were any missteps," Chase said. "You stayed with it until you got the killer. To me that's all that counts."

DALTON ARRIVED AT Sheriff Martinez's office on Stock Island about ninety minutes later. Several employees exited the building as he entered. Probably the administrative staff leaving for the day. The sheriff's secretary, a pretty woman of about twenty-five looked up and smiled as he approached her desk.

"Are you Detective Dalton?"

"Yes, I am."

"Go on in. She's expecting you."

When he entered, the sheriff stepped over and shook his hand. "Thanks for coming. Hold on a minute." To her secretary, she said, "You can go now, Carol," and then she closed the door. "Have a seat." She pointed to a chair in front of her desk.

When they were settled, she gave him a smile. "Good work on the case. I knew you were up to it."

Dalton nodded. "Sure, glad it turned out like it did. The sisters could've hired high-priced lawyers and cost the county a lot of money."

She nodded. "Yes, a good possibility. Sounds like with the confession, the other sister could fold, too."

"I think she will."

After staring for a moment, she said, "It's bad about Kevin."

"Who?"

"Lieutenant Cobb."

"Oh, yeah, that was bad. Pretty shocking, too."

"What you told me he said to those women, demanding part of the stolen money? You said Deputy Chase heard it, too?"

He wondered where she was going with the questions. "Yes, he heard it."

"Can he be trusted to keep a lid on it?"

"Hmm. Don't know. You could ask him."

"I'd rather you do that."

Dalton felt his face heat up.

"What I want to do is place you in Kevin's position. I could hire somebody else, but I don't know anyone more qualified. And it would be a promotion for you." She gave him a big grin.

He just stared for a couple of beats, and shook his head, "I don't think so. I'm pretty happy where I am."

Her face appeared to flush as the smile leaked away. "I understand, but I need you in that position. And first order of business I want you to do a press conference. You have a real knack for dealing with those folks. You can tell your story about how you ferreted out these killers. When it comes to Kevin, just say he got shot in the line of duty and give him some kudos on his bravery and heroism."

She wanted him to gloss over the situation. Make everything rosy. "You're talking to the wrong person.

I don't want the position, and I'm not going to lie about what happened with Cobb."

She rocked back in her chair and crossed her arms, a frown on her face, apparently unaccustomed to not getting what she wanted. "You don't seem to understand. I can give you a direct order, and fire you if you don't follow through."

"Sure, you can do that."

"So take the promotion."

After eyeing her for what seemed like a long time, he sighed. "You have my answer." He stood and headed to the door.

"You're going to regret this."

THE DRIVE TO Little Torch seemed to pass in a flash, and then he walked onto the deck with Eric, Sam, and Simone.

Eric stood and handed him an icy beer. "We thought we should celebrate you solving your case. What took you so long to get home?"

He drank from the bottle and sat down. "I had to go see the sheriff to close things out."

After an hour or so, Sam and Simone drifted off to Sam's boat, and Eric and Dalton headed to their respective cabins. As Dalton finished feeding Cupcake, his phone rang. The number looked unfamiliar. He answered.

"Is this detective Dalton?"

"Yes, who's calling?"

"This is Gloria Cobb, Kevin Cobb's wife. I got your number from a phone list Kevin kept here."

"Oh, hello Ms. Cobb. So sorry about your husband."

"Well, thanks. We hadn't gotten along in years, but I was still broken up about him dying."

"What can I do for you?"

"I went to the bank late this afternoon and opened our deposit box. There was something in it I didn't expect, and I wondered if you might come over and take a look at it?"

He wanted to say *No*, but the woman's husband had just died. "Sure, when did you have in mind?"

"How about right now? I know it's late, but I don't think I can stand to wait until tomorrow."

"Okay. I'm on Little Torch Key, so it'll take a while for me to get there."

An hour later, Cobb's widow opened the door and invited him inside. She gave him a nervous smile, and he didn't notice any signs of grief over her dead husband. When they got seated in the living room, she said, "This is what I found." She picked up a memory card from the coffee table and inserted it into a laptop computer. The screen sprang to life with a grainy video that appeared to have been photographed with a spy cam. Three men sat around a table. Dalton recognized them as Joseph Pound, Leonard Orlov, and Boris Ivashin. The two Russians glared at another person who sat at the end of the table and out of view of the camera. After a few seconds, a door on the left opened and Sheriff Martinez entered. She stepped over to the table and reached out to shake hands with Orlov. He hesitated for a moment, but took her hand. "We have been waiting."

"Yes, sorry for the delay. It was unavoidable." She took a seat next to the crime boss.

"What are you going to do about this Detective Foskey?" Orlov asked.

She shook her head. "Stop worrying about him. He won't be a problem anymore."

Orlov gave her a scowl. "How can you be so sure?"

Smiling, she said, "Dead men don't talk."

The Russian nodded and seemed to relax. "All right, then, we will continue as before."

"Not so fast," Martinez said. "We've incurred additional risk because of your sloppy operation. Eliminating Foskey could bring additional attention to us. I want ten thousand more for each shipment."

"You always want more," Orlov said. "How can we do business like this?"

"If not for us, you would be in prison."

After seeming to fume for several seconds, Orlov said to Pound, "This will come out of your end."

"Then we have a deal?" Martinez asked.

"Yes, we have a deal." Orlov nodded to Ivashin, and the two stood and left the room. The video stopped.

Robin had told Dalton that Detective Foskey's murder had never been solved. The video explained why. The sheriff hadn't detailed other detectives into Islamorada long enough to make any headway on it.

Tears ran down Gloria Cobb's face. "Kevin took this video, didn't he?"

Since Cobb had the card, Dalton was pretty certain he had been the photographer. His widow likely knew nothing about his involvement in the drug business.

"Probably. No need for you to worry about it, though."

She wiped her face with the back of her hand and extracted the memory card. "I didn't know what to do with this. Kevin had mentioned you and said you were a good detective."

"I'll make sure it gets to the right place."

THE NEXT MORNING, Dalton turned into the parking lot of a café in Key Largo. Inside, he ambled over to a booth and took a seat across from Daniel Crown, an agent with the Florida Department of Law Enforcement. The two had become friends while attending an FBI course in Quantico a few years earlier. Dalton had touched base with him when he got to Florida, and Crown had encouraged him to apply for the position with the sheriff's office. He'd also asked him to be on the lookout for somebody in the office who might be feeding DEA raid information to drug smugglers. There had been no significant drug busts in the area for a couple of years.

A waitress appeared and they both ordered coffee. When she returned with the steaming cups and left again, Dalton handed over the memory card and said, "I think this is what you wanted."

Crown plugged it into a computer tablet lying on the table, inserted an ear bud, and watched the screen. A few minutes later, he jerked the bud from his ear and smiled. "This is great. I had no idea she was the ring leader. Who took the video?"

Dalton shook his head. "Doesn't matter. He's dead now."

DALTON AND CHASE worked on the murder files for a couple of hours and closed them out. Robin came by as they finished. "Did you see the news? The sheriff has been arrested. Something to do with Leonard Orlov. Apparently, the FDLE has a video incriminating her in his drug business."

"Huh," Dalton said. "Where did you see that?"

"It was on channel six. Lola Ann. She said she'd have more details on the evening news."

TWENTY-SEVEN

ERIC STOPPED DALTON on his way into his cottage. "I heard the sheriff was arrested. You know anything about it?"

"I heard. Sounds like she was mixed up with Orlov somehow. Too bad. I kinda liked her."

"Me, too. You up for a couple of beers? Sam and Simone said they would be up here before sunset for drinks."

That sounded good to Dalton. "I want to catch the news at six and see what they say about the sheriff. I'll be out right after that." He went inside and heard the pet door flap. The cougar bounded over, reared up and almost knocked him down with a hug.

"You hungry, big boy?"

Cupcake dropped to the floor and purred. Dalton opened a pack of ground meat and gave him half of it. The big cat gobbled it up and looked up at Dalton, as if to ask for more. Being a softie, he gave him the rest of the meat and made a mental note to buy some more the following day.

He opened a bottle of beer and turned on the TV. The news began, but Lola Ann didn't show up for about twenty minutes. She looked as beautiful as ever. Although she didn't show any of the spy cam video involving the sheriff, it was apparent from her report that she had viewed it or had it described to her.

Finishing up, she said, "The Florida Department of Law Enforcement received the video anonymously, but they suspect it came from a disgruntled former employee of Leonard Orlov. Our investigative staff learned a few minutes ago that Sheriff Martinez has been released on bail. We also have a report, though not confirmed at this time, that she has resigned her position."

Dalton turned off the TV and headed outside. He didn't think the sheriff would be issuing any more orders about concealing Cobb's involvement. It would be all she could do to stay off death row, especially if she pulled the trigger on Detective Foskey.

When he arrived at the office on Friday, the night watch commander, a lieutenant, had moved into Cobb's office.

"We have a new leader," Dalton said.

Marvin Starr rocked back in the chair. "Just temporary. You hear about the sheriff?"

Nodding, Dalton said, "Sure did. That's sad."

"She called yesterday, before the arrest, and asked me to sit in until we have a formal assignment. Said you turned it down."

Dalton shook his head. "Not my strong suit."

"I'm not too excited about it either. I left some case files on your desk. What I plan to do, for the time being, is send you all the investigations and you can divvy them up with Steve Chase. That sound okay?"

"Look forward to working with you." He turned to leave.

"Oh, yeah," Starr said. "The psychologist will be calling you for counseling on the shootings."

Dalton nodded. "Gotta keep the brass happy."

At his desk he looked over the files. There was a bar robbery a few miles south, a couple of stolen vehicles, a home invasion, and another body found floating. Maybe the death wouldn't lead to others as the Carl Myron case had. After studying the reports, he decided to keep the floater and the robbery and took the rest to Steve Chase's desk. The deputy hadn't arrived yet so he left a note.

While getting coffee in the break room, Robin came up behind him and said, "Hey, you have a minute?" Sadness pinched at the corners of her eyes.

"Sure, you want to talk in here?"

"Yeah, that's fine."

They took cups to a table and sat. She gave him a pained smile. "I'm going back to Miami. I talked with my boss from before and he said I can have my old job back."

He frowned. "I thought you liked it better in the Keys."

Nodding, she said, "I do, but with all that's happened…" Her eyes glistened.

"Don't worry about what's happened. None of it involved you."

"I know, but it's for the best."

So much deception had swirled around him, and he knew his own paranoia had played a part in pushing her away. All she had done was follow orders. A gnawing pain grew in the pit of his stomach. "You sure you want to do this?"

She nodded. "Yeah, the paperwork has already been submitted. I hope you'll drop by to see me when you're up that way."

He sighed and tried for a smile. "You can count on it."

THAT EVENING, Dalton went with Sam and Simone on a dive of the wrecked Spanish galleon Sam had mentioned a couple of weeks before. A friend of Sam's, Gunner Deet, had discovered the wreck. He was in charge of the operation and took them out on his boat. Deet assured Dalton that the dive would be legal, and anything they found would be filed with the State of Florida. They went into the water shortly after dark and searched the site for about ninety minutes, changing their air tanks once during the excursion. The ship's hull had remained in remarkable condition for a vessel submerged for a few hundred years. When they finished, they had found gold and silver coins, jade figurines, and a gold art object that appeared to be Aztec in origin. Gunner, a veteran treasure hunter, estimated the worth of their find at close to a hundred thousand. After the state took its twenty percent, Gunner would give each of the divers five percent. It would amount to a few thousand each. Not bad for a night's work, and a lot of fun.

THE NEXT DAY at breakfast on the deck, Sam and Simone said their goodbyes. Dalton told Sam how much he appreciated him coming to Islamorada. "I really needed your help, and you came through."

Sam waved the comment away. "Glad I could help. I'm still in your debt, so call if you ever need anything."

"You more than paid any debt you had to me. Please thank J.T. for me, too."

Eric said, "Anytime you want to visit this area, let me know and I'll find a spot for you."

"I might take you up on that," Sam said.

Dalton and Cupcake walked with them down to the boat, and Sam shook Dalton's hand. Simone scratched Cupcake's ears and then pulled Dalton in for a hug. The two travelers boarded *Slipstream* and Sam started the engine.

Dalton threw the lines to Simone and stood on the dock as they pulled away. Cupcake lay at the edge staring at fish swimming below. As Dalton turned to leave, the cat jumped up and followed. One of the marina residents, a woman of about fifty, said from the stern of her houseboat, "I wish you would give me Cupcake. Such a cutie. He let me pet him yesterday." The big cat turned and stared at the woman for a moment. He seemed to smile.

"Sorry, no can do."

LOLA ANN CALLED late in the day. "I thought I'd hear from you by now," she said.

"Yeah, sorry. I've been really busy."

"I know, and I appreciate you steering that FDLE agent my way."

"What makes you think I steered him your way?"

She chuckled. "He said so."

Dalton sighed, "I told him not to mention that."

"Yeah, well, he did." After a short pause, she said, "How about dinner tonight?"

* * * * *